THE LAST
LAVENDER SISTER

Reviewers Love Melissa Brayden

"Melissa Brayden has become one of the most popular novelists of the genre, writing hit after hit of funny, relatable, and very sexy stories for women who love women."—*Afterellen.com*

Exclusive

"Melissa Brayden's books have always been a source of comfort, like seeing a friend you've lost touch with but can pick right up where you left off. They have always made my heart happy, and this one does the same."—*Sapphic Book Review*

Marry Me

"A bride-to-be falls for her wedding planner in this smoking hot, emotionally mature romance from Brayden...Brayden is remarkably generous to her characters, allowing them space for self-exploration and growth."—*Publishers Weekly*

"When I open a book by Melissa Brayden, I usually know what to expect. This time, she really surprised me. In a good way."—*Rainbow Literary Society*

To the Moon and Back

"*To the Moon and Back* is all about Brayden's love of theatre, onstage and backstage, and she does a delightful job of sharing that love... Brayden set the scene so well I knew what was coming, not because it's unimaginative but because she made it obvious it was the only way things could go. She leads the reader exactly where she wants to take them, with brilliant writing as usual. Also, not everyone can make office supplies sound sexy."—*Jude in the Stars*

"Melissa Brayden does what she does best, she delivers amazing characters, witty banter, all while being fun and relatable."—*Romantic Reader Blog*

Back to September

"You can't go wrong with a Melissa Brayden romance. Seriously, you can't. Buy all of her books. Brayden sure has a way of creating an emotional type of compatibility between her leads, making you root for them against all odds. Great settings, cute interactions, and realistic dialogue."—*Bookvark*

What a Tangled Web

"[T]he happiest ending to the most amazing trilogy. Melissa Brayden pulled all of the elements together, wrapped them up in a bow, and presented the reader with Happily Ever After to the max!"—*Kitty Kat's Book Review Blog*

Beautiful Dreamer

"I love this book. I want to kiss it on its face...I'm going to stick *Beautiful Dreamer* on my to-reread-when-everything-sucks pile, because it's sure to make me happy again and again."—*Smart Bitches Trashy Books*

"*Beautiful Dreamer* is a sweet and sexy romance, with the bonus of interesting secondary characters and a cute small-town setting."—*Amanda Chapman, Librarian (Davisville Free Library, RI)*

Two to Tangle

"Melissa Brayden does it again with a sweet and sexy romance that leaves you feeling content and full of happiness. As always, the book is full of smiles, fabulous dialogue, and characters you wish were your best friends."—*The Romantic Reader*

"I loved it. I wasn't sure Brayden could beat Joey and Becca and their story, but when I started to see reviews mentioning that this was even better, I had high hopes and Brayden definitely lived up to them."—*LGBTQreader.com*

Entangled

"*Entangled* is a simmering slow burn romance, but I also fully believe it would be appealing for lovers of women's fiction. The friendships between Joey, Maddie, and Gabriella are well developed and engaging as well as incredibly entertaining...All that topped off with a deeply fulfilling happily ever after that gives all the happy sighs long after you flip the final page."—*Lily Michaels: Sassy Characters, Sizzling Romance, Sweet Endings*

"Ms. Brayden has a definite winner with this first book of the new series, and I can't wait to read the next one. If you love a great enemies-to-lovers, feel-good romance, then this is the book for you."—*Rainbow Reflections*

Love Like This

"Brayden upped her game. The characters are remarkably distinct from one another. The secondary characters are rich and wonderfully integrated into the story. The dialogue is crisp and witty."—*Frivolous Reviews*

Sparks Like Ours

"Brayden sets up a flirtatious tit-for-tat that's honest, relatable, and passionate. The women's fears are real, but the loving support from the supporting cast helps them find their way to a happy future. This enjoyable romance is sure to interest readers in the other stories from Seven Shores."—*Publishers Weekly*

Hearts Like Hers

"Once again Melissa Brayden stands at the top. She unequivocally is the queen of romance."—*Front Porch Romance*

Eyes Like Those

"Brayden's story of blossoming love behind the Hollywood scenes provides the right amount of warmth, camaraderie, and drama." —*RT Book Reviews*

Strawberry Summer

"This small-town second-chance romance is full of tenderness and heart. The 10 Best Romance Books of 2017."—*Vulture*

"*Strawberry Summer* is a tribute to first love and soulmates and growing into the person you're meant to be. I feel like I say this each time I read a new Melissa Brayden offering, but I loved this book so much that I cannot wait to see what she delivers next."—*Smart Bitches, Trashy Books*

First Position

"Brayden aptly develops the growing relationship between Ana and Natalie, making the emotional payoff that much sweeter. This ably plotted, moving offering will earn its place deep in readers' hearts." —*Publishers Weekly*

By the Author

THE LAST
LAVENDER SISTER

by

Melissa Brayden

2022

THE LAST LAVENDER SISTER

ISBN 13: 978-1-63679-130-2

This Trade Paperback Original Is Published By
Bold Strokes Books, Inc.
P.O. Box 249
Valley Falls, NY 12185

First Edition: July 2022

Credits
Editor: Ruth Sternglantz
Production Design: Stacia Seaman
Cover Design by Jeanine Henning

Acknowledgments

This is my twenty-first book. The first book I've written old enough to buy itself a drink. I don't know how that happened, but here we are. The journey with this particular novel was such a positive one. I enjoyed getting up to write each day, and this particular story unraveled at just the right time. Plus, the characters became friends of mine, making the good-bye bittersweet. I hope you enjoy a glimpse into Aster and Brynn's world and their story.

Now for what I like to call hugs in writing. I always seem to end these acknowledgements by thanking you, the reader, last, but I would like to start with you this time. There are a great number of fantastic books out there, and I have so much joy, humility, and gratitude that you've chosen to pick up one of mine. I hope I make it worth your while.

I would like to thank the short people in my home for giving me twenty minutes of writing time here, and then six minutes there, and then another twelve when I'm lucky. The extra keys you mashed were also a big help. We have a solid partnership. Many thanks also to Alan for short people support as well as letting me bounce ideas around at the least convenient times. You are the best.

To all the professionals at Bold Strokes, I'm immensely thankful for the always-available help and kindness. It truly does take a village, and you've built a pretty great one. Thank you also goes out to the proofreaders who have become invaluable to the process. Ruth, my editor, gets a hug and a cup of coffee in front of a theatre for guiding me through my time writing Homer's Bluff. Cindy, Toni, Stacia, Jeanine, and more for your talent and hard work.

There are literally too many writing friends to thank! Georgia for keeping me focused on the words and smiling along the way. Nikki and Rey for the friendship and escape. Carsen and Paula for the laughs. Kris and Fiona for the generosity. Ali for the hysterical stories. And so many more of you who are there with an encouraging word or small act of kindness. I'll never get used to the strength of community. Looking forward to more talks and laughs and amazing times.

For the Bench Readers.

PROLOGUE

People who thought small towns were cute and cozy certainly never lived in one. If anything, Aster Lavender thought they were overrated and slow. She'd grown up smack in the middle of stagnation in equally comatose Kansas her entire life, just waiting for something exciting to happen. Verdict? It was never going to. Homer's Bluff didn't even come with a cute name like the small towns in the heartwarming little TV movies. Unfortunate.

The town did have one thing going for it. Frequent storms. Aster loved them and their exact lack of predictability. That morning, she stared through her shop's drive-through window, captivated by the show as one crept in. Lightning that streaked across a darkened sky was a beautiful occurrence that stole her heart and made her breath hitch. Aster watched a jagged line of it shoot through the sky and fracture into a million little unpredictable bursts.

How she longed to be like lightning.

No time for dreaming. She rolled her shoulders, snapping out of it. This weather was going to slow down business this morning, but that didn't mean there weren't a ton of doughnuts to make for those who did venture out. Aster didn't mind a quiet morning here or there. Gave her time to catch her breath and get creative about the shop and its future. She loved coming up with more flavors and recipes for her artisan doughnuts in what had truly become not just a job but a passion project. Hole in One was her baby. She'd personally opened the tiny shop three years ago now with money she'd saved in a savings account since she was six plus a little bit of inheritance from an uncle—and the rest she'd borrowed from her mom, who'd always believed she'd be successful at whatever she set her mind to. Being able to pay back every cent of that loan after two years was a true source of pride for Aster.

It helped that the shop was a success. The place had immediately found eager customers among Homer's Bluff residents who didn't mind paying a little extra for special. She carried four flavors of doughnuts a day to ensure top-notch quality and care. The best part was choosing what those flavors would be. The combination was key. The shop needed to offer a variety but also provide a complementary foursome in case her customers chose to consume them in sequence. Like a good wine pairing, a savory flavor partnership was critical. Plus, keeping the number of options small not only made her shop manageable for only herself and two part-time employees, but it kept her customers in suspense. What would be offered today? When would their favorite doughnut pop up on the menu board? Of course the best-loved doughnuts made more regular appearances. After all, she was also a businesswoman who needed to make her mortgage. For example, whenever word got out that she had Piggly Wigglies—her own take on maple bacon doughnuts—on the menu, people showed up in droves. She'd have a line of cars patiently waiting because they didn't want to miss their chance. The scarcity tactic was effective. Who knew when Piggly Wigglies would be back? Better hurry and get over to Hole in One before they sold out.

Aster exhaled with pride and dusted the flour off her hands. All by design.

It was ten minutes to six, and daylight hadn't even been hinted at yet. The town was slowly starting to wake as folks climbed out of bed in search of coffee. They'd jump in their cars, head to work, and think how nice it would be to enjoy a hot, fresh doughnut. Hell, maybe they should bring a dozen in for their coworkers to enjoy on a rainy day, boost morale. She'd be ready for them, always the first one to work, with trays of piping hot doughnuts made with only the freshest dough. Tori would be in soon to back her up, and Drew was scheduled for an hour after that when the midmorning rush hit hard. For now, Aster enjoyed the peace and quiet of the moment and the aroma of fresh fried dough.

Ten full trays lined the sheet pan rack. The first car, anticipating her opening, ambled its way up the uneven road toward her window just as Aster hung her chalkboard sign outside her drive-through, announcing the flavors of the day:

1. Glazed and Confused
2. Pistachio Rodeo
3. Strawberry Romance
4. Nutella My Secrets

A balanced partnership she was proud of. Traditional, sweet, decadent, and savory all represented on her board like a well-matched group of friends.

"Hey there. I'll take a mixed dozen," Mr. Landry said when she opened her window at six a.m. sharp. "But maybe toss in an extra Strawberry Romance." He came by at least three times a week and preferred her fruit leaning offerings. Aster checked her line. Two more cars. She would be on her own for the first hour, and then Tori and Drew would be in to back her up when the rush got going. Drew would take over the fry station. Tori would handle the drive-through and Aster would top the doughnuts and man any counter business. The Hole in One was designed as a stop and go. She did the lion's share of business from her drive-through window, but the stand did offer counter service inside, along with two very petite tables that became overcrowded when there was a line. Her place was small, but she liked that about it. People came and people left. The pressure was minimal.

"Coming right up, Mr. Landry," she told the pharmacist, already wearing his white coat. She assembled her most popular box, three of each flavor, accepted his payment, and waited as the next car drove forward.

"Oh, it's Strawberry Romance day!" Mrs. Rule exclaimed as she checked out the menu. "I've been waiting. Oh, this is shaping up to be a good day already. I was just going to order one, but now I'll need three. No. Make it six. An even half dozen is a stronger number and probably better luck, right?"

"I think that's a good call," Aster said. "How are the taxes coming?" She wasn't great at small talk but longed to be better, and the practice helped. The window was a great way to work that muscle until Tori arrived and took over.

"March has certainly been busy, but with April looming, I can hardly complain. Don't wait too late to bring me all of your receipts," she said. "We don't have a ton of time."

Aster nodded. "Got them all ready for you. I'll make an appointment next week." She handed over the bag of cream cheese stuffed strawberry doughnuts and made a mental note of how many had been sold. She'd need to start borrowing bits of time between cars to bolster her supply until backup arrived. She had the fryer hot and her dough rounded and ready. Just a little bit of multitasking to keep the engine chugging away.

Once early morning shifted to late morning, the doughnut dash slowed to a doughnut stroll. She had a car here or there but earned time to start cleanup and prep for the next morning. That's when she saw the large gray and white pickup lumbering her way. Her father. Probably heard she had his favorite, pistachio.

"Hi," she said as he slowed to her window. "Looking for a fix?"

"I'll take six pistachio," he said, grinning like the lumberjack he resembled. "Your mom wanted me to ask you to swing by for lunch. She made chicken salad and is real proud about it. Keeps going on about how it has..." His fingers moved as he searched for his words. "The little crunchy things. She says it's your favorite, and you should come before your brother scarfs it all, and you know Sage. He will clobber it."

"Grapes," she supplied, smothering a smile. Her father was a burly man with graying hair, pink cheeks, a close-trimmed beard, and big hands that used to scoop her up onto his shoulders. He shied away from things like chicken salad, opting for burgers and turkey legs or anything that might lead to a heart attack or be found at a Renaissance Fair.

He nodded. "Yep. Those."

"Perfect. I love it when she adds grapes."

He seemed upset. "Grapes or nuts on a sandwich make me suspicious."

"Don't you also hate cotton?"

He raised his shoulders to his ears, a sign he had the willies, which made her grin. He was the most sensitive giant man she'd ever met. But that's what made him pretty great.

His clothes were dusty, which meant he'd likely been at work on the farm early, getting ahead of the sun. He spent a lot of his time outdoors with his crew. The Lavenders had built a solid reputation off their semifamous lavender farm and the rustic two-story gift shop that featured a variety of products manufactured with lavender straight off the farm: soaps, oils, candles, culinary spices, and even lavender infused firewood. The commitment to standing out didn't end there, however. Her parents had named her and all three of her siblings after flowers. *Sigh.* Yes, flowers. They meant well. Her two oldest siblings, Violet and Marigold, were vivacious go-getters who did most everything together. Three years younger was her brother, Sage, who was probably the best-looking human anyone had ever seen. He was also affable and smart, which didn't seem fair.

Then there was her, Aster Nicole Lavender. The youngest sibling. The doughnut traitor.

Quiet. Less exciting. Not often talked about. The also-ran of the Lavender family, who came late and made the smallest impression on, well, most everyone.

She was also the only Lavender without a job on the property, not that they hadn't offered her about eight. Luckily, her family was fantastic and warm and treated her with the supportive kindness lots of folks longed for from their families. But she had never been as comfortable in her own skin as the rest of them seemed to be, and that left her feeling off to the side. So she stayed in the background by choice, cheering them on, reading as many books as she could get her hands on, riding her bike on nice days, and going home to her quiet house.

They'd sold out of doughnuts shortly after noon, which left her available for a late lunch. Chicken salad time. On nice days, she traded her car for her bike, preferring the feel of the fresh air on her cheeks as she pedaled through the main stretch of town to the east end of Homer's Bluff. Her childhood home was located just a little ways down from The Lavender House, tucked behind a long and winding driveway, which she and Sage had used as their own personal racetrack growing up. He generally won every time regardless of whether they were on foot, skates, or bikes. Big brothers were like that. Not that she hadn't given him a run for his money.

"You got close this time, Aster. You're getting fast." He'd been ten. She was seven.

"I almost caught you!" she said gleefully from her scooter, out of breath and carefree.

"Next time," he said, throwing her a high five.

Nowadays, the driveway had a few large cracks. Bits of grass grew through the open patches, reminding Aster that she was all grown up and time marched on. Twenty-eight and counting, which made *baby of the family* feel like such a misnomer.

"Aster Lavender. There you are," her mother said, beaming. She had her dark hair pulled up into a pile on top of her head. Her eyes were big and expressive, accentuated by mascara that she always seemed to apply expertly, a skill Aster didn't have. Her mother was pretty. Everyone thought so. Aster had been told a million times how much she resembled her mom, Marilyn Lavender, and she held on to the words like a guarded treasure, the best compliment she could imagine. Proud to carry a little piece of the woman she long admired.

"I heard there was free lunch?" She looked up and down the kitchen.

Her mother, always up for fun, slid a plate down the counter to Aster like a barkeep, with an already made chicken salad sandwich. "For you. My baby child. Try it." She held up a victorious finger. "Grapes."

Aster caught the fast-tracked plate and nodded her gratitude. The sandwich was hearty and tall. "You don't mess around."

"Not when it comes to feeding my family." Her mother hooked a thumb. "You just missed Violet. She's all dolled up for a date with Tad Jourdan. He's taking her mini-golfing, so I'll be covering the store." Violet, the firstborn, dazzled people with her ability to put any human at ease. She had beautiful curly brown hair that reminded Aster of one of those Italian paintings. "Oh!" Her mother's face lit up. "We got in a new batch of the lavender shea butter you like so much. I set some aside for you. Two tubes." It was a Lavender family perk. Free merchandise. Aster wasn't about to complain. It did make her skin extra soft.

"I will find a way to repay you."

Her mother placed a hand on her hip. "How about working that praline doughnut back into rotation? It's been three weeks."

"Deal," Aster said. She hadn't realized her mother had liked that one or she'd have brought it back much earlier. "I'll whip some up tomorrow and set aside a dozen."

Her mother squeezed her cheeks as she passed. "You are a good daughter. I'm keeping you forever and ever."

Aster leaned against the counter. "Don't tell the others I'm your favorite." She was only half joking. In a town that didn't often register her existence, her mother did. She looked after Aster, checked in on her, and truly listened to everything she had to say. In a world where it was hard to feel seen, where people forgot her name, instead referring to her as *that last sister*, her mother truly did *see* her, and she would never take it for granted.

"Hey, kid." She glanced behind her. Sage. He wore a blue ball cap and flashed his dimples. In addition to turning up as one of the blonds in a family that was divided by hair color, he had inherited their father's slight curl. He and Marigold repped their dad's side of the family, while Aster and Violet, the brunettes, took after their mom's.

Sage gave her head a soft knock, his custom, as he rounded the kitchen island, opened the refrigerator door, and stole a carton of their parents' milk, chugging what was left of it.

Aster frowned. "Do you still let him do that? It's barbaric."

"I don't. No," their mother said, eying him. Sage got away with everything. Good thing he was generally a sweet person, if not a little cocky.

He flashed her puppy dog eyes, the same ones that got him out of most of life's repercussions. "I'll never do it again."

"He lies to you blatantly," Aster said. "Do not fall for his puppy dog looks, either. It's criminal that he's still trotting them out."

Sage's mouth fell open.

"On it. You remember your manners, sir," her mom said, followed by a hip bump to Sage. "Or I'll have to wallop you." Aster grinned. A walloping generally meant covered in aggressive and embarrassing kisses where their mom was concerned, but the threat still worked.

"Yes, ma'am." He trashed the carton. "Tad's here. Picked Violet up in the shiny BMW, too. She's beaming, probably hoping to Instagram the whole experience."

Her mother's cheeks colored with pride. "Good for Violet. Tad seems like quite the catch from what I hear." Her eyes slid to Aster, who had no catch. Who rarely fished. The Homer's Bluff pond was virtually free of lesbian and bisexual women of any kind. Disastrous. Well, except for Nicola and Mindy, who had married each other five years ago in the park with half the town dressed in rainbow. Aster was a lesbian without a match or hope of finding one unless she expanded her search area. The internet had seemed like a viable option at first. But if Aster was awkward in person, her online persona was worse. She'd chatted with a few different women, but those dancing dots were a lot of pressure, and coming up with the perfect response ate up a lot of her free time. She wasn't good at smooth and flirty and eventually had taken a step back.

"Good for Vi," Aster said by way of support. Though her sister needed no help. She'd been the homecoming queen and voted most likely to marry a millionaire. "What about you?" she asked her brother. "Still dragging your heels with Tyler? I'd really like her to be my sister-in-law sooner rather than later. She's the best, and you know it." Tyler Lawson had been her brother's best friend all the way back to childhood. They were a perfect match, which he refused to see. Oblivious to what was right in front of his damn face.

Sage grimaced, but it was overdone. "Stop that already. I told you. It's not like that with me and Ty. She's my pal."

"She's your wife," Aster said matter-of-factly. "You just don't seem to know it yet." The truth was her brother was terrified of Tyler. Smart, successful, pretty, and likely made him feel things he didn't know what to do with. Tyler had his number, and that left him on his heels. One day, he'd come around. Aster took a bite of her sandwich. "You're too good at chicken salad," she told her mom, who nodded.

"I'm going to enter the chicken salad Olympics and win."

"I know it. I'll bet cash." Aster continued eating.

Sage eyed them. "You two are weird." He glanced over. "And you can't bet on the Olympics."

"Can so," Aster shot back, just to mess with him. "And will. And at least we don't drink milk from someone else's carton and deny our very real feelings for someone awesome."

Sage flipped his ball cap around, flashing curls. "Doesn't matter. Tyler is up and fleeing town next week. You hadn't heard?"

That had Aster's attention. They'd known Tyler her entire life. She was a fixture in Homer's Bluff, their all-around sweetheart. Aster couldn't imagine this place without Tyler to wave or offer you half her lunch. "What are you talking about? Where is she going?" Aster asked, squinting.

He scratched the back of his neck. He didn't seem to like the idea either. "Headed to Chicago for some sort of specialty certification in veterinary dentistry. She wants to treat teeth now, too. Not sure why her regular vet practice isn't enough."

Aster sighed. She hated this news. Tyler Lawson was at the helm of the town's one veterinary clinic, and she was great at it. Everyone loved her and the gentle time she took with each and every animal. This would be quite a loss for everyone.

"Well, good for Tyler," her mother said. "We'll all miss her, but we can root for her, too. She can go out and learn all she can and bring it right back here to us. Hopefully, soon."

"That's her plan," Sage said. "Six-month commitment for school. Let's just hope she doesn't get a wild hair and never returns." He looked royally pissed off and terrified of the possibility.

Aster swallowed. She recognized Tyler's trajectory as similar to what she'd envisioned for herself someday. She loved Hole in One, but she'd always imagined it would be a stepping stone to something bigger. Aster dreamed about life beyond Homer's Bluff and what it might be like to chase down a little excitement. Live theater. A train ride. One of those hip wine bars where she could establish herself as a regular and sip merlot and read fancy poetry while pretending to be more of an intellectual than she likely was. Hell, even somewhere with a few more traffic lights would be an improvement. She had a tentative plan for an escape in her back pocket and had quietly been looking into culinary schools with a focus on pastry arts. Aster wanted to get better at what she loved, challenge herself in ways she couldn't on her own. In fact, she'd already received an admittance letter from one of her top choice schools in Boston and would have to accept or decline their offer within the next two months. She kept that part to herself even as they discussed Tyler.

"What about the clinic?" Aster asked. She clocked the next available veterinarian at over forty minutes away. Quite the haul for a simple case of the dog sniffles.

"A friend of hers from school has agreed to fill in. Tyler says she's dynamite, so Buster Britches will be in good hands." Sage walked through life with a bull terrier by his side. Buster had swagger and a fan club of his own around here. People clamored for the laid-back dog with the ability to smile. When Sage walked Buster in a smart blue bandana, the duo set off alarm bells in the home of every single woman within a five-mile radius. As if beckoned by an unseen force, the women grinned and smiled and appeared right on cue to chat up her brother, who—bless his heart—didn't know anything other than universal female adoration. Aster had to wonder what that must be like.

"When does she go?" Aster asked. Nothing ever changed in Homer's Bluff, so a new vet, even temporary, was quite the shake-up.

"Soon," Sage said. "Six months without Tyler...man, gonna be weird around here." Sage and Tyler spent a lot of time together, watching football, laughing at movies, or just taking Buster for long walks. She wasn't sure what Sage was going to do on his own. Tyler was his right hand.

"You could bite the bullet and propose now. Give her a big romantic send-off." Aster set down her sandwich and placed a deliberate hand on her hip.

Sage gaped. "Not that easy and you know it. We're just friends." Her brother was clueless.

Aster and her mother exchanged a look because Tyler certainly had shown signs to the contrary. In fact, maybe those feelings were what prompted her to flee town. Aster rocked back on her heels, feeling bad about that now. "Just don't blow a good thing because you're stubborn, okay?"

Sage scoffed and took off his cap. "I'm gonna miss her is all. Doesn't mean we're meant to be or whatever." He held up a hand. "Tyler is...Tyler. She's pretty great."

Aster resisted an eye roll. "Well, I hope I get to see her before she leaves." Tyler had become a bonus big sister, sometimes a touch kinder and gentler than her own sisters, who, for years, tried to pull Aster into their world of clothes, hair, makeup, boys. It was only recently that they seemed to finally understand that she truly wasn't interested. Tyler, though, had taken the time to learn and understand Aster from early on. She'd been more than welcoming when a younger Aster followed her and Sage around like their pesky little shadow. It was in those days that she'd witnessed the soft way Sage had looked at Tyler and the looks she stole right back. Maybe they weren't meant to be in a romantic sense, but there was an undeniable bond between the two that didn't come around every day.

"There's a going away party for her tomorrow night at Larry's," Sage said. "You can ride with me. Leaving at seven."

Larry's Last Stop was the semi-broken-down bar smack in the middle of town, a stuffy notary's office on one side, and a neon lit ice cream parlor by the name of Lick Luster on the other side. That was Homer's Bluff, a hodgepodge that didn't always make a lot of sense. "Great. I'll bike over."

"You be careful on that bike after the sun goes down," her mom said, stirring a pitcher of lemonade. "You terrify me. I'm serious."

"I'm always careful," Aster said. She wasn't a risk-taker or a go-getter. She preferred to watch life's action from a safe distance. She dipped her toe into life's pool every once in a while, like with her short stint in the online dating world, but more often than not, she pulled it right back out again.

Underneath it all, she longed for...something. Whether it was school in Boston or just a change of pace, Aster wasn't quite sure. But something important was calling her name. She could feel the tug and, more than anything, wanted to follow it.

She just didn't quite have the courage.

Yet.

PART ONE

CHAPTER ONE

W hat the hell was she doing? This was crazy. Brynn Garrett wondered if she was making a mistake. When your world went up in smoke, you didn't just pack your bags and leave town. At least, that wasn't how she normally operated. In fact, doing so now left her feeling like she'd walked out of her house without any pants. Except in her case, she was leaving with all of them. She was the type who dotted each *i* and crossed every *t*. Not one of hers had any dots or crosses, yet here she was, fleeing the scene in impulsivity.

Pausing her very clichéd pacing, she stared at the voice mail notification waving at her from her phone like a pesky toddler seeking attention. Unable to put it off any longer, she pressed her thumb over the play button, leaving the voice mail to play on speaker as she continued packing like her life depended on it.

"Babe. Please don't ignore my calls."

First of all, *babe*? Tiffany hadn't called her that in months. Since well before the breakup. She bristled at the way the word made her feel now, after everything had fallen out of place. *"We have a lot to talk about and sort through."* Tiffany sighed. Brynn knew that sigh well and the voice that went with it as closely as she knew her own. But it was all wrong now, familiar or not. They were broken and gone forever. *"I saw that you signed over the lease, but can we take a moment and make sure this is what we want? What* you *want."*

She squinted in mystification. "What I wanted is someone who wants me and only me," she said to the empty room. Most of her belongings sat in boxes along the wall, thrown together in a less than organized packing job. This move had come on so fast. She looked around. Art still adorned the walls. She didn't want it. Just reminders. She'd leave it for Tiffany and her new life, which was such a surreal concept. She tasted bile in the back of her throat, the trauma still so prevalent. She'd once believed they'd spend forever in this house, celebrating milestones and Christmases, bringing home their first child. The first time she'd caught her girlfriend on the phone with that woman, Erica, she should have known. She'd given her the benefit of the doubt, because Tiffany was trustworthy, kind, and solid. There was no reason to think otherwise.

Distantly, the voice mail continued to play. *"Anyway, I've come to realize something important. Erica and I don't have what you and I do. That says something, right? Maybe I need to pay attention to my gut."*

"Oh God," Brynn said, dropping her head all the way back. "Are you kidding me?"

"Maybe what we have is special, and I think that deserves a second look."

Brynn squinted. Was she making this call from Erica's apartment where she'd been living for the past six weeks? It was likely. There was no chance of a reconciliation. Hell, no. Brynn still mourned their relationship, for the loss of what could have been, and her imagined future. But she was well beyond wanting them to work out. The sad part was that her trust had been shaken. She saw the world differently now. Instead of letting the voice mail finish, she silenced her phone with the push of a powerful button, bringing peace back into the room.

And also stillness. Loneliness. Hurt.

When Tyler had called with a temporary job offer, it almost felt like the arrangement had been ordained. Her good friend from vet school popped up and offered her the perfect opportunity to escape all of this? She couldn't say no. It was as if the universe had sent help in the form of a perky brunette woman.

"I immediately thought of you as the ideal person to step in and take over the clinic," Tyler explained over FaceTime. The two of them chatted frequently, but this news had her surprised.

"Wait. Where are you going?" Brynn had asked.

"I'm headed to Chicago. You're there now. While I would adore spending the next six months hanging out with you there and reliving our wine infused study sessions, we could essentially trade out for a bit and you could save my ass. I won't trust my practice to just anyone. But I trust you. Say yes."

Brynn nodded. "I'm still on staff at a clinic here in Chicago."

"So? They'll replace you in a week. Here? You'll matter, and the pets need you and your soft but logical approach to care. I keep waiting for a yes. Am I getting one?"

She could feel the hope in Tyler's grin through the damn phone. That's how adorable she was. Brynn chewed her check in thought. "It is a pretty big operation, where I work, which can feel less than validating." She rarely saw the same patients twice, and the clinic was so large that she barely knew the names of some of her colleagues. Once she did, they were often replaced. Turnover was high.

"Then this will be a palate cleanser for you. A one woman show here in Homer's Bluff where you can get to know my clients personally. They will bake you pie. *Pie*, Brynn. Are you hearing me?"

That actually sounded really refreshing. Connecting with people. Getting to know the animals. And what an interesting name for a town. Something out of a TV show from the sixties. "I will admit that your timing isn't bad. But Homer's Bluff? That's literally its name?"

"It's ridiculous but true."

"I may need to think on this."

"I get it, and I realize this is probably out of left field. You've always been thoughtful, and I would expect nothing less with a decision like this one. I'm just relieved you didn't hang up on me."

"I can't stand your sad face. Never could. Your little lip drops on the side, and your eyes get so big and Bambi-like."

Tyler laughed. "Let's both avoid my sad face. I can give you a few days, but then I need to find other arrangements. Less perfect ones, because you're awesome."

"Thank you, and I completely understand." She thought back. "Hey, what about that guy you're always telling me about. Sage. I thought things were looking up on that front, and now you're leaving?"

Tyler went quiet. "Well, I was dead wrong. A good reason for me to take a break from this place."

She could certainly understand the sentiment. "Are you okay?"

"I will be," Tyler said. "And maybe one day soon we can talk about it."

"I'd like that because I love you and love sucks. We're both smart to remember that."

"Oh, it's already tattooed across my forehead."

After mulling over Tyler's proposition for a mere twenty-four hours, Brynn accepted. Now it was time to quickly make plans and get herself to Kansas. She'd heard Tyler speak fondly of her hometown for years but couldn't find it on a map if she tried. And since the call, she had. Twice.

She'd get to know it soon enough, though. Her bags were now packed, a storage company was coming for the rest of her belongings, and her flight to Wichita took off in two hours. She'd miss Chicago and her favorite cup of coffee from Overflow's down the street, but she had to be honest. She was lonely, shattered, and not at all herself. She needed a change, a chance to catch her breath and pick herself back up. Then she could return home a stronger version of herself, ready to take on the difficulties of life again. Because quite honestly, the woman in the mirror—blond hair pulled up in a poorly executed ponytail, yoga pants that had seen better days, and green eyes that had lost their spark—was unrecognizable. She touched her hair, pulled the rubber band out, and watched it fall to her shoulders. She sighed.

Yeah, time for a change.

"Make it a double," she said dully to her empty house.

An adventure awaited, and she for one was ready to hop on board that plane and get a new chapter of her life started.

"This place is crowded," Aster murmured to Sage as they shouldered their way inside Larry's. *Crowds.* Her stomach sank at all the future small talk ahead. The normally sleepy bar was bustling with folks standing in groups, leaving not much room to maneuver. Apparently, the whole town had crammed itself into Larry's for a beer and a hug from their favorite veterinarian. Country music played loudly from the throwback jukebox in the corner, Larry's pride and joy. He refused to update the place, and it still matched photos on the walls from the eighties. The one room establishment was shaped like a rectangle that stretched from front to back with the beat-up bar along the wall on the right, a pair of dimly lit restrooms at the back, and a hodgepodge of somewhat stable tables and chairs throughout the middle.

"Damn. People love Tyler," Sage said, his jaw a little tighter than she was used to seeing. Mm-hmm.

"That's what I've been telling you. You're just too boneheaded to appreciate her, and now she's leaving. Is this your fault?" She eyed him.

"Of course not, and I do appreciate her. It's not like I want her to leave. Hell, it's the opposite."

"Have you told her that?" Aster asked.

"Who, me?"

Tyler had snuck up on them, and damn if she didn't look like a million bucks. Entirely by design, Aster was sure. A navy and white polka dotted top with off the shoulder sleeves. Slim jeans and a killer pair of brown heels that gave her five-foot-three frame a generous boost that brought her eye-to-eye with Aster. Her brown hair was in a ponytail, and her matching eyes were done the hell up. Lashes for days. *Nice work, Tyler.*

"Exactly you," Aster said and received the hug Tyler offered. "I can't believe you're leaving." She stared hard at her friend. "Take me with you." She half meant it.

Tyler grinned and her eyes crinkled. "You're in. Show up at six a.m. tomorrow morning, and I'll tuck you into my suitcase. I could use a little sister like you to cheer me on. I've heard rumors about this program. The classes are supposed to be fast paced and insanely difficult."

"But you're the smartest person I know," Aster said, rocking on her heels, still not entirely comfortable at a large gathering. She'd warm up soon.

"You mean next to you, the town whiz kid?" Aster demurred at the reference to her successful days in school. While people could be hard for her, academia had not been. She missed it.

"Tyler, no," Aster said. "You're going to do great in Chicago. I just know it. Please come back, though. Without you here..." The sentimentality of this event was not in her comfort zone, so she kept it light. "I'll probably end up talking to a brick wall on Fifth Street, asking it for friendship."

"You're gonna be just fine," Tyler said, pulling Aster in for a half hug.

"We're all proud of you," Sage said, standing there forgotten. "You're gonna knock 'em on their heads."

Tyler's eyes flicked to him. Her smile cooled, and she nodded conservatively. "Thank you, Sage. I appreciate that."

"Anytime."

Aster watched in mystification. These two were off. She wasn't sure what had transpired between them, but something had clobbered their easygoing best-friend-I-might-sleep-with mojo. Sage and Tyler were like peanut butter and jelly. The people standing in front of her were miles apart. It was sad in so many ways.

Sage shifted his weight, and then did it again. *Look at that.* He was uncomfortable, which Aster knew to be rare. He flicked his head at the bar. "Gonna grab a brew."

"Enjoy," Tyler said a little too distantly.

Once they were alone, she leaped for Tyler's hand, one of the few people she felt comfortable enough grabbing. "Everything okay? You two are freaking me out."

"We're gonna be fine. But sometimes people outgrow each other," Tyler said, but her inflection was flat, lifeless. "But I would never speak poorly of Sage, especially to his little sister. That's a promise."

Aster leaned forward, determined. Concern flared. "Maybe you should rethink that strategy, so I can knock him in his head if he's wronged you."

Tyler tossed an arm around Aster's shoulder and gave her a squeeze. "You've always been such a sweet person, Aster. You take care of him for me. Promise me?"

"I'll try. He's a lot. Drinks milk out of the carton."

A faint smile hit. "I'm not kidding about that suitcase. I'll make room."

"Neither am I," Aster said, admiring Tyler's ambition and the adventure she had ahead of her. She longed for one. The days were beginning to blend to an alarming degree. She wondered if life was just going to pass her by like a freight train if she didn't leap soon. "I guess this friend of yours will have a lot to live up to at the clinic. Does she know that?"

Tyler's eyes lit up. "Brynn. I forgot. You have to meet her. You, Aster Lavender, are one of my VIPs." She went up on tiptoe and motioned above the crowd, beckoning someone. Aster couldn't get a good look, but she cringed internally. She wasn't good at introductions. Even when she tried to be natural, easygoing, it was awkward city. She took a deep breath, determined to just get through this part. "Aster, meet Brynn Garrett, one of my very best friends from veterinary school."

Aster took a breath, but the air refused to exit her lungs. Standing next to Tyler was a woman about three inches shorter than Aster, with a really great smile. That wasn't all. She was also the most beautiful woman Aster had ever seen in her entire life. A little bit like a friendly looking movie star, but right here in person. Staring at her warmly. She wore dark jeans and a purple scoop-neck top under a really cool looking black jacket. Her blond hair was longish with those lazy curls that all those Instagram tutorials made look easy to achieve when they so weren't. Not that Aster had tried. Okay, she had. And failed. A lot. That didn't change how important this moment felt. She wasn't used to moments announcing their weight so overtly. This one was.

"Aster? So nice to meet you," the woman said and held out her hand. She had light eyes. Green? Yes. Big, beautiful green ones that actually sparkled. Aster always thought that description was a cliché. Not true. Eyes could sparkle. These did.

This would be the appropriate moment to extend her own hand and say hi like civilization called for. That's what humans did, but Aster fell short when it came to behaving like one of those, and instead wasted time on self-analysis, like now. Dammit. *Be present.* "Hi," she managed way too late for normalcy.

"Aster, you okay?" Tyler asked. "You look pale all of a sudden."

"What?" Aster blinked.

"How about some water?" Brynn offered, turning in the direction of the bar. So she was thoughtful, too.

"No. I'm really, really good." She looked around, attempting to play it off. "It just seems warm is all. Larry is probably still running the heat. March is tricky." Tyler's friend had finally dropped her offered hand altogether. Oh yeah, Aster had failed miserably. First impression with the new really pretty doctor was in the books, and it wasn't a good one. Totally normal, though. Just another day at the office of awkward.

"Sorry about the handshake that I missed."

Brynn smiled and raised an amused eyebrow. She knew how to sculpt them expertly. "No crime. It's still available."

Aster took the cue and extended her hand. Brynn reciprocated with a firm but not too firm handshake. Of course she was the perfect handshaker. Of course her hands were unbelievably soft. "So, you'll be the new vet in town. All set?" *Better. Breathe.*

"Yes! I just got a look at the office today. Beautiful space. Tyler showed me everything. I even got to meet the staff, who are super warm. Looks like a fantastic place to work."

"Why, thank you," Tyler said. "I designed the remodel myself." Prior to Tyler, the building had been an old insurance office and had sat empty for close to two years. With a loan from the bank, Tyler had snatched it up, knocked down some walls, put up others, until the place felt brand-new with top-of-the-line equipment, lime-green walls, and a friendly feel. She had a staff of three that kept the clinic and small kennel afloat. She ran a fantastic operation.

As they chatted, Aster doing her best to not be weird, she noticed a line of people forming to their right. She felt silly now for probably overstaying. "Hey, I think there are a few people who'd like to wish you well," Aster said. "I'll get out of here and let you say hi." She nodded to Brynn.

"It was nice meeting you, Ashton."

Oh no. Aster blinked, catching the mistake, but didn't have it in her to correct Brynn. She'd happily live as Ashton for the rest of her life rather than suffer through another inelegant moment with a woman who made her entire mouth go dry. "Nice meeting you, too." She added what she hoped was a confident smile. "I'm sure I'll see you around. Small town and all."

"Oh, you will," Tyler added. "Brynn's a sucker for baked goods. And it's Aster," she said quietly to Brynn who, if Aster wasn't mistaken, blushed at the mistake.

"I'm sorry about that—*Aster*. It's loud in here."

"It's okay. Not too many people get it right anyway." She had a million other names. *The youngest Lavender. The doughnut shop kid. Sage's little sister. You know, the quiet one with the bike.*

They didn't have a chance to finish the conversation because Tyler turned to attend to her well-wishers, whisked away by adoration and love. Aster ordered a beer from Larry and watched from the bar as their neighbors gathered around Brynn equally, fawning over her, gathering information, and passing it around. A new person in town was an exciting event, and unless she broke some sort of unspoken small-town rule, like forgetting to say hello on the sidewalk, she would remain their collective best friend for a time. Aster smiled into her glass because Brynn would be double the entertainment for them. Not only was Brynn a smart doctor, she was unlike anyone else in town. Gorgeous, eons more sophisticated, and from what Aster had seen, incredibly warm. The clamoring went on for the next half hour as the town of Homer's Bluff got to know her.

"Did you meet Brynn?" Aster asked as Sage drove her back home since it was so dark out. She'd pick up her bike the next day.

"Huh?" he asked, studying the road. His mind was clearly elsewhere.

"The woman stepping in for Tyler at the vet clinic."

"Oh yeah. She seemed nice, right? Blond." He was distracted. Troubled. He let most everything roll off his back like an unaffected duck. But the way his jaw moved as he drove told Aster that he wasn't okay at all. She didn't know what transpired between him and Tyler, but something had. "Yeah, I liked her. Good people. Blond."

"Right. You said that."

"Yeah."

They drove in silence for a bit. She looked over at her brother, her heart hurting for him. "She's coming back, you know. Tyler."

"Totally," he said energetically, faking nonchalance. "Just weird to imagine not seeing her face around every corner, even for a little while. That's all. She can be pesky as hell, but she's Tyler."

"She's Tyler," Aster echoed. Her brother was struggling, and it was clear she just had to let him lick his wounds for a bit. Hopefully, he'd come around. He was literally losing his best friend, and that would be hard on anyone.

Aster went home to the house she rented on Baker Street, just a handful of blocks from the center of town. She liked being close to things, not just for convenience purposes, but she was someone who liked to observe and take in as much activity as possible. There wasn't a lot going on in Homer's Bluff, so every little bit mattered. She could report that the laundromat had three broken washers the week before, which nearly incited a laundry riot. That was good stuff. She'd read her book on a nearby bench and watched the drama as she sipped her iced vanilla latte. Seven people vying for two washing machines over the course of a three-hour period was the *Days of Our Lives* she needed. The bench had served her well. She took a late lunch there most days after closing down Hole in One. Watching the world go by was her favorite pastime, and that was a little sad. Most notably the word *watching*. Because that's all she ever did. She was off to the side, removed from the action, and inconsequential.

As she brushed her teeth before bed, Aster regarded herself in the mirror, taking stock. Standing there in her gray shorts and black tank top, her eyes moved down her body. The dip of cleavage in her shirt led to medium-sized breasts and a waist that flared to hips. She touched her stomach, in decent shape from the time she spent on her bike. She could work on her abs, but then again, she'd rather spend the time in a science fiction book. Her dark hair was pulled into a standard ponytail. She liked that it was thick. A familiar freckle dotted the side of her right eye. She knew the face looking back at her intimately, but also not at all. There was a longing in her for something greater than what she had going, but cowardice held her back. For the life of her, Aster had no clue what to do about that. Pull a Tyler and head out for the big bad world without a net? Accept the spot at the culinary school in Boston, or find a way to make peace with all she had? Her shop, her customers, her family, and a handful of friends. She didn't lead a bad life, but she did feel invisible. Her social floundering in front of the new vet was par for a course she was tired of. Aster knew that somewhere in her, she had more to give. "Here I am," she said to her reflection. "Maybe I need to work on letting other people know it."

It wasn't such a bad idea.

❖

Well, well. Homer's Bluff Veterinary Clinic turned out to be the well-organized operation that Tyler had advertised. Brynn nearly wept with relief, shelving half her fears that she'd be walking into a monster of a task. The records were all easily accessible on the electronic network. The small staff of exactly three was made up of friendly, helpful people, and absolutely everything was labeled. That part was going to save her. She could kiss Tyler, quite frankly, all across her cute little face.

It was Monday, and after spending the weekend acquainting herself with the ins and outs of the practice, she was ready and appropriately nervous for her first official day in the clinic. This would be her professional introduction to Tyler's clients. Big shoes to fill.

"All right. Who's up first?" She checked the morning lineup. She had an eight a.m. with a poodle with a possible respiratory infection.

"Waiting for you in exam room A," she was told by Eve, the office manager. Brynn scrunched her shoulders. "This is a pretty big moment," Eve said, her eyes wide. "You can do this, Dr. Brynn. Know that we're all cheering for you. We will do so silently, however, to not disturb your exam."

"Thank you," Brynn said, picking up the printout of the chart as she headed in.

"Best wishes," Eve whispered loudly. "You are a hero. A towering giant. Go, go. Stomp the enemy."

"Eve, were you a cheerleader?" Brynn asked, pausing with the door handle in her hand.

Eve blinked, mystified. "How did you know?"

"Lucky guess." She headed into exam A, brightening. "Mr. Dobbs?" she asked as she opened the door.

"Hey there," a man about forty said, standing and straightening when she entered. He had short brown hair and a nice enough smile. He also sucked his stomach in, which had her smothering a smile. "You can call me Ray. Ray Dobbs. I work at the auto body shop up the road if you ever need any dents banged out of your car. You just give me a call. Yes, sir." He stood in that gentlemanly way.

She nodded. "Ray it is, and I will certainly remember that offer. And this is Sprinkles?"

He glanced at the little white dog walking in circles around his feet, clearly more interested in his shoelaces than anything else going on. "Yeah, yeah. That's Sprinkles, all right." His gaze returned to hers. He smiled big and held it. Huh. Interesting. Extra friendly fellow.

"And what made you bring Sprinkles in today?" Brynn knew full well he'd reported to the staff that the dog had been coughing, but she liked to hear the firsthand account from the patient's owner. She often picked up more specific details that way, and the little things mattered. They helped create the bigger picture and flag potential issues.

"She has a cough." Ray left it there, preferring instead to gaze at her with a big dopey smile again.

"Got it. Poor thing." She knelt and gave Sprinkles a scratch behind the ears. "When did that start and how frequently? Tell me the whole story." She also kept an ear out, should Sprinkles give a demonstration. Most notably, Brynn wanted to hear if she was dealing with a wet or dry cough, which could make a difference in treatment.

"I heard her cough yesterday morning." He seemed distracted by her questions, as if his focus was needed elsewhere. More specifically, on Brynn's face. He puffed out his chest like an afterthought. He now looked like one of those manly statues in front of an old-fashioned hardware store. What in the world was happening?

"And it's continued since?" He didn't answer. Confusion on his face. "The cough."

"No. Just that one time, but I thought I should definitely have it checked out by you. And say hi."

"Oh." She paused and pressed the chart to her chest. "Is it possible Sprinkles just needed to clear her airway, or maybe encountered some dust? It's not sounding like a chronic cough from your description."

He made a big show of relaxing, as if the weight had been lifted off his shoulders magically. "You're really good at this, Doc. And you know what? I bet that's what happened. Since there's been no more coughing after that time. I feel a million times better now that I've talked with you."

"Right. Well, I'm so glad." Brynn squinted, a little confused. "But since you're here anyway, why don't we do a brief exam and make sure Sprinkles is doing well. Give her a little checkup just to be sure."

Brynn scooped up the cutie and placed her on the flat surface of the exam table. Ray immediately countered around to the other side, not wanting to miss a moment. She checked her mouth, her eyes, her ears, and did a quick assessment of her weight and vitals from the chart. All looked perfectly normal and healthy. Sprinkles was in fine shape. "She's looking great," Brynn reported. "We should maybe look into a teeth cleaning in the next year."

"What about dinner?" Ray asked.

"Well, most dogs like to eat around the same time each day. Splitting her food into two meals a day can help with metabolism. She's at a healthy weight and her coat looks great, so I'm not concerned about diet. Whatever you're feeding her seems to be working." Brynn took a moment to build rapport with the dog, offering a few well-placed pets and accepting the wag and wiggle she got in return. Cute baby. Happy, too.

"Right. I'm not really sure. She's actually my mom's dog. What about having dinner with *me*? I was thinking burgers. Beer. We can shoot the breeze. I have a tractor. Not sure if you knew that. It's pretty big. I can show you."

"I did not know that." Brynn took a moment to follow the thread of the conversation until it dawned on her. Ray Dobbs, fake father to Sprinkles, had borrowed a dog to ask her out. "You are so thoughtful to invite me for beer and tractor viewing, truly. But I'm dedicating my free time to settling in. Getting the lay of the land."

"Understood. Maybe once you've had time to do that. I could give you a ride on the tractor. It's real red." He said it like a soap opera actor, as if the color would turn her the hell on. How interesting the morning was turning out to be.

"Maybe. You never know. It's nice to have friends, right?" She nodded, hoping he understood the thesis statement, but decided to make it a bit more clear. "I'm not really looking for more than that, though. I'm just here for a short time and all. Six months."

"Yeah, I hear you." He picked up Sprinkles. "You might change your mind. It's been known to happen when women spend time with me."

Oh? Was Ray Dobbs a sought-after fella? She tried not to cringe visibly at his statement, feeling that he meant well but was woefully overconfident. Should she tell him the last time she'd dated someone of the opposite sex she'd been fifteen and the results had been disastrous? Nah. She wasn't even sure it would deter him.

"You let me know if Sprinkles has any more issues. Okay?"

"You got it. I'll tell Mom."

Brynn gave her head a shake, marveling at the entire appointment. Had he really just used his mom's healthy dog to get him through the door? Who did that? She couldn't wait to tell Tyler all about it.

❖

It was a good thing she did wait. Because there was so much more to come.

The next three days were remarkably similar. Brynn, in mystification, saw one healthy pet after another while listening to overtures from three more single men, accepting baked goods from women who dropped by, not only to welcome her to town, but to meticulously take down her story, probably for passing around to their friends. Two older women who came in together with an equally elderly turtle just wanted to show him off and hear who Brynn's parents were and where they lived. She smiled and obliged, but omitted the part about not having seen her father since she was small and that she and her mother didn't talk much either. Brynn was apparently a hot topic, and people were lining up to learn every little detail they could. Where were the sick pets when you needed them?

She decided to take a walk on her lunch hour one day, her second week on the job, hoping to clear her head and get to see a little bit more of Homer's Bluff up close. She'd yet to truly explore all it had to offer. She decided to start in the center of town where there were three very cool clothing shops in a row that, refreshingly, seemed to all be friends with each other. When she asked one of the shop owners about zip up hoodies, since the weather still had one foot in winter and one in spring, the owner, Tessa, happily referred her to the shop two doors down.

"I will tell you what, Bella Beautiful has a great selection of zip ups. Quality stuff, too. Tell Heather I said hello. We need to grab breakfast soon. I'm a big fan of country sausage. She likes omelets."

"I will do that. I like omelets, too." That seemed to delight Tessa. "Oh, and Doctor…?"

"Garrett. But you can call me Brynn. In fact, please do."

"Dr. Brynn, you should pop in to Tammy's shop, too. Don't want her to feel left out. Next door. She's got the store between Heather and me. Tammy owns Spaghetti Straps, and it's got the cutest skirts and tops. Not just for summer, either. I know the name of the shop sounds like it's just a mess of summer clothes." She shook her head as if it was the most unfortunate turn of events. "We all have noticed that part and just don't say anything, because who wears spaghetti straps in the winter? But really, it's got year 'round clothing. I promise." She punctuated her speech with about eight follow-up head nods.

Brynn's brain buzzed with amusement as she sorted through the chaos. "I will definitely visit Spaghetti Straps as well as Bella Beautiful. What's the name of your store again?" She looked around for a reminder.

"Yay Clothes!"

Brynn took a moment to decipher if Tessa was cheering on her merchandise or offering the name of her shop. She went with the latter. "Nice! Great name. Very direct."

"Festive, too, right?" Tessa exclaimed, her eyes dancing.

"Really cheerful." Brynn had to give her kudos on that. "I'll definitely be back to Yay Clothes! as well."

"You've just made my day, Dr. Brynn. I need to bring my goldendoodle in for an appointment. Jimmy John."

"Oh yeah? What's wrong with Jimmy John?"

"Nothing really, but you need to see him. Such a gorgeous curly coat."

Brynn swallowed a smile, accepting the healthy pet visit as the culture of the entire town. "I look forward to it."

Brynn continued her perusal of the businesses in the area. She didn't have another appointment until after two, giving her time to enjoy the day. A quaint café. A coffee house. Ice cream shop. Diner. Dry cleaners. Convenience store. Farm supply. Three of those, actually. They had it all. Curvy streetlamps stood at the corner of every block, and every third or fourth business had a bench out front. At the end of the row of shops, Brynn recognized the person sitting on one. She'd met a lot of people at Tyler's going away party, and most of them blended together. Not this one.

"Hey there," she said pausing at the bench. "Aster, isn't it?"

The young woman sitting on the bench had her nose in a book. At the sound of her name she looked up and blinked as if being ripped from the world of the book and thrust into the real one. "Right. Hi. That's me." She sat up tall as Brynn approached, rolled her lips in, and then smiled. She was really very pretty. Younger than Brynn. Maybe midtwenties. Soft brown eyes that matched her dark hair that fell past her shoulders. Full lips. A sweet smile.

Brynn touched her chest. "Brynn. Tyler's friend."

Aster brightened. "I remember. I'm Sage's sister. Most people remember him more."

It was possible new people made Aster nervous. She seemed a touch uneasy, similar to their encounter at Larry's. Tyler spoke highly of her, though, and Tyler was a great judge.

"Nice day for an outside read."

Aster looked around as if just noticing the sunny day. She'd really been deep into that story. "You're right. Yeah. I, uh, sit out here a lot. You can watch the whole world go by, and well, no one bothers you." Her eyes widened. "*You're* not bothering me. I definitely didn't mean that." Her cheeks went rosy, flamed. "It's nice that you said hi."

To prove that she hadn't taken the comment poorly, Brynn took a seat, doubling down. "In that case." Aster nodded, then looked at her book and back at Brynn, seemingly torn on whether to read or make small talk. Brynn decided to help. "I had nine appointments at the clinic today, and I'm pretty sure only three of them were for the pets."

"Oh." Aster closed her book entirely, following Brynn's cue. "I would say I'm surprised, but when someone new comes to town, everyone clamors to get a good look, learn what they can, see how they might factor into the grand scheme of the town."

"That was my working theory. I think you've just confirmed it."

"Are you going to cause a scandal or just lend carrots to those in need? That's their question."

Brynn nodded, thoughtful. "Carrots, huh? Would not have guessed that."

"It was the first example that popped into my head." Aster squinted. "People like carrots, right?"

"I suppose that's true." Brynn paused, reflecting on Aster's earlier comment. "There's a grand scheme to the town?"

"No, but people like to pretend there is. Small towns tend to be romanticized."

Interesting take. "From within?"

Aster sat taller. She clearly had opinions. "Big time."

They paused a moment as a car pulled to a stop in front of Mailbox Mania. A woman carrying an armful of packages stopped her progress on the sidewalk as it did. An older gentleman leapt from the car and took the packages from her and carried them into the store. Brynn gestured with her chin. "I don't know. That was a pretty unique gesture. You wouldn't see that happen where I'm from in Chicago."

"Well, there's probably a little bit more anonymity in a big city." Aster mimicked the chin gesture. "See the guy that took the packages? That's Hank Devers. The woman he was helping is Beverly Martin. He's married to her sister, Claire, but is secretly in love with Beverly. Stares at her across every room he's in. She loves him back, too, but refuses to hurt Claire, who—if I'm being honest—isn't the nicest human alive. But they care enough to keep their feelings restrained." Aster sat back. "So it's down to carrying boxes."

Brynn balked. "Wow. And here I thought this was just some nice stranger helping another stranger with her packages."

"That's the thing. Nobody is a stranger here, which is what you got a little taste of today. They're bringing you into the fold. Welcome to Homer's Bluff, where your business is waved in front of your house like a flag."

"That's a colorful description."

"It's also accurate."

"Huh." She looked over at Aster just as the breeze lifted her brown hair and set it gently on her shoulders. Serene. Maybe it was the topic, or because they sat facing the same direction rather than each other, but Aster seemed to relax the more they talked. There was something nonthreatening about her presence that Brynn appreciated. "I could be wrong, but I'm not sure you like it here, Aster."

"Sorry." She rolled her lips in. "I didn't mean to give off that impression. Especially when you just got here." She studied the bench, running a thumb across a splintered piece of the wood. "I do wonder about other places, though. I've never lived anywhere else. You're from Chicago, right?"

"I am."

She took a breath, her interest hooked. "What's it like?"

"Busy. Everyone has somewhere to be and quickly. Crowds are pretty common especially at the beginning and ending of business. Downtown, where I worked, you could find yourself shoulder to shoulder on the sidewalk, shuffling along like a group of sardines. People don't take a lot of time with each other. Transactional. But..." She took a moment to find her words. "It always feels like something important is happening in a big city. There's a hum in the air that comes with people collectively living their lives and making important things happen. I really like that about city life. I feel like I'm selling it short."

"No," Aster said. "You're not. You paint a striking and vivid picture. I've thought about Boston. Moving there." She immediately looked down at her hands, and Brynn understood that this was a confession.

"You have?"

Aster seemed a little embarrassed, like the information had flown from her lips without permission. She gathered herself and pressed on, a little quieter now. "I've thought of going to culinary school there." She took a breath.

"That's fantastic. You should do it."

She looked up and smiled. Brynn's encouragement had landed. "Maybe."

It seemed a little bit like the topic was a stressful one, so Brynn pivoted and tried to steal a peek at the cover of Aster's book. "Can I ask what you're reading?"

"Oh. No. I can't say." She held the book tight to her chest.

Brynn scoffed through her laughter at such a blatant rejection. "Why not? Top secret mission?"

"Yes," Aster deadpanned. "That's exactly the case. I'm highly important—if you couldn't tell from my midday bench sitting in the middle of a sleepy town."

Endearing. Different. This woman was something. "Well, now I know. Better let you get back to it." She stood. "Take care, Aster. Hey, what's your last name again?"

"Lavender."

"Right. I remember now." She paused, letting the *Aster Lavender* combination roll around. "What a great name. Is there a story there?"

"Oh yes."

Brynn laughed again because Aster made no move to tell it. "Let me guess. If you tell me, you'll have to kill me."

"Hardly. Maybe one day."

"You'll kill me?" Brynn feigned surprise. Aster's eyes went wide, and Brynn laughed harder. Oh, this was fun. *Aster* was.

"No. I'm not the murdering type. Please don't put that out there. My mother will have me on the phone in under an hour."

"Okay, but only because you asked."

"I meant maybe one day for the story. Not the homicide."

"Well, now you're dangling it like a carrot, which we've established most people around here like and want to borrow." Brynn looked forward to more chats with Aster Lavender, woman of mystery. "I'll have to find you on this bench again sometime."

"Well, now that you know the location of my favorite bench, how can I, you know...Damn. I forgot the word." There was that blush again.

"Escape?"

She exhaled. "Evade."

"Well, you can't. You owe me a story now, Aster Lavender. As you were." As she walked away, she had a much more energetic spring in her step and a small smile upon her lips. It was one of the more distinctive conversations she'd had since coming to town, but also really enjoyable. What a character. When she found herself thinking back on the exchange hours later, she wondered if she might have herself a new friend.

Time would tell...

CHAPTER TWO

Even though the family business hadn't been for her, Aster couldn't deny the welcoming effects of The Lavender House. The soft aromas of the many lavender and vanilla products could easily have overwhelmed, but didn't. They said a gentle hello, enveloping the visitor in a palatable swirl of relaxing sensations. Somehow, her sisters, who dually managed the store, had made sure of that with product placement and the strategic layout. The two-story rustic log house was all exposed beams and dark woods, perfect for showcasing the equally natural lavender wares, from infused scarves to homemade soaps. The room was full, packed to the brim with all sorts of products to explore. The fact that the store was located just yards from the actual lavender farm was a huge selling bonus and got folks in the mood to fork over their cash even at premium prices. And they were premium. Authenticity sold well.

Aster was feeling more energetic than usual when she arrived at the store that day. She wasn't sure why. Except maybe she was, and it was the silliest reason. Brynn Garrett and the conversation they'd had on the bench earlier that week had really affected her. Not in any crazy sense, but kinda like when you're going about your day and remember you're in the middle of a really good book and have it at home waiting for you to finish. That's what Brynn's arrival in town felt like to Aster, like there was something to look forward to now. They might never have another one-on-one conversation like the other day, and that would be okay.

But they might.

And she could admit to herself that it was a welcome prospect, a new friend to jazz up her less than exciting daily slog. She smiled at the memory of their back-and-forth. Even the embarrassing parts. Her shoulders had gone a little swirly when Brynn first sat down on the bench next to her. She'd lacked the ability to control them and hadn't known that was possible.

"How does one person give another swirly shoulders?" she asked, feeling naive, as she lingered behind the cash register while her sister replaced the receipt roll.

Marigold squinted. "I've never heard of it. Swirly?"

"Swirly," Aster said. "Affirmative."

"Like a dance move?" Her sister kicked her hip against the counter and rolled her shoulders around with flair.

"Except you don't actually move them. They just feel swirly."

Marigold shook her head. "I've not had swirly shoulders. I want to now. God."

"Naturally." Her volume took a dip. "It's not awful. A little foreign maybe."

A pause. Marigold eased a strand of curly blond hair behind her ear. Aster had always been a fan of that honey-gold color, not to mention the versatility that came with those curls, and her sister didn't waste the potential. She knew all the best hairstyles and products like some sort of divine wisdom had been imparted to her from the heavens. "Who's giving you the shoulders?" Marigold asked. "This is getting good."

"Hmmm?" Aster stalled and applied the pale pink gloss that kept her lips hydrated. While she didn't pull a lot of attention on average, she had been told she had gorgeous lips, a compliment she'd tucked away. "No one. I'm just talking."

Marigold turned to her fully. "Are not. You're the only kid sister I have, so I need you to be more forthcoming. How am I supposed to counsel you without context?"

Aster looked around, gawking at imaginary people to showcase her indignation. "Who says I need counseling?"

"Oh, but you do," Violet said, strolling up to the counter, back from her break. She turned to Marigold. "Do you remember when she used to eat peanut butter from the jar with a spoon?"

Marigold nodded. "Oh yes. It still hurts that we let it come to that."

"Hyperbole. Plus, it was quicker that way," Aster offered. "And I was six. And I might still do it."

"I had a feeling," Marigold said, patting her head with sympathy.

Aster ducked out of the pat. "All right. That's enough of that. Give me the shea butter Mom promised, so I can flee this judgment laden zone."

"You can't leave," Violet said, enveloping her in a warm hug. "We love you too much."

"We do and we must shower you with affection until you agree to stay," Marigold said, joining the hug, smothering Aster further as she squirmed to free herself of her sisters' affection. They gave her a hard time regularly but made their love known just as often. A nearby shopper raised an eyebrow, eying the overhugging, probably wondering if the young woman in the middle of the forced hug huddle required assistance. She made sure to grin and assuage the man's concern. He went back to sniffing soap.

"Okay, okay. I'll hang out for a minute if you'll halt the lovefest."

"I agree to the terms," Violet said, kissing Aster's head and releasing her. "But you're really cute. Just look at you."

Marigold also let go. "I'll eat your face, though. Postponed. But it might happen. So don't get comfortable."

"I'm good and warned," Aster said, shoving her hands in her pockets.

Marigold took a minute and tapped her chin, remembering her detective work was unfinished. She tossed Violet a look. "I think Aster's met someone online."

"A girlfriend?" Violet said, delighted, her eyes wide and celebratory. "Bring her over immediately. You've never brought a girl home before. Oh! Even better, we can double with Tad."

"Can't. She doesn't exist." Aster liked having a little secret. The source of her swirly shoulders was strictly her knowledge, and she planned to keep it that way. Plus, she and Brynn weren't even close to romantic.

"So you say," Marigold said in a singsongy voice as she rang up the soap sniffer. "That will be thirty-seven dollars and fifty-six cents."

"For three bars of soap?" the man asked, brow furrowed.

"Fresh lavender soap," Marigold reminded him, pointing behind her. "Just off the farm over there."

He huffed and finally thrust forth two twenties as if parting with members of his family. He clearly wanted that soap, and who could blame him? Heavenly stuff.

When their customer took his leave, Violet frowned. "I'm worried for you, Aster."

"Me? Why?" Aster asked.

"Because you keep to yourself too much. You sell your doughnuts until lunchtime. You read. You ride your bike. What else?"

Ouch. "I never claimed to be riveting."

"Oh, leave her alone," Marigold said. "Aster is Aster. She likes things that way."

Aster slung her arm around Marigold's shoulders and stared at Violet. "I'm a boring lone ranger and just fine with it." She wasn't, but she was trying to improve her circumstances quietly.

"Speaking of alone, Sage is walking around like a lost puppy," Violet said with a wince. "He misses Tyler. I saw him aimlessly riding the tractor in circles yesterday. Lost in his thoughts."

Marigold rubbed her hands together. "I have a plan for that. Knock him back into the real world."

"What would that be?" Aster asked.

"The new vet. Have you seen her? Gorgeous. Dr. Brynn Garrett." Marigold wiggled her fingers as if casting a spell. "You guys, she's the perfect distraction, and just what Sage needs. I plan to set them up. Sexy, blond, smart, and—from what I hear—single. Totally put together, too. I'd kill for her clothes."

Aster blinked as Marigold watched her expectantly. "Oh, have I, you mean? Met her. Me, specifically."

"You are the person I'm staring straight at with love."

She nodded, playing it cool and probably failing miserably. Brynn did have great fashion sense. "Yeah. I met her. She was at the going away party, I think. And I saw her in town for a minute." She made it all seem totally inconsequential when it felt like anything but. Deflation time. Every woman fell for Sage, and Brynn would likely be no different. But honestly, she'd be okay with Marigold setting the two up. Yes, it felt a little weird. But maybe it would save Brynn from the onslaught of overtures, and Sage from his own pensive tractor festival. As practical as that all sounded, it also didn't feel great. Maybe because she'd always imagined Sage would end up with Tyler one day. She still hoped for that but shook off the discomfort. That kind of thing wasn't her call.

"What do you think? Might they hit it off?" Marigold asked the room.

"I think so," Violet said. "I mean, if you can get Sage to focus on something other than the Chiefs at playoff time." Her brother's favorite pastimes included sports, watching sports, hanging out with his dog, hanging out with his boys, and driving the tractor all over the farm in his favorite blue ball cap, now threadbare. He pulled hard hours and soaked up the attention that women paid him, while rarely putting forth the effort he should. It was unfair and something he needed to grow out of. Good thing she had a soft spot for him.

"Maybe Dr. Brynn Garrett with her gorgeous blond hair could be the one to make it happen."

Marigold had forgotten to include her green eyes that weren't even a normal shade. They were a deep green with little gold flecks that were more noticeable when the sunlight caught them just right. "I look forward to seeing if your magic plan works. But maybe check with Tyler first."

Violet leaned against the counter. "Did you forget the time Marigold organized her entire junior class into walking out of school at eleven a.m. because they'd discontinued pizza on Fridays in the cafeteria?"

"How could I forget?" Aster asked. "In school, I was always known as the little sister of the pizza vigilante. Every teacher kept an eye out for any signs of a marinara-laced overthrow. Couldn't shake the shadow."

"My point exactly. She'll make it happen," Violet said with an arch of her dark brown eyebrow.

"I love the confidence," Marigold said. "And hopefully Brynn will love Sage. All with Tyler's blessing, of course. I'll play this right. No one's toes shall be stepped on." She softened. "Even their names sound amazing together. Sage and Brynn Lavender."

Aster exhaled, feeling less energetic than she had when she'd walked in. Must have been her long morning catching up with her. Surely nothing else. "Shea butter?"

Marigold glanced around. "Wherefore art thou, shea butter?"

"That actually doesn't mean what you think it means," Aster said gently.

Marigold pointed at her. "Don't be so smart all the time. It makes the rest of us look mundane."

"You could never be that, MG. Shea butter is over here," Violet said, snatching up a box and placing it in Aster's arms. "It's a great batch. You're gonna love it. Tell all your friends."

"I will inform the throngs. Bye. Sell lots of stuff."

"Same to you and the fancy doughnuts," Violet said, giving her hair an affectionate ruffle. Why did they all do that? Underneath, Aster understood that she was still that little kid trailing after them all in many ways, forever the kid of the group. "Bring me one of those bacon ones someday? The ones that wiggle."

"Wigglies. On it. You're getting a dozen hot ones soon. Only because you supply me with free skin care products," Aster said with a gentle lift of the box. "Say hi to Tad for me. Kiss his lips off. Isn't that what the kids say?"

"I'm a lady," Violet said with a knowing smile. Yeah, she was sucking face with that guy, all right, and Aster was likely to have a new brother-in-law before too long. A rich one.

"Whatever you say."

"I heard you were making out in the back of his golf cart after hours," Marigold said coyly.

"I always did enjoy his swing." Violet dabbed the corners of her mouth.

"I can't take the girl talk," Aster said. "I can't. Must leave the premises now."

"Maybe one day it will be about you," Marigold called after her.

Aster held up a hand as she exited, refusing to look back. "Send me a memo if we ever get there."

She rode her bike back to her house, a comfortable two-bedroom one-story that she'd made her own. Her place was tucked away on Baker Street, lazy enough that there was a decent amount of space between her and her neighbors but close enough to dodge recluse status. Six houses in a circle, all with beautiful live oak trees lining the walks. She waved each afternoon to Mr. Anderson across the street. Lena and Rick Jacoby from three doors down brought her cookies at Christmas and pie for Thanksgiving. She'd been generous with her doughnuts right back. A dozen for this birthday or for that holiday.

The street was a good one to live on as far as streets went. People were friendly but not intrusive.

As for Aster, she didn't have people over much. But she still kept the place neat and tidy. The fifteen hundred and eighty square foot house was mostly white, and that worked for her aesthetic. She preferred things clean and simple and straightforward. She wasn't the best at traditional decorating, always leaning toward the more in-your-face motifs like she'd given Hole in One, black and white and full of loud art. But she knew how to use available resources and found a few photos online of professionally decorated homes she liked and did her best to duplicate them, down to the small details, because those seemed to matter most. Some blue pillows on her cream-colored sofa. A framed and matted photo of the waves crashing onto the shore, an image she'd grown to love. Curtains that swooped and grabbed accents of the blue in their diamond pattern. The swooping was very popular these days, so she made sure hers did.

Then there was her overused stainless-steel fridge. It was odd to garner so much happiness from an appliance, but she did. Aster regarded her fridge as an extension of her family. It had been one of her few splurges when business at Hole in One really started to take off. She had room for fresh fruits and vegetables, of which you could purchase a lot in this town, not to mention all sorts of ingredients that kept her experimenting with creative recipes she found online. Cooking was a favorite pastime of hers. Almost as much fun as creating the perfect doughnut. In fact, with the whole night stretched out in front of her, Aster thought she might put on a little classical piano music and make a nice chicken cordon bleu. Practice her technique. As she pulled the ingredients from her fridge, there was a knock on her door. She frowned. *Interesting.* It wasn't a holiday.

She glanced down at her clothing, half of which she'd shed when she'd arrived home, leaving her barefoot in faded jeans and a black tank top. Good enough for a neighbor chat. Maybe Mr. Anderson needed someone to pick up his mail.

She opened the door, small smile in place because that was friendly. But it wasn't Mr. Anderson at all. In a plot twist, she found herself standing in front of Brynn Garrett, who looked just as surprised to see Aster looking back at her.

"Hi. Aster. Was not expecting you. Wow."

"Yeah, hi." She glanced behind Brynn for some sort of explanation. Had someone brought her here? Her brother? Mr. Anderson and his mail? Not that either would make much sense.

"Well. I *was* stopping by to say hello and introduce myself. But I think I can throw that out the window now."

Aster took a beat, still lost. "We've already met."

Brynn laughed. "I know. We have. But I didn't realize you lived here. Wait. Do you really live here?" Brynn took a step back and looked up at the house. She had one strand of hair behind her ear and looked really pretty.

"I do."

"That's crazy." She hooked her thumb. "I'm renting the place next door."

"No you're not." She'd blurted it, too. It wasn't the warmly stated *Welcome to the neighborhood* that should have come out of her mouth, but the idea of Brynn turning up as her actual next-door neighbor wasn't something she could absorb fully.

"I am. Do you want to see the rental agreement?"

"No." She should have said more. She'd work on it. Talking to Brynn was a new skill she'd yet to master, though she was making progress. But it made sense. That Brad guy who always kept to himself had moved out months ago, and the house had been sitting vacant. She'd somehow missed Brynn's move in. Though she wouldn't have come with much for a temporary stay.

Brynn offered her a half smile. It was a thing she did where one side of her mouth pulled up, and a hint of a dimple showed on her right cheek. Just a hint. One couldn't call it a full dimple. She liked it. A really good look.

"You're a funny girl, Aster."

Aster shifted from her left foot to her right. "That's me. Everyone says so. My comedy is famous across town." She shook her head adamantly to let Brynn know that wasn't the case at all. She had a feeling it hadn't been necessary.

"Well, I guess you're *my* new very funny neighbor."

"You're not staying at Tyler's house? I figured this was one of those friend swaps like in the movies. You trade lives for a few months and rediscover yourselves by the end of your respective journeys."

"You'd think. But Tyler's place will be undergoing heavy termite treatment while she's away. The little guys have become a problem, and she's taking advantage of the empty-house time."

"Well, that ruins the whole premise of the movie," Aster said seriously.

"Unfortunate, too." Brynn straightened. "So, what are the Baker Street rules? I want to be an upstanding citizen. All carrots are up for grabs, obviously."

Aster rocked back on her heels. "We meet on Tuesdays and argue politics."

"Oh no."

"Oh yes. Saturdays are decorate-your-mailbox day, and on the fifth Sunday of the month, we dance naked at midnight."

Brynn didn't hesitate. "I can meet those terms."

"What about your pets? Friendly?" Aster asked.

"I have no pets."

"Not possible." That didn't seem right. "You're a vet. You have pets. Surely. It's a rule."

Brynn pointed at her. "I get why you'd think that. I am an animal lover. Don't get me wrong, but I was a stepmom to my dog, and when the relationship broke up, he went back with my ex. A shepherd. Really sweet guy."

"Well, that sucks. I'm sorry."

"More than you know. But I'm sure another kind and furry soul will make their way into my life. When it's right. Probably sooner rather than later."

"Well, don't go stealing any from your clients." Wait. Was that okay to say? She'd been shooting the breeze, loosening up when she went and said something probably awkward. She closed her eyes, and braced for the humiliation that arrived on schedule. "I was trying to kid with you, but I'm not the best at it in spite of how much I practice. I know you surely behave with a level of professionalism at work that's beyond admirable. Ignore me."

"I will not," Brynn said. "Because of your advice some adorable dachshund will avoid wiener snatching."

Oh, that just scored points. So did the way Brynn's whole face lit up when she laughed. There were those dancing eyes again, and she had the softest looking skin, probably without having to use lavender shea butter. It was currently wet, however, which was not ideal. How had Aster missed that? "Oh, wow. We're standing here talking, and you're being rained on."

"I know. Do you mind if I just…" Brynn hopped beneath the small covering over Aster's front step which left them sheltering in the same small space. This was rude, and Aster knew better.

"No. Come in. Come in. My mother would kill me."

"Are you sure? You might be busy or have somewhere to be."

"Neither happens to be true. I'm woefully, uh, free. Just follow… yeah."

Brynn Garrett was in her house. Not only was it rare that she had anyone over other than her family and occasionally Tori, but the fact that it was the woman who made her mouth go dry was exponential news. Her hands were now tingling and, yep, shaking a little, too. A lot to keep track of. What next? She focused on hostess duties instead of her biological reaction. "Would you like something to drink?"

"No, thank you. I won't stay. I just wanted to say hi and meet the person I'd be living next to for the next few months. I feel like this is one of those small town movies where I should have known it would be someone I already knew."

"Clichés tend to be based on at least some element of truth. We're all on top of each other in this few mile stretch. That part's true." She'd seen those TV movies, the ones where the town was cute and adorable and seemed to dote on Christmastime for some reason. She'd stopped watching them because of the myth they perpetuated.

"Well. It's a very foreign happenstance in my world. It's actually really nice." Brynn tapped the counter. "And now that I've stolen a glimpse of your house, my ultimate mission, I will dash away victorious." She raised her shoulders. "I'm a naturally curious person."

Aster looked around, trying to see her place through someone like Brynn's eyes and failing. She didn't have a clue what it was like to be Brynn or what kind of design aesthetic she might find appealing. "Basic stuff."

"I wouldn't say that at all. You have a great sense of space and composition."

"I do? I like to draw. That helps."

"I can tell. You've made such great use of that corner over there, for one." Brynn walked in that direction. "The height of the plant pulls up the eye, but the corner shelf adds texture and functionality." Brynn swiveled back. "Speaking of, you never told me what book you were reading. We're neighbors. I'm owed."

Aster crossed her arms and laughed. "Fair. It's called *The Sixth Season of a Saturnite*. A sci-fi meets historical fiction. I'm into that kind of thing. A space nerd."

"Wow. Very cool. I'm always impressed at how involved those narratives are. But I've only read a few."

"I wouldn't have guessed you'd read any. Really?"

Brynn eyed her with those big expressive eyes. "I think you just tried to sum me up and failed."

"I did." She grinned. Held up three fingers. "Won't happen again."

"Good. I plan to keep the world guessing."

Brynn seemed to mean it. On a list of traits, Aster was able to fill in a few for Brynn already. She was fun, for sure. But kind also topped the list, and that made her even more pretty. *Oh.* Aster swallowed the realization that she had a little crush on Brynn. Nothing she couldn't handle. Nothing that required action. It was just that she couldn't remember the last time that had happened to her outside of a random celebrity. She'd misdiagnosed it as the excitement of a new friend at first, someone who really knew how to make an impression. But when that person gave you swirly shoulders and tingling palms and stripped you of your ability to think through sentences in your own living room, but also put you right at ease and made you laugh, it probably meant more was afoot.

"Well, anything you need, you know, carrots, I'm just a text away," Aster said.

"Right." A pause. Brynn was waiting for something. "Except I'd need your number."

She was a weirdo on steroids. "That might help."

Brynn handed over her phone, and Aster typed in her number. "So, what do you do? For work."

"Oh. I own a doughnut shop. Not far from the clinic, actually. About three blocks, on the outskirts."

"What? Doughnuts?" Her whole face lit up. "I happen to adore a good doughnut. Why haven't I seen this place?"

"We're tucked away, but if you follow Homer's Bluff, the street not the town, all the way past the bank, you'll see us a little ways down on the left."

"Do you get a lot of traction out there?"

"We do really well. Plus, I'm not a center of town kind of business."

Brynn smiled. "No. You wouldn't be. That's a compliment." She looked around as if remembering herself. But from what? "I guess I should get outta here and let your life resume as scheduled." She pointed through the wall to the left. "I'll just be next door."

"And I'll be in here."

"Neighbors."

"That's us."

They shared a smile and Aster's cheeks went hot. She resisted the urge to cover them with her hands. Shoved 'em into her pockets instead. Brynn's smile faltered and then rebounded. "Okay, um, I'm off." And she was. Like a mother who'd just remembered she'd left a toddler alone with the peanut butter, she was through the door and on her way.

"My neighbor," Aster said to the empty room, as her brain tried to absorb this new dynamic. She'd be running into Brynn a lot more than she'd originally expected. She'd be literally feet away. This was certainly going to liven things up. Aster just couldn't decide if it would be for good or to her own personal detriment. Either way, it wouldn't be boring. *Be careful what you wish for*. Because they just might move in next door.

❖

Okay, what was that?

Brynn closed the front door and leaned back against it, her eyes finding the tan ceiling and holding on, an anchor. There she'd been, minding her own business, when a harmless conversation had shifted on her in the strangest way. Somewhere between science fiction and Aster's doughnut shop, Brynn took acute notice of the way her new neighbor looked in a black tank top. Most notably, the way the fabric followed and clung to the curves of her breasts. Not to mention her fantastic and perfectly toned arms. Were those genetic or from the gym? Because good God. Really? Who knew Aster had such an amazing body, and why was she allowing herself to remember every detail she'd glimpsed of it? Water. That would help.

Also, also, also, where was this all coming from exactly? She stalked to her sink, knowing what had to be the answer. She'd gone without sex for far too long, and now she was lusting after innocents who just wanted to sell doughnuts and hang out in their homes unbothered by lustful new neighbors.

But she wasn't actually interested in Aster Lavender. No. Not in a romantic sense, anyway.

Aster was nice enough and clearly very smart. Okay, really pretty too with full, heart-shaped lips. But she wasn't at all the type Brynn went for. The opposite. She was drawn to life of the party types. Loud, talkative, gregarious. The kind of person who took Brynn's hand and dragged her onto the dance floor in spite of her protests, sharing a little bit of her tenacity and flair. Aster, cute as she was with her sci-fi novels and dark wit, was not really what Brynn was pulled to.

This was clearly a sign that her libido was not dead, however. That was something to celebrate. It had just taken a little hiatus after an unforeseen breakup that had tortured her heart for far too long.

Her phone rang, saving her from her lust. That better not be Tiffany, she thought to herself, seeing her ex's face in her mind. A pang of sadness slashed at her. She envisioned the eyes that used to do her in, bright blue and bursting with life. "Uh-uh," she said out loud and took a step back as if the physical distance would tame her wayward nostalgia. She looked down at her phone in relief. Tyler.

"If it isn't the new Chicagoan."

"City mouse reporting for a check-in," Tyler said.

Brynn laughed. "Country mouse is happy you did. How's Chi-Town?"

"You know? A lot less scary than I was imagining. My classes so far have been really interesting as well. I've made a new friend even."

"What kind of friend? Are we talking a boyfriend? Spill it."

Tyler laughed. "Time will tell. But so far, we're just classmates who enjoy studying together. But he does have good hair."

"Keeping my eye on you." Honestly, she was impressed. Tyler had only been in Chicago for a short while, and she was already forging relationships. But intense coursework had a way of bringing people together.

"How's my practice?"

"I have yet to burn it down accidentally. You're welcome." They hadn't spoken since Brynn's first day on the job when she'd come up with a list of questions. Since that time, she'd learned the ins and outs of the office procedures and oriented herself on where the supplies lived. She even knew which of the three employees was the most knowledgeable on any given subject. "But in all seriousness, I think I'm finding my stride. Yesterday, Peggy the Pug had some porcupine quills that needed extracting. That was our exciting case of the day."

"Again? This is not Peggy's first rodeo with quills."

Brynn shook her head. "She just can't quit the porcupine, it seems. Her parents think it's the same one as last time."

"Just another lesson on the dangers of love," Tyler said wistfully.

"Sing it. We could all benefit from Peggy's lesson."

Tyler exhaled. "So how's Sage?"

"We mention love and you mention Sage. Interesting."

"It'll pass. Right?"

"I'm hoping on your behalf."

"So give it to me straight. We sleep together for the first time. He practically pretends it didn't happen. I leave town. And he…what?"

She winced at Tyler's retelling. Sage seemed like a nice enough guy, but he was behaving like a fool. "I haven't seen much of him, honestly. I get the impression he's lying low. I'm living next door to his little sister, though. I could ask."

"No. Don't burden Aster with Sage drama. She loves him to pieces. How is she?"

"Seems great. She's fun. Aster."

"She is that. Also brilliant."

"Yeah?" Brynn wasn't entirely surprised. "She's definitely an intellectual. In her own head a lot, too."

"Yep. The kid had straight As in everything without trying. That's not an exaggeration. A near perfect SAT score. And some people theorize that she dropped an assignment or two her senior year on purpose, just so she wouldn't be named valedictorian and have to make a speech."

Brynn smiled. All to dodge a speech, huh? Oh, Aster. "I picked up on the less than comfortable with people part. She's sweet, though." She left out the detail about how perfectly she filled out a tank top.

Some things were best held on to. Especially when this was Tyler's bonus little sister she had inadvertently objectified. She'd have to make sure never to do that again. Boundaries were important.

"She's a good egg," Tyler said. "But I worry about her sometimes. She gets lost in the chaotic Lavender shuffle. Watch out for her while I'm gone, will you?"

Brynn took the request seriously. She softened to sincerity. "I will certainly do that. You have my word."

"Thank you. You have no idea how much easier I can breathe here, knowing you have everything taken care of back at home."

"You know, it's fun to be you for a little while. I have to admit, the change of pace has been refreshing." A pause. "Any other tips for the clinic? Sometimes I feel like the human patients need more from me than I'm giving. They want to stick around. Hang out."

Tyler chuckled. "Welcome to small-town practice. Everything moves at a slower pace, and part of the service is being neighborly and discussing the way insects are invading their gardens, what their son likes to eat for breakfast. But there are exceptions. Don't let Mrs. Bartlett tell you any of her book club stories. They don't end, and you'll never get out of the exam room. And Mozzie's mom, Katrina, will act like she's concerned about Mozzie's weight, but it's often a ploy to sell you Mary Kay cosmetics. I'm down two hundred bucks and have way more mascara than I could ever use. Stay strong. Refuse the samples politely, or you're sunk."

"Too late." She winced at the order she'd reluctantly placed just yesterday. She should really work on her holdout skills. "I thought Mozzie was looking too svelte for genuine concern."

"The devil works hard, but Mary Kay works harder. Better run. I have a study session in five."

"With the good hair. Love you, Tyler. And all is good in Homer's Bluff."

And it really was. She hadn't fixated on her broken-to-pieces life nearly as much. She thought less of her happiness with Tiffany, and how it had been ripped away like a slap across the face. In fact, discovering Homer's Bluff and all it had to offer had been the best kind of salve. It reminded her that the world had a lot more to offer than just what was right in front of her. If her old trajectory hadn't worked out, there were plenty of new ones waiting for her to give them a test drive.

She would do things differently here. Rely on herself. Stay out of any and all potential fires. She smiled and exhaled slowly. She was going to be all right—a sentence she'd said to herself more than a few times over the last few months, but this time she actually believed it.

CHAPTER THREE

Some days, you were just in the mood for a warm, fresh doughnut. When Brynn woke that Friday, she knew there would have to be an extra stop on her way into the clinic. She had a staff meeting scheduled for eight a.m., and a box of doughnuts would help get them started on the right foot. People loved breakfast at work. Plus, she'd get to see Aster's business and find out if these doughnuts were any good.

When Brynn drove up to Hole in One early that morning, she was struck. She'd never in her life encountered a doughnut shop with as much character as this one. The building was small, but on the side facing the street, a doughnut mural covered the entire side of the structure. An honest-to-goodness masterpiece that would make anyone pull over for a dozen. The painting featured three doughnuts—chocolate, glazed, and strawberry frosted—along with a tall glass of milk with a curvy straw. It was eye catching and simple enough that you wouldn't miss the details when driving by. The message was clear. Doughnuts could be found inside, and didn't you want one with this lovely glass of milk? She really did. Brynn, already enjoying the vibe, decided to go inside rather than joining the drive-through line, four cars deep.

When she opened the door, she had to pause a moment because the heavenly aroma of fresh fried dough about brought her to her knees. What was it like to work continuously in a room that smelled so wonderful? When coherent thought returned, she took in her surroundings. The place was *petite*. That was for sure. Black and white subway tile adorned the front of the counter from the floor on up. Framed photographs of individual doughnuts accentuated the walls like celebrities at Sardi's, and two small tables sat on either side of the room, leaving space in the middle for a potential line, of which there already was a small one.

She surveyed the menu displayed on a chalkboard with colorful chalk illustrations of each doughnut. She remembered Aster liked to draw and smiled. Today's flavors included Glazed and Confused, Blueberry and Sweet Corn Chaos, Lavender Lemonhead, and Chocolate Murder. She blinked at the less than common offerings, understanding that this was not her grandmother's doughnut shop. Aster was flexing her creative muscle with her business, and Brynn was here for it. In the glass case behind the counter, she saw large sheets displaying the four kinds of doughnuts in all their glory. Her mouth watered, and her senses overloaded in the best way.

"Good morning, new person! What can I get you today?" a red-headed woman asked from behind the counter. She had both arms stretched out and wore a red Hole in One T-shirt with a matching black baseball cap. Behind a tall cart of some sort, Brynn thought she glimpsed Aster in the exact same black ball cap, which she happened to look fantastic in. A little sporty with the feminine sway of her dark ponytail hanging out the back.

"Good morning. What do you recommend?"

Just as the woman opened her mouth to answer, Aster's face appeared partially from behind the cart. She finished sliding a full tray onto a rack and came around front. "You stopped in." She turned to the redhead. "Hey, Tori, I'll take this one." The bouncy redhead hopped over to the drive-through service and went to work.

"Of course I did," Brynn said, grinning at her new friend. "I had a doughnut craving. I have ever since you told me about this place." She glanced behind her. "Speaking of, I have to ask, who did you commission for the mural on the side of the building?"

Aster blinked. "Yeah, no one. That was me."

Brynn quirked her head. "You're telling me you painted that mural. Ladder, brushes, and all."

"Uh-huh. Easier than trying to explain to someone what I wanted depicted and in what style when I could just do it myself in an afternoon."

Brynn balked. "Aster, it's really good."

"Thanks." She tossed a thumb behind her. "Do you want a doughnut? First one is on the house."

"Really? Okay. Yes. Let's see." She tapped her chin. "I'll take a dozen to go and maybe a Chocolate Murder for me to eat here? Attention-getting name, by the way."

"Murder? Well, it happens in life. Best if it's by chocolate." Aster had a way of saying things plainly, which Brynn was beginning to find fantastic. This was a woman who said what she meant and thought. After dealing with someone like Tiffany, who clearly held information back, Brynn could really get used to up-front declarations.

"I'm grappling, but I can't come up with any argument."

"Perfect. Your order's coming right up."

In under thirty seconds, a black and white checkered box that reminded her a lot of the subway tile was slid her way. As she picked it up, she noticed the warmth emanating from the box. Dear father God in doughnut heaven. Next, Aster presented her a plate with a scrumptious looking chocolate doughnut with dark as night chocolate frosting and what looked to be white chocolate shavings covering the top like snow.

"Let me know what you think," Aster said. She flashed a smile before moving on to help the next customer.

Occupied by Aster's devastating smile, one she only let you glimpse for a moment, Brynn bumped into the table, which screeched across the floor, pulling stares. "I'm okay," she said and held up a hand. "Just enjoying my murder doughnut and crashing into stuff."

She settled in and took a bite of the doughnut, surely leaving some of the frosting on her lips. Didn't matter. This doughnut, this angel kissed creation, was worth every second she potentially looked like a chocolate bandit. Aster Lavender and her team belonged in the doughnut hall of fame. She gripped the table. She slowed her chewing. She savored and lingered over the doughnut longer than she ever intended, wanting to enjoy every last bite before the experience was over.

"Well?" Aster asked, approaching her table and retrieving the plate. She had a white towel over her shoulder and paused for an answer, the ball cap shading her eyes slightly. She begrudgingly admitted how sexy it was and then remembered that she was a sex-starved woman and stopped it.

"I've never enjoyed a doughnut that much before."

Aster nodded. "Good. So come back. We have more."

"Oh, I don't think you have to worry about that. I'm a little in awe of you."

"Me? Why is that?" Now she seemed a little shy. A very sweet person.

"A magical doughnut maker who also has mad painting skills. You keep me guessing."

"I do?" Aster said, blinking.

"Just an expression." Brynn retrieved her doughnuts for the staff meeting.

"Hi again," a voice said. Brynn looked around Aster to see the redhead grinning at them. "I'm Tori. A friend of Aster's. I also work here. That was me, waiting on you briefly just a few minutes ago."

"I remember. Nice to meet you. Brynn Garrett. I'm the new vet filling in for Tyler Lawson. At least for a little while."

"Oh, I know. Everyone knows about you." Tori's eyes were sparkling, and her smile spread out across her face. "We're all thrilled to have you—and pause that for one milli because, oh my God, you are even more beautiful up close. Just gorgeous. I'm in love. Not really, because I'm dating someone long distance, but you know what I mean. Sorry for the gushing." It was like one long run-on sentence of happy feelings. Tori was extra exuberant, which was quite the contrast to Aster's quiet calm. She wondered how that working relationship played out on the daily. "Did Aster give you a free doughnut? We often do that for new people."

"Yeah, and I murdered it. Pun intended."

Tori laughed extra loud and pointed at her. "I like you even more now. Don't you, Aster?" She nudged Aster with her elbow.

"Oh yes." Aster smiled conservatively, that same smile that made Brynn wonder what was really going on in that head of hers. Such a mystery to unravel. Not that she'd be unraveling it. Her stomach dipped. Just the doughnut.

"Well, you've found yourself a new fan and customer. I'll be back." Brynn held up her twelve doughnut score. "See you soon, neighbor. I'll be stalking you from my driveway."

"You got it," Aster said.

Brynn stole one last glimpse of Aster in the ball cap, her ponytail swaying slightly as she made her way back behind the counter. It was a good look on her and added a hint of swagger. She did own the place, after all, and between these four walls, she carried herself like she did, exhibiting a level of confidence Brynn hadn't seen from Aster before. But this was her space, and she seemed very much at home.

As she exited the small shop, she heard Tori exclaim to the next customer, "Did you see her? The lady leaving. That was the new vet. She's real, real nice. You folks need to take your pets on over next time they have the sniffles." Brynn paused on the sidewalk, feeling like a character in a film because did actual people talk like that? The small-town chatter was real! She'd just experienced nothing comparable in bigger cities. No one was interested beyond a few niceties on their way somewhere. Nothing personal, just a truly different pace and culture.

"You went to Hole in One?" Eve shouted when Brynn walked in the back door of the clinic clutching her box of treats. "Joan, Dr. Brynn went to the goddamn Hole in One. Get in here." Tyler's office manager, Eve, was a woman in her fifties with lots of blond hair and mascara. She didn't mince words and had sharp attention to detail. Brynn understood why Tyler kept Eve around, even if she was a little brash. Luckily, that intensity extended to her joyful side as well. "Oh, dear Lord, did they have the chocolate homicide thingy today? Get out right now. They did. Joan!"

Joan, a short brunette in charge of the front desk, raced around the corner and came to an abrupt stop like the Road Runner himself at the edge of a cliff. "We got Hole in One?" she asked in her customary high-pitched voice.

Brynn grinned. "I thought we could use a snack for our staff meeting."

"I'd say we could," Joan exclaimed. She was the quieter type, but sweet as could be, and did a nice job of handling the clients as they arrived for their appointments. "Well, this is just so nice of you, Dr. Brynn."

"Is it time for the meeting?" Freddy asked, coming around the corner. He was a devoted vet tech and also handled most of the kennel work. Youngish, with a short beard likely designed to make him look older. Brynn had only known him a short time but was already impressed with his gentle demeanor with animals. That skill set went a long way to ease what could be a scary time for pets.

"You're three minutes early, Freddy, and you've earned a gourmet doughnut. Yes, you have," Eve said, taking the box from Brynn. She placed it in the center of the table in the small break room and broke out plates and silverware from a magical cabinet organized to all of her preferences.

"Well, let's all have a seat, grab some breakfast, and get started," Brynn said. Was it weird that she was nervous? She'd attended a million staff meetings over the course of her career and had contributed consistently. This was the very first one she'd run entirely by herself, however. Tyler's three employees each grabbed their pick of doughnut and blinked back at her expectantly. *Deep breath.*

"Right. Well, I don't think we'll be long, but I did want to keep afloat Dr. Lawson's tradition of having a staff meeting once a month. It's good for us to touch base and share our thoughts." All three heads nodded eagerly, and she appreciated how much they seemed to care about their jobs and the clinic. "First of all, I think we're doing a great job of patient flow, and I appreciate the system you have in place, Eve, for the exam room rotations."

"It really is the most efficient way," Eve said, nodding. "To float you around while Fred and I prep in between. Should we offer bagels to those who are waiting? That's been a question I've had for a while. Years even. I always thought that would be a nice touch that Dr. Tyler never went for."

Brynn understood why. The cost for daily bagels would be huge. She saw what Tyler billed, and it was a fraction of what you could charge elsewhere. From a financial perspective, Tyler could barely afford those red and white mints she had in a dish on Joan's desk. "I love your ambition, but I think our budget might be too tight for bagels."

She watched as Eve's face fell. "Maybe I'll just make them at home then. I could learn."

"It's something for maybe down the line." Brynn refocused. "I would like to address charting admin and how important it is for us to prioritize it above things like organizing the sample closet."

"That was Eve's call," Fred said, referencing their big project the week before, as charts stacked up. He caught Eve's challenging stare and backpedaled. "But I supported her decision."

"That it was." Eve tented her hands on the table. "We are only as strong as our most organized cupboard, Dr. Brynn. I believe that."

"Me, too," Joan said dutifully.

Brynn swallowed. "Yes. I hear you, but our charts are backed up, and the health of our patients is more important than anything. Right?"

The three of them checked in with each other before collectively nodding. "Can't argue with that," Joan said.

"We love our patients. God bless 'em," Eve said.

"I'd do anything for those little guys," Fred offered, and the depth of emotion behind his eyes said he meant it.

"Updating the medical records after I've added my notes will help them immensely."

"On it, Dr. Brynn." Her new name. She'd never been called *Dr. Brynn* in her life until Homer's Bluff. It had pulled her up short at first, but the more days passed, the more she tried it on. Wasn't so bad now, especially since she knew they meant it with affection. *Dr. Brynn* was feeling like a brand new persona, and after her year, that felt good. She stole a bite of her Lavender Lemonhead doughnut before glancing at her notes for the next agenda item. "How on earth…?" she asked no one in response to the immense flavor that hit her tongue. She was off topic and knew it, but smack her ass, that doughnut was too good to be real. How was the dough so soft?

"Hole in One gets better each time I try one of their doughnuts," Joan said in her meek tone, nodding with immense understanding. Everything she said dripped with honest-to-goodness sincerity. "They're an asset to this town. Before them, we had a little doughnut shop in town center, but they lacked innovation and closed up after just two sad years. That lady quilts now and attends shows in all the little surrounding towns. I have one of her patchwork deals. She's better at quilting than baking. I'll say that."

"Sometimes her doughnuts were not so fresh," Eve said as if she was confessing something delicate. "I didn't want to say anything, but it's true. Bless her anyway, and her mama."

"Those doughnuts sucked," Freddy said outright. "But it's all we had. Then the, uh, Violet's little sister stepped in, and damn. We were in business."

"Aster," Brynn supplied, surprised that Aster had been right about folks not remembering her name. How? Aster Lavender was a memorable person. At least to Brynn, who'd already flashed back to her in the ball cap more than once that morning. That's when she noticed that the three initial doughnuts selected by her staff had quietly disappeared as they'd talked, and a second doughnut appeared on each paper plate. Her offering was a hit. "Well, anyway. As much fun as doughnuts are, we should get back on task."

"Anything you say, Dr. Brynn," Joan said, admiring her Chocolate Murder doughnut like she'd just met a new best friend. "Fire away."

Brynn's nerves had been calmed, and they went on to have a balanced, productive staff meeting, everyone high on a little sugar and enjoying their morning a bit extra thanks to her pit stop on the way to work. She'd be sure to let Aster know that her doughnuts had greased the wheels of her first staff meeting in Homer's Bluff, no pun intended.

Well, maybe a little one.

❖

Aster was a hundred and twenty-two pages into her book and pretty certain that the alien leader, Krylie, was lying to her subordinates and the reader, making her the most unreliable narrator in history. She couldn't turn the pages fast enough, taking a bite of her apple and flipping the page.

"Is there room for another?"

She looked up, ripped from the planet Pentagargo, trying to remember who she was and where she sat. After a minute, she returned to Earth, shocked and happy to see Brynn Garrett standing there, clutching a hardback book in both hands. "You want to read your book on this bench, too?"

"Look. I get that this is your bench, but I heard reading on it was the thing to do at lunchtime." Brynn flashed a smile and her perfect teeth. She wore a peach and black striped shirt that made her look preppy and cute. Aster never in a million years would have guessed that she'd find preppy attractive, but here she was.

"It's not bad. You can give it a try. See if you like it."

"It just looks like a really peaceful way to read a book, which I've been meaning to do more of." She flashed the cover. "*The Girl on the Train.*"

"That's a relatively good one."

"You've read it?" Brynn seemed surprised.

"It's not a space opera, but the character study is intriguing."

"I've been turning pages pretty aggressively for two days now. Translation: I'm hooked."

Aster smiled. "Don't let me stop you."

"Likewise."

They read side by side for an hour, and in that time Aster vacillated between engagement in her book and preoccupation with little things about Brynn. She smelled liked oranges with a side of vanilla. Her legs were long, even though she was shorter than Aster. She was capable of deep concentration developed in a short amount of time, something that Aster found attractive for reasons she couldn't quite explain.

"You dog-ear your pages?" she asked when Brynn finished reading and marked her spot. She stared in sadness at the book.

"I know. I know. Most people think it's barbaric. I don't. I think it's a map of my own journey with the book."

"You relationship with it. Interesting. That's certainly a new take." Aster liked looking at things another way. However, dog-earing was inherently wrong, but Brynn made it right. How?

"What can I say? I prefer my books to look read when I finish with them. I need to see my work on display."

Aster turned this over as she used a bookmark to log her own progress, closing her book. "I'm not sure how I feel about that. Your explanation isn't a bad one, but I have principles."

"Mull it over. Can I come back? This was a nice break in my day."

"Yeah. Sure."

"See you soon, Al."

"Al?" Aster paused, then grinned. "My initials?"

"You have good ones. Off to see a woman about an anxious schnauzer with an appetite for cardboard."

Aster watched in complete fascination as Brynn headed off on foot through the center of town on her way back to the clinic, walking with the slightest sashay, hips back and forth in a swish. It had been a really nice way to spend the midday, doing something she loved in a low pressure social situation with Brynn, of all people, who demanded so little but offered quite a bit.

"Whoa," was all she could murmur two days later when she stumbled upon good luck once again. She found Brynn already sitting on her bench, nose in her book. Aster paused feet away. "I don't know whether to say hi or glare in accusation at my bench competition." She tried to add a smile to let Brynn know she was kidding. In honesty, she'd been hit with a rather warm sensation when she'd spotted Brynn there, and it hadn't left her yet.

"You shouldn't have sold it so effectively. Hi, Aster."

"Hi, Brynn."

There was a new book cracked open this time. Brynn held it up. "*Poisonwood Bible*. I'm told it's a different side of Kingsolver."

"It is." Aster took a seat. "As someone with three siblings, she captures a certain dynamic that resonated."

Brynn balked. "Have you read everything?"

"Definitely not. But I do read a lot. It makes up for my lack of a true social life."

"I find you social enough."

"Really? Mostly I'm just inept when it comes to peopling. Hole in One has helped some in that department. I even smile now. See?" She demonstrated and Brynn laughed.

"Truly impressive. And it's a really nice smile. Now quit talking. We need to read." Aster grinned, sincerely this time, because it was clear Brynn was cutting her a break, letting her off the small talk hook, which was not only kind, but insightful.

The next day, she brought a fresh-baked loaf of raisin bread, hoping more than she would care to admit that Brynn would be there on the bench. The gods were smiling.

"Did you bake this?" Brynn stared at the sliced loaf and then Aster.

"I did. Tell me what you think." She slid a slice down the bench, noticing how brightly Brynn's eyes shone when she was delighted.

Brynn chewed happily. "I think you're a food genius, and this just confirms it. Are the other members of your family as good with food? Is it passed down?"

"Just my mom. When the other kids were off playing, I would hang back and be her little kitchen helper. I even got my own apron for Christmas. It was the coolest thing that had happened to me in a while. Where's your family?" Aster asked, and then realized it might be too personal a question.

Brynn opened her mouth and then closed it. "My dad, well, who knows. He's not been in my life much. Don't feel bad."

"That doesn't mean I can't feel bad. That kind of thing can leave a hole."

Brynn turned to her. "You're right. Thank you for saying that." Her gaze lingered on Aster's face like it belonged there. Aster, to her own surprise, didn't look away. No part of her wanted to. "My mom tries. We haven't lived in the same city since I was a high school kid, though. We touch base here and there. She's remarried. Likes to travel."

"Do you?"

"I want to see as many inches of this world as time will allow."

"Does time get in the way actively?" She wrinkled her nose. "I'm asking a lot of questions."

"That's okay." Brynn seemed thoughtful. "I guess maybe I let time take over. This is maybe a good reminder."

The bench reading became a semiregular happening. On days when Brynn was too busy at the clinic, Aster felt the pang of loss reading alone, something she used to embrace daily. Brynn had brightened everything since. Her presence had become something Aster looked forward to. She cherished the snatches of conversation, even if they were never too long, and would take them out later in the day and turn them over again, like a precious stone in her hand.

"Favorite book?" Brynn asked one afternoon.

Aster thought hard. It was chilly out after a storm the night before and they were sitting closer together, a decision neither had really voiced formally. It was nice. "I don't have one. That's too much pressure. No."

"Aster. Book lover that you are?" Brynn turned fully so that the full brunt of her disbelief could land. "C'mon."

"It feels wrong to single out a favorite. A literary betrayal. I won't sleep."

"There's no such thing."

"Ask one of the characters that. They're my imaginary friends."

Brynn studied her. "That's actually really sweet."

"See? Don't ruin this for me. I'm fragile."

"Mm-hmm."

They read on.

Aster's world had never felt more full, and for the first time in her adult life she was excited for each new day. She prepped her dough each morning with a pep in her step and found herself laughing a lot more with her customers, her coworkers. Life now came with a spark, and it was because a certain someone was becoming more important to her than she ever dared imagine. It felt a lot like lightning dancing.

CHAPTER FOUR

It was a sunny Saturday afternoon in late May, and Aster couldn't deny the call of the outdoors for a second longer. It had been her day to close the shop, and that would have had her at Hole in One an extra hour, but Drew had volunteered to fill in and stay late. He'd been searching for extra hours now that he had a baby on the way with Monica Henry, the blond nurse from the clinic. The town had scoffed when there was no announcement of marriage, and that made Aster roll her eyes. Why were they stuck in the 1960s when the rest of the world had clearly evolved? They wanted everyone coupled up, married, and living on their front porches for the rest of time. Even the handful of gay people, whom the town claimed like a badge of honor, were expected to settle the hell down and commit. That made folks happy for some reason. Maybe they craved solid ground under their feet.

Aster, however, craved the warmth of sunshine on her face. She hopped on her bicycle and set out for a ride. The early summer temperature was just what she needed. She'd opted for joggers and a short-sleeve white shirt, leaving her hair down so it could blow in the wind, wild and free. She rode the perimeter of town twice, enjoying every second of the exercise. Her muscles pulled pleasantly, and the wind soothed. And just because she was feeling ambitious, she decided to push a bit, taking one of the trails that wound its way through a wooded area a couple miles to the north. She knew enough to keep her eyes peeled for stray branches that had a tendency to droop, and *bam!* She was flat on her back, gasping for air, having run face-first into one. Her bike lay in front of her, wheels to the side and still spinning. She blinked and sputtered, choking on air after having the wind completely knocked out of her on landing. Alone on the wooded trail, she found herself staring up at intermingling tree branches with a few rays of sunshine poking through in consolation. The unexpected view was actually kind of pretty, and Aster let herself lie there a moment, taking it in, trying to ignore the strange squeaks infiltrating the peaceful moment. Wait. What was squeaking? She raised her head. Not her. Her bike? No. She looked around. The sound was closer to quiet cries now that she listened closely, and it was coming from somewhere to her left. Interested, she pushed herself up, ignoring the fact that her elbow was scraped to hell. Her own fault for not wearing her full pads. She followed the insistent sound. The crying grew louder as she got closer, and her mind filled with concern for what she might be walking into.

Her fear was misplaced because about ten feet off the trail was a box with three very small black and white puppies inside. Aster almost couldn't believe what she was seeing. She went up on tiptoe to survey the area, swiveling in a three sixty for who could have left them here. No sign of anyone, which was downright awful. She knelt down and took in the scene, her heart thudding. The tiny pups mewled. Well, two of them did. The third was pretty still other than some shallow breathing. She dropped her face for a closer look. Oh no, no, no. He didn't look so good. Where was the mama dog? Another swivel. They were quite a distance from anyone's home, and even if the mama dog did come back, this box was way too tall and cramped for her to get inside to nurse the pups. Aster had a horrible feeling that someone had just dumped these puppies out here as a way to get rid of the responsibility, and that made her want to cry and maybe throw a punch. "Hey, it's okay," she told the mewling duo, but it was the third puppy she couldn't take her eyes off of. She didn't know a ton about puppies, but he didn't look like he had much longer. And without his mom, he didn't have a shot. None of them did. Hell, it looked like their eyes were only just newly open. Springing into action, she made a quick decision. Time mattered. She wheeled her bike off the path and into brush, out of sight. She couldn't bike and keep the pups safe. She lifted the box and gave the area one last good look. "Anyone out here?" she yelled to no response. She dropped her focus to the box. "Okay, you three. Let's get out of here." The only problem? They had quite a few miles to walk, and time was in short supply if her instincts were right.

"Please stay with me," she told him. "Please."

❖

Homer's Bluff Veterinary Clinic was open half a day on Saturdays, which meant Brynn had finished with her last patient hours earlier. As the sun set, she'd hung around the clinic to enjoy the turkey bacon avocado sandwich she'd picked up from Kip's Diner and to take a little time to organize her work life. Her desk looked like a bomb had gone off after the week she'd had. The welcome-wagon nature of her appointments had definitely shifted to legitimate needs, most importantly an outbreak of kennel cough that had hit the dog park. They also had all four boarding runs full that weekend as residents embraced summer getaways, three regular clients who'd left their dogs while traveling and a stray that had been dropped off the day prior. She planned to make a last loop to check on each dog and make sure they had plenty of food, water, a chew toy, and a comfy blanket to go with their bed.

Snoogie, the spunky beagle, bellowed as she approached. He tossed his bone in the air in celebration, one of his favorite ways to express himself. He'd just be staying overnight and had already received a nice long walk and a ball session with Freddy. "I hear you, Snoogie. It's a hard-knock life." She gave his ears a hearty scratch. "But guess what? You're sprung tomorrow." He chased his tail and offered her another bark.

"I know it. It's like vacation for the best dogs ever."

Before Brynn could move down the line to distribute a little more TLC, her attention was pulled by a loud rapping on the door up front. She didn't so much as pause, recognizing the insistent nature of the knock as important. Her emergency instincts kicked in, and she hurried to open up, already getting herself ready for whoever might need her help. She was surprised to see Aster standing there, pink cheeks and worried eyes. She held tightly to a cardboard box making lots of noise.

"Can you help us? We need help."

"Of course. Come in. Come in," Brynn said automatically, stepping out of the way.

"I have puppies. Three of them," Aster said, hurrying in. She turned back to Brynn, eye contact unwavering, a new form of intensity from Aster that she'd not seen before. But this was Brynn's world, her area of expertise, and she could be calm enough for the both of them. Always best in an emergent situation.

"You came across them?"

Aster nodded and gulped air. She was worn out, clearly. "From off the trail in the woods. I don't know what they were doing there, but I think someone dumped them."

"Okay, let's see." Brynn took a look inside the box. A trio of black and white pups. "They're young. About a week and a half, maybe two weeks old." She scooped up the least active puppy and turned him over gently, giving him a good rub back and forth. He was clearly weak, likely cold and dehydrated, which caused her concern. He needed his mama for a good chance at survival, but they would do what they could. Twelve hours without food for a puppy this young could easily be a death sentence, and who knew how long these guys had gone. That's when she remembered. She swiveled and faced Aster. "You know, a stray that the postman dropped off here yesterday had recently given birth. I wonder if we have a match."

Aster's eyebrows went up, hopeful. Her brown eyes went wide. "You might have the mom?"

"Let's find out. Follow me."

Together they walked back to the boarding room and found the black and white little girl who happened to match the puppies' color scheme to perfection. Jack Russell mixes was her guess. When the box of puppies neared the stray, she started turning in circles and whining frantically. "I'd say we got her attention." They watched as she put her paws up on the door and barked once to confirm their suspicion before turning in circles again, anxious.

Aster turned to her. "We should reunite them, right?"

"Yes. She's probably been a total wreck without them." Brynn took the box into the run with her while Aster watched from outside. "Hi, baby girl. I have some pups that you might be looking for." She removed each of the three puppies from the box and placed them on the white blanket folded into a large rectangle. The mama dog immediately began to lick her pups in greeting, and the two active ones wasted no time in the pursuit of milk, suckling without prompting. "I think we have a winner," she said to Aster.

"But the little guy. He's not eating."

Brynn had noticed that, too, but also knew he might just need a little help. "Here you go, puppy," she said, ushering him to an available teat and offering support. "You can do it." Unfortunately, he wouldn't latch, even at the mama dog's encouragement as she licked and helped reposition him.

"Damn," Aster said, hand through her hair, gripping it.

"Be patient," Brynn said, knowing these things could take time. But after a few minutes of trying, in which the littlest puppy only seemed to grow weaker, she knew it was time to intervene. Hypoglycemia was a concern that could lead to other problems. And dehydration in puppies was dangerous and nothing to sit on. "Well, we all tried. I think it's time to feed him with a catheter and syringe," Brynn said. Aster had slid to a seated position on the floor, her eyes glued to the unresponsive puppy.

"Yes. Good. We have to do something," she said, standing up and following Brynn into the supply room.

Brynn located the milk supplement and everything they would need along with a fluffy towel for warmth.

"Would you like to do the honors?" Brynn asked. "After all, you are the one that brought him for help."

Aster's big brown eyes blinked back at her. "I could feed him? You think that would be okay?"

"Mm-hmm. I'll show you how."

They sat together, side by side on the concrete floor in front of the run, as the mama dog happily took care of her two rescued babies. While Snoogie put two paws on his door and looked on with concern, Brynn gently inserted the catheter toward the back of the puppy's mouth and pushed the plunger to expel the tiniest bit of milk, hoping he would reflexively swallow. It took a few tries but after they found a little rhythm, she handed the operation over to Aster, who looked nervously reverent as she accepted the blanket wrapped pup.

"Oh. Hey there. Me again." Aster's voice had gone soft and quiet as she spoke to the puppy. Adorable. Brynn watched as she fed the pup, exercising such gentle care with him. "Am I doing this right?" Aster asked.

Brynn nodded. "You're doing great. Just be patient with him and go extra slow. He's weak and will tire out easily."

Aster nodded and exhaled. "Be honest. Do you think he's going to make it?"

It was a difficult question, because he was in danger. He was young, malnourished, and rejecting his mother. It wasn't a promising combination for a young puppy. "Tonight will be telling. If he can make it through, he'll have a much better shot."

Aster's gaze picked up intensity. "Then we have to get him through tonight. I'll do whatever you tell me."

"Well, he'll need pretty frequent feedings, every two to three hours, and lots of cheerleading. I can call Freddy."

"No. I'll do it." Aster met her gaze evenly. "I mean, would it be all right if I stayed with him?"

It was the sweetest sentiment. "Oh, Aster, you've already done your part and brought them in. I can call in Freddy. He overnights with the sick pets, or if it makes you feel better, I can stay with him myself."

Aster didn't waver. In fact, her brown eyes carried even more conviction. "I really want to be here. Can I stay?"

"Of course." She paused, making a call. "I'll stay with you."

"Yeah?" Aster brightened with relief. "That would be amazing. I worry I wouldn't know if something was wrong. But I won't sleep tonight not knowing how he is."

"Well, with both of us clocking in, we're going to make sure he has the best care possible. We got this. I'll grab some snacks, and we'll settle in."

Luckily, Eve kept a really handy pantry, fully stocked for such an occasion. Brynn was able to scoop up some chips, Oreos, candy bars, apples, and salt and vinegar almonds. All the essentials, really, to help with the hours ahead. Because she was no fool, she also put on a pot of coffee. Brynn had pulled plenty of all-nighters in vet school and knew that caffeine was key. The mission actually woke her sense of purpose the hell up and had her determination in overdrive. It was satisfying to have boots on the ground and not just hand off supportive care to a vet tech the way she would have at her last practice.

When she returned to Aster and the boarding runs, she'd found the pup had taken half the food he'd been offered. It didn't look like a lot, but it was a true win. Yet Aster looked worried, and Brynn rushed to reassure her. "It's not bad. It's not unusual for them to start small, especially when they've gone without for a while. He'll need to work up to taking more." She placed the puppy in the swirled pile made up of his siblings and took her seat next to Aster on the floor. "So we have a couple of hours to kill. What's new?"

❖

"What you're saying is that you've never had a dog. Not even a family dog as a kid?" Brynn asked. She seemed truly shocked. It was the middle of the night, and after hours of talking, not talking, feeding the puppy, talking some more, they'd come out of their shells, learning more about each other. Aster learned that Brynn had grown up in North Carolina and sometimes imagined moving back there, but she wasn't quite sure for what. Most of her family had moved away. She was five feet five inches and used to love eating snow as a child. She was great at math but struggled with philosophy in college, often getting into imaginary debates with her professor in her head. Aster could stay up another whole night listening to this kind of trivia about Brynn. Her favorite was hearing that Brynn would hoard library books until the library would threaten to revoke her card if she didn't return what she'd borrowed. A fellow feisty reader!

Aster shook her head, her cheek resting against the cinder block wall behind her, facing Brynn. "Dogs? Not a one. My oldest sister was allergic. I've always wanted a pet, though. Sage adopted Buster as soon as he was old enough for his own place, so I got to be a dog aunt. My turn. What do you do for fun?"

Brynn smiled. "Easy. I love exploring old movies. When you find a little gem of a film that's brilliant or insightful or romantic or suspenseful, and it's been there all this time—as in *years*—just waiting for you to one day discover it?" She shrugged, bringing her shoulders to her ears. "It gets me energetic. My turn. Favorite social media outlet?"

"I don't do social media. It has the word *social* and that stresses me out before I even open the app. I gave it all up. You?"

"I dabble, but since my breakup, I stay off."

"Oh, I'm sorry."

"Don't be," Brynn said. "It's always best to know the truth. I'm taking another turn."

"That's downright cheating, but okay."

"Did you have a high school sweetheart?" Brynn asked.

"No. My turn. Did you?" Snoogie began to snore.

"Yes, Austin Johns." Brynn gave her head a shake. "He was self-centered and obsessed with his hair. We broke up in the eleventh grade. My turn. Last person you dated." She watched Aster with interest.

"Uh, *dated* is a strong word. I talked to a woman online named Lacey who seemed really great. Funny, too. But I think she met someone in Dallas and it ended there."

There was a long pause. Brynn's voice went soft. "You date women."

Aster swallowed. Brynn didn't seem to be the judgmental type, but the temperature in the room had sure shifted. "Yeah. I'm gay, so… there's that."

Brynn nodded. "That's great, Aster. I didn't realize."

"I should probably advertise it more. Maybe that's my problem."

"I don't think you have a problem at all. You're a catch." She touched Aster's leg in assurance. "You just have to be patient. You'll meet the right one someday, and *bam*, it'll smack you in the head like a two-by-four. Your shoulders will get all loose, and your insides will tingle." Brynn laughed.

Aster didn't. She turned. "Swirly?"

"That's a good word for it."

Aster swallowed, not sure what to say. She knew who made her own shoulders swirly, and the person's hand was on her thigh provoking all kinds of responses. Brynn seemed to notice at the exact same time and slowly removed it, touching the back of her own hair. They were quiet for a long moment.

"Your turn," Brynn said.

Aster's brain had temporarily stalled, and she rushed to cover her tracks. "Um. Same question." Not that she even remembered what it was anymore.

"Well, my ex was my last relationship. Tiffany. She had a whole secret life."

Aster turned to her slowly as the most unexpected realization swam and settled. Tiffany. "Wait. So that means…"

"Yeah. Me, too." Brynn offered a gentle smile and shrug. They stared at each other for a moment, taking in that recognition of seeing a part of yourself in someone else. They'd clicked before as friends in conversation, but they now had something truly in common.

Brynn wasn't straight. Aster didn't know how to organize that information. She'd have to sit with it. Turn it over carefully. It made everything feel different. The idea of Brynn with a woman, kissing her, holding her hand, looking into her eyes, turned Aster's world on its head. In fact, that head might explode.

"I think it's time for our next feeding," Brynn said, pulling her out of it.

"Brynn?"

"Yeah?" She turned back with a soft smile that about knocked Aster over. A new tension radiated.

"Nothing."

Though it seemed like not much could top the news Brynn had leveled on her, something else remarkable happened. The puppy began to mewl, making nearly as much noise as his brother and sister. Aster almost couldn't believe it. It was working?

Brynn smiled. "He's found a little bit of strength."

"That's good news, right?" She sat up straighter, daring to hope.

"It's really promising. He's acting like a puppy, and that's what we want to see."

A huge weight came off Aster's shoulders as the little guy yawned and closed his eyes, intertwined in the warmth of his siblings. He was doing all right. They just might have saved him. "That's the best news. You know what you're doing," she said. "You're a good vet, Brynn. Really."

"Yeah, well, it's *you* who saved the day. It was a good thing you did, racing them here."

"Well, they weren't staying out there on my watch." Aster smiled and leaned back against the wall, tired from the long day and just now realizing it. "I think I'm going to close my eyes for just a minute."

Brynn nodded. "He doesn't need to eat again for a little while, and I can take that one. Not to worry."

It had to be close to five a.m. when Aster stirred. Her body seemed to know that it was near time for her to head to work and get started on her first round of doughnuts even though her alarm hadn't gone off. She opened her eyes anyway, startled to learn that she wasn't where she thought she was. Not only was she upright, but her head rested on something warm, and her cheek was being tickled by a soft strand of what felt like hair. She blinked and took in her surroundings. Dogs. The vet clinic. Brynn. She was snuggled up against beautiful Brynn Garrett, her head resting on Brynn's shoulder. How in the world had she landed here? Also, there should have been mayday sirens going off in her brain. There weren't. Her body felt heavy, warm, and beyond relaxed.

"Hey there, sleepyhead." Brynn had the sweetest morning voice.

She lifted her head and met green eyes. It wasn't a bad visual to wake up to. At all. "I didn't mean to crash on you. Especially in the literal sense."

"Totally okay," Brynn said softly.

"You have a nice shoulder, though. Five stars." And for a very strange minute, Aster considered staying right where she was. She didn't feel physically comfortable around too many people, but being near Brynn like this felt not only comfortable, but very nonthreatening.

"I honestly didn't mind."

"We're friends, right?" Aster studied Brynn. She felt like they were, hoped.

"We are. Yes."

Their faces were still very close together, and she couldn't help but notice that neither one of them made any move to separate, which would have been the natural thing to do. Brynn reached up and brushed a strand of hair from Aster's forehead before her gaze fell to Aster's lips. Whoa. Okay. The entire thing made Aster's stomach muscles tighten.

"You are a really peaceful sleeper," Brynn said quietly.

"You were holding me," Aster said, remembering the feeling of someone's arms around her. "Weren't you?"

Brynn nodded. "Just keeping you warm. It did the same for me." She gestured with her chin. "Like the puppies."

"What's going to happen to them?" Aster asked. The mama dog was awake and grooming the pups, who were all still out like lights. The little one already looked chubbier, his belly round and full.

Brynn approached the run to watch the interaction. "The puppies will still need their mother for another few weeks. After that, we'll look for good homes."

Aster didn't hesitate to announce what she'd been thinking since she'd arrived at the clinic. "I would like to adopt the little one when he's ready." She stood, shifted her weight. "Would I be able to do that?"

Brynn smiled. "Feels fitting to me. I like the idea."

Aster joined her in that smile. "Okay, good. I'll start making arrangements. And I can apply formally. Fill out a background check. Fingerprints. Interview. Whatever you need me to do."

"What you need to do is go home and get some rest. Let me take care of the brood."

Aster rocked back on her heels. "Can't. It's Sunday. People need their doughnut fix, and it's my job to give it to them."

"No way. You're going to work?" Brynn laughed. She had a really melodic tone. Aster could listen to her laugh a lot more. A new goal.

"Someone has to keep the church crowd fed." Aster looked around. Waited. It felt strange to leave Brynn now, especially after what they'd been through together. She felt like a teammate. "Thank you for all your help. Letting me stay." She hesitated but just decided to say it. Life was about putting yourself out there. She could try that. "I liked getting to know you better." There. Done. It was out there.

"It was a good night," Brynn said.

"Eating snow, huh?" Aster asked.

"Nothing is quite as refreshing. Trust me on this."

They stared at each other. Aster, still feeling brave, moved to Brynn and pulled her into a hug, and something amazing happened. They fit together perfectly. No awkwardness that often came with the first time two people tried to maneuver a hug. Everything about it simply felt…right.

Aster left the clinic still clinging to the high, reliving that moment several times over. She didn't experience that kind of connection too often, and now she craved more of it. Was it romantic, the nature of her feelings? Maybe. But maybe not. Maybe Brynn was brought into her life for a reason. The reason had yet to reveal itself. In the meantime, Aster seized the new energy, ready to take on more of this world, bolstered by the night she'd just spent on a concrete floor. She went about her morning, made her doughnuts, chatted with her customers more than she ever had before, and as she sat at home later that night, she opened her laptop and filled out the commitment form for the Cambridge School of Culinary Arts. She'd heard Boston was a beautiful city, one worth spending a little time in.

CHAPTER FIVE

A ster was beside herself with anticipation. She'd always wanted a dog. She'd just never imagined it would be happening so soon. She was a planner and geared up for most big decisions in life with days, weeks, or months of forethought, only to have a tree branch and a box of puppies upend the practice entirely. She was about to be a dog mom and took the job very, very seriously, was thrilled about it even. She'd read three books, found an online forum for new pet owners, and purchased a membership to a subscription box service for toys and food.

And now the day was here.

"He's a smart little guy," Brynn told her as she arrived with Dill for his official move-in. The puppy wiggled crazily in her arms, so much bigger than when she'd first met him, and straining desperately to get to Aster to lick her face. She'd visited him most every day at the clinic, and they'd developed quite the bond. Plus, he was adorable and handsome. She'd grown to love all his little markings, three black spots on his back in sharp contrast to his white fur and a black patch over his left eye. She'd chosen the name Dill because this little guy was a fighter and came with a kick. She liked his spicy little spirit already. She accepted him into her arms and let him kiss all over her face. "Oh, hi. You're home. This is where you live now."

"Ah, young love," Brynn said and folded her arms to watch.

"Drink?" Aster asked, not wanting to ignore her guest, as if that was even possible when Brynn was in her presence. She'd come from work and looked a little bit tired. It never seemed to dampen her spirit, though. She was someone who was always friendly and warm.

"If you have a bottle of red open, I'll steal one. If not, no need to go out of your way. I'll suffer in silence."

"The red is open," Aster said with a laugh. They hadn't spent any long stretches together since the night they'd nursed Dill back to health, but the little exchanges they did have—at the grocery store once in passing, whenever Brynn came into Hole in One, or chats from their driveways on the warm June evenings—now felt different, weighted, in a good way. Aster noticed herself looking for Brynn when she walked to her car, hoping to catch a glimpse, disappointed when too long went by without an interaction.

She deposited Dill in the bed she'd purchased for him and grinned when he lunged for the grouping of toys just outside. Aster poured two glasses of red wine and handed one to Brynn.

"To new adventures with Dill." Brynn's green eyes sparkled. A wonderful view.

Aster touched her glass to Brynn's. "I'll drink to that."

"Oh! And I have news of my own," Brynn said, before drinking. "I've decided to keep Pickles. I'm adopting her."

Aster's mouth fell open. Pickles was the name they'd given to the stray mama dog. No one had come forward to claim her, and her future had been in question, tugging at Aster's heart. "You're keeping her? She has a home?" She loved the idea and shot a fist in the air. "That's the best news I've had in so long." She just couldn't celebrate enough. Relief flooded. She'd been up nights, wondering whether she should take them both, but knowing her lack of experience should probably limit her to one until she knew what she was up against.

Brynn shrugged, glowing now. "I thought about it. There was no way I couldn't take her. She's the sweetest girl, and when I look into her eyes, I can tell we're a match. Plus, mom and son will get to spend a little time together as neighbors now."

Aster swallowed her wine and knew she had to contribute her own update. "I have news, too. Dill and I will be leaving for Boston at the start of fall."

Brynn's beautiful eyes went wide and she set down her glass. "Shut the front door. You're enrolling in the culinary school. You're doing it?" She covered her mouth with both hands.

Aster nodded, trying to suppress her grin but too excited to do so. "I decided that life is short, and I should live it. They have student apartments, and with a deposit I can bring a pet. I checked it all out, and there's a dog park just a few blocks away and a pet store around the corner."

"This is amazing. I'm so happy for you, Aster! The best news." Brynn opened her arms as Dill ran a lap around the kitchen. "Come here."

Aster moved to Brynn and accepted the hug, holding on for a moment longer than was probably normal because of the insane rush that came with it. She didn't care. She missed touching Brynn and the jolt it gave her, making everything feel extra vibrant and alive. When she finally did let go, she realized Brynn's hand was still on the back of her neck and everything tingled. *Steady now.* Brynn met her gaze and seemed to acknowledge the charged moment with the softest of smiles. Aster's focus fell to Brynn's lips. Glossy and parted. Her stomach clenched and her shoulders tingled.

"I'm really proud of you." She took a step back then, and something about it felt reluctant. Was it? Like Aster, she didn't want the moment to end. That part seemed clear.

"Have you noticed we touch a lot more now?"

Brynn paused, glanced at her wine and back at Aster. "Yes, Aster. I did notice that." She didn't offer anything more.

Maybe she wasn't supposed to just come right out and say it. But how could she not? "It's nice."

Brynn rolled her lips. She was either amused or embarrassed. Hard to tell which. "Yeah, it is." She placed the wine on the counter. "When do you leave again?" She folded her arms. Was Brynn making a point or moving on?

"In about three months. The semester doesn't start until mid-September, but I wanted to have time to settle in. Catch my breath." She shrugged. "I've never lived anywhere but here before."

She smiled, genuine. Warm. "You're going to love it."

Aster exhaled. "You know, I think you're right. But I'm nervous."

"Don't be. Focus on the excitement." A thought seemed to occur to Brynn. "Oh no. What about Hole in One? You're closing shop?"

"No. Not at all. Drew and Tori are stepping up and taking over. They know that place backward and forward. They're pros and want the extra cash. I trust them. We'll hire someone for extra help. Interested?"

"Don't tempt me." A pause. "You'll be missed. I'm sure."

Aster felt courageous. Dill pulled at her shoelaces as if encouraging her. And since she'd felt like a stronger, more confident version of herself lately, she embraced it. "Will you miss me?"

Brynn nodded. "I really will."

No one said anything for a moment. All Aster wanted in the world was to sit in her living room and talk with Brynn until the wee hours of the morning again. Hold her, maybe. Press her cheek to Brynn's. And was there a tug to do even more? Sure. But Aster limited that kind of thinking, because the idea was wildly overwhelming, even entertaining a sliver of those details.

"Well." It's what people said right before they left.

"Yeah," Aster said, sad now.

"I should let you and Dill get settled in."

"Okay." Aster wished Brynn would stay longer but realized that she maybe didn't want to. That was all right, too. "Thank you for bringing him. I've been counting the days."

Brynn walked to the door, turned back, and squeezed her hand. "You two are gonna be great together. But you, Aster Lavender, all on your own, are going places. I can tell."

Oh, that hit her hard. She felt the blush. Brynn's opinion mattered. "You really think so?"

"I know so as confidently as I know tomorrow is Wednesday."

"Wow. That's a nice endorsement."

"I mean it."

The smile faded from Aster's lips because she understood that Brynn absolutely meant it, and she wasn't sure anyone had ever had that kind of faith in her. It resonated. It mattered. It made her chest warm and her heart full. "Brynn."

"See you soon." *Dammit.*

And Brynn was out the door, now a glimpse of blond hair across their lawns, leaving Aster happy, confused, and quite honestly longing for more of whatever pinged between them. Brynn Garrett was special, and she'd already left a lasting handprint on Aster's life. That's the part that mattered most, and what she would focus on. It felt like that's what Brynn wanted.

Dill danced around her feet, bringing her back into the moment. "Hi, Dill. Hi." The dog yipped. "It's you and me, now, against the world. Wanna help me draft a packing list for our new adventure? We have to start planning." She scooped him up, accepted a puff of puppy breath and a lick to her nose, and started brainstorming her list. Did she feel the energy from the house next door? Most definitely. And it brought a smile to her lips. She was a lucky person.

❖

Brynn was out of control and really not sure what to do about it. She'd shrugged off the Aster phenomenon repeatedly. Ordered her mind and body to stand down. Multiple times.

It wasn't working.

Moments ago, a harmless visit to drop off a puppy to his new owner had turned into a droolfest. At least for her. She'd gone and objectified Aster Lavender, her innocent, youthful next-door neighbor, yet again. She pinched the bridge of her nose and begged the universe to stop making Aster more attractive each and every time she saw her. Going next door specifically was exponentially dangerous, however, because in her own home, Aster tended to wear fewer clothes, and the end result left Brynn's hands anxious to reach out and touch that really fantastic body with the impressive definition and the complementary feminine curves that, even in this moment, had Brynn wanting to explore.

Going to hell on a highway paved with lust. No question there. Aster was her friend, for God's sakes. Her very hot, younger, gay neighbor whom she'd *promised* Tyler she'd look out for, not scandalize.

In an attempt to calm her humming body, she pulled out her phone, ready to *Candy Crush* her traitorous mind into submission. But she paused, because there was a voice mail from Tiffany waiting. Huh. Fate was angry with her tonight, apparently, and decided to inflict all kinds of torture. It had been a couple of weeks since the last one. She sighed but allowed herself to listen.

"I miss us. Our life. And you. That's all. Give me another shot? No secrets this time. You can have access to my phone, my passwords, my mind, body, and heart. All of it. I love you, sweetheart. Always."

She closed out of the message, because even just the sound of Tiffany's voice took her back in time, and that meant reliving the way things ended, too. She couldn't do it again. It was important that she stay strong. But little thoughts crept in, tickling the back of her brain. What if this whole thing had been a true wake-up call for Tiffany?

No, no, no. Brynn couldn't allow it in. What if this was her shot to truly have it all back? No. She rejected the notion...or at least tried to. Wouldn't it be nice to just fall back into the ready-made life she knew so well? On the one hand, yes. On the other, no. She'd found a new part of herself since arriving in Homer's Bluff, and that told her that this place had a lot more to offer her. She should explore it.

And she would.

But she had to be honest. Aster heading off to Boston would leave a hole in the life she'd formed here. They'd only known each other a couple of months, but there was no one out there quite like Aster, and she would miss their unique friendship.

When Brynn left her house on the way to the clinic the next morning, there were a dozen artisan doughnuts on her front porch in a black and white box. No note or explanation. She didn't need one. Her heart swelled. She glanced over at Aster's house as she made her way to her car in her work clothes. For the unassuming woman that she was, Aster was leaving quite the impression on Brynn. She'd made her feel special that morning, like someone was thinking of her. In fact, not since before her breakup with Tiffany had Brynn floated on air, and that's exactly what she was doing.

This town. The pace. And one very unexpected new friend had made that happen for her.

She smiled as she drove, feeling like maybe her groove was on its way back. She focused on the doughnuts, the gesture, and not on the very intriguing woman who'd made them both.

CHAPTER SIX

There are days where it feels like the day is having you. Brynn had not only handled thirteen patient appointments but even managed to squeeze in two emergencies, only one of which had ended happily. Her soul felt as heavy as her shoulders did, and she just needed to limp her way home and nurse her heart.

"Are you okay?"

"Holy shit." Brynn placed a hand over her heart as she walked from her car to her front door. "I had no clue you were there."

Aster stood in the side yard between their homes, eyes wide. "I am so sorry I scared you. I was pulling weeds. I bet my car hid me from your view."

Brynn managed to pull in some air, hand now on her knee in recovery. "You're like a pop-up book. Yard version."

"Wearing that one like a badge. Bad day or something? You look…less than happy."

Brynn sighed. She was exhausted, but talking to Aster gave her a hit of unexpected energy. She walked over to her. Correction, was pulled over like a magnet, really. "That's a good classification. Run ragged. Had some equipment break on me, and I lost a patient that I did not expect to lose. That's the worst part of my job. I hate it. I've never been one to shake it off the way some of my colleagues have learned to."

"I don't like that part for you either. It must be so hard. I'd be a mess."

She made a circular gesture around her head. "I replay all the things I could have done differently, even if there really wasn't anything."

Aster sighed. "I hate hearing that. You should come over. Maybe it will help to shelve it. Bring Pickles. The dogs can play."

Brynn only hesitated for a moment because she was a fish chasing a baited hook at the idea of spending a little time with Aster, who in her experience didn't host a lot of people intentionally. The honor was not lost. "What if I brought a book over? Benches and couches are similar."

"You're talking my language now."

Fifteen minutes later, Pickles and Dill, who was already three-quarters his mother's size, raced around the small kitchen table while Brynn and Aster read quietly on the couch. Brynn went through periods of enrapture with her book and others where it felt like all she could do was notice Aster, two seats down the couch. She had her legs stretched out and resting on the coffee table, no shoes, the hem of her jeans frayed. As she read, she tended to run her forefinger across the open cover of the book, a tiny action that Brynn found fascinating.

"Are you hungry? I could make us something."

Brynn looked up from her book, a romance novel she'd heard about from a patient's human, who'd brought her cat in for compulsive stealing, not really something Brynn could help with. "Yeah. That'd be nice."

Aster got to work making them a couple of BLTs and homemade fries. The aroma of the sizzling bacon after the day she'd had almost brought Brynn to happy tears. She'd skipped lunch entirely. Who knew bacon was the ultimate comfort food? Aster, apparently. They ate on the couch while they read, the quiet domesticity of the evening like the warm hug she needed to come down from her stresses.

After that night, something shifted. Unspoken. Their get-togethers increased. Living next door made it easy. Brynn now knocked and entered without waiting for Aster to answer. They'd become that casual, and she loved it. She began looking forward to their evenings together, and Pickles agreed, racing into the house each time they visited, finding Dill and heading off on an adventure in the square backyard or a cuddle on the floor under the table. She and Aster had grown closer in that sense, too. It had started when she'd granted herself permission to be more affectionate with Aster. Brynn was tired of ignoring her instincts. Her arm briefly slung around Aster's shoulders as she perused the fridge. Her fingertips on Aster's forearm when she made a point. They also sat a little closer together on the couch because it allowed them to share a blanket. Blanket coverage was important, after all.

"Why are men always such jerks in these things?" Brynn asked, holding up her fifth romance novel in a row. She was on a kick, likely because of the lack of action in her bedroom. Vicarious living had perks.

Aster looked up from her biography of George Washington Carver, something she'd called a palate cleanser in between sci-fi binges. "Got me. I don't know how you can read those things."

"You just don't like them because they're all feelings."

"I don't mind feelings, but shouldn't there be more packed in? Wars? Failing societies? Flight?"

Brynn leveled a stare. "See? I knew you'd say that. You're just as predictable as my books."

Aster tried for wounded but came up cute. "Gotta work on surprising the world more."

"I have no doubt you will. There's nothing you can't do. I'm convinced. Art? Check. Food? Check. Trivia? Double check."

"I can't save animals the way you can." Oh. She'd said it so sincerely. There was that sweet side of Aster peeking out again. "You make a kind of difference that I can't."

"Thank you." And with the warmth that enveloped her, she snuggled in a little closer.

"Tired?" Aster asked. Brynn had worked late again and wondered what it would be like if the clinic took on a second doctor. With the amount of breeze the folks of Homer's Bluff liked to shoot, they could sure use an extra pair of hands to see more patients. She'd decided to mention it to Tyler.

"Mm-hmm. A little, yeah."

"Well. You can lay your head down if you want." The indication was Aster's lap, which looked incredibly inviting. She wore black joggers that were not only soft looking but accentuated her athletic form almost too perfectly. She watched the pulse in Aster's neck shift after extending the offer. Brynn noticed something. Her proximity made Aster nervous, but not to the extent that she didn't ask for more.

"Okay, yeah." Brynn lay back, her head in Aster's lap as she continued to read about stoic men and the bedroom activities of people who sadly weren't her. Then she got to thinking about the fabric of those joggers beneath her head and what was beneath. The smooth skin of Aster's legs. Her thighs. Their apex. She sat up. "It's getting so late."

"Is it?" Aster murmured, lost again in the pages. That was the thing about Aster and books. They swept her deeply away into the worlds and lands she read about. She gave herself over so fully to the activity. All activities, really. Brynn wondered what she'd be like in the midst of passion—just as thoroughly committed? She had a feeling. Meanwhile, Aster ripped her gaze from the words that clearly had her riveted. "No. Do you have to go?" The implication was *This is nice*, and God, she wasn't wrong by any stretch. Which was what had Brynn putting space between them. She had a feeling that slipping her hands beneath Aster's shirt and exploring her breasts might put their friendship in a precarious spot, and honestly? Their friendship had been the best thing that had happened to her in a long time. She felt the need to preserve it and hold on to this oasis of happiness. Taking things farther could easily ruin the purity of what they had going. In fact, it likely would. Romance had a way of scattering the good parts of life like pieces of a broken vase. No, thank you.

She planned to do things differently this time. No rolling the dice.

"I'm sorry. Didn't get much sleep last night and I should probably catch up. 'Night, Aster."

"'Night," Aster said with a touch of bewilderment behind her voice.

Brynn hated that she had to lie, but the truth was a daunting reality she wasn't ready to face. The second she voiced her feelings to Aster out loud, the more real they'd become. And, well, she simply couldn't have that.

❖

It was close to midnight on a warm evening in August, and both she and Brynn had work in the morning.

In fact, Aster would be rolling out of bed at four thirty to open Hole in One, but there was no way she was moving from where she sat on the couch. Tonight, Brynn sat next to Aster with her feet folded beneath her like an adorable person. She'd memorized the image, the shape of her, cozy and tucked in like that.

Aster had started clinging to moments like this one more and more, knowing their value and that once she left for Boston, she would sorely miss this kind of quiet time with Brynn. She'd miss everything about Brynn. In many ways, it felt like they'd carved out their own little quiet refuge from the world. Aster had been someone who didn't mind time spent on her own, preferred it even, but Brynn had changed that. She waited each day until their stolen time together, literally counting down the hours. Sometimes she cooked for Brynn, who was the absolute best food audience. Even when Aster had overcooked the sautéed chicken and mushrooms because she got lost reading the recipe originator's backstory instead of watching the pan, Brynn refused to acknowledge the problem.

"It's fantastic."

"It's not," Aster said, embarrassed. "I'll make us something else. Give it back."

Brynn had whirled around, taking the plate with her. "Hands off. We're in love."

"You can't love damaged chicken. Hand it over."

"Aster. Look at me." Intensity flashed. "You can try and take this plate out of my hands"—she turned back, green eyes glistening in challenge—"but you will lose."

Aster rolled her bottom lip in and ran her tongue across it, resisting the urge to tackle Brynn right there on the kitchen floor and allow herself to do a few of the things she'd forbidden her mind from imagining in detail. It's not that she didn't feel every part of Brynn when they were together. Her instincts, the pull, the continuous tension, a gushing waterfall without an off switch. Brynn overwhelmed and consumed, so of course she *felt*. But Aster had grown very adept at restraint. She should be nominated for an award, in fact.

But that night on the couch, she couldn't take the sidestepping what was right in front of them for one second longer. "Brynn?"

"Yeah?" She blinked twice and dog-eared the book. The horror slashed. Aster let it go, swallowing an affectionate smile, because Brynn could make something that offensive endearing just because it was all her.

"I'm going to say something."

"You already are, but go on." A proud grin.

She was being playful. Aster wasn't. "I have a crush on you. I think you know that."

She watched as Brynn's eyes widened almost imperceptibly. "I know that we've gotten…close."

"That's one word for it. We touch a lot. We cuddle. We stare at each other when the other isn't looking and sometimes when they are."

Brynn hugged the book to her chest. "I've caught those things, too. I think it comes very naturally for me to touch you. I wish I had a better explanation. I look at a lot of people."

"Fair enough. Do you have a crush on me?"

Silence crashed the party and decided to hang out awhile, which Aster allowed. For what felt like a lifetime, she watched as Brynn's face filled in pink as a myriad of emotions crossed her features. What a journey she was taking. "I guess I do. Yes." Defeat won out, toppling the other emotions and taking up residence on Brynn's face.

"And we're adults."

"Who are doing really well right where they are."

Aster exhaled, loudly. Purposefully.

"You don't like that answer," Brynn said. She articulated the words like an older, wiser woman who was ready to explain a few things about life. Nope. Aster wasn't about playing the role of child. Not when it came to her and Brynn.

She leaned in to honesty. "I don't know what to do with all the energy I feel bouncing between us. I like you in my space."

Brynn swallowed and that was telling. "Do you?" She was using the question to buy time. Aster felt a little bad for putting her on the spot, but the cause was a good one. A desperate cause.

"I just said so. Yes. I want you here all the time. In a lot of capacities. Do you feel the same?"

"Do I like being in your space? Yes." She lifted her shoulders and stared at the wall. "Why are you asking me loaded and dangerous questions?"

"Because I can't not anymore. Do you understand? I can't sit here with you and feel you all over and love who we're becoming without acknowledging the fact that I want more. And maybe you're not supposed to just blurt that stuff, but I have to."

Something flickered behind Brynn's eyes, and Aster saw the resolve crumble. Finally. All she needed from Brynn was an honest moment devoid of pretense or evasion. "I need this, Aster. What we have going. You matter to me every bit as much as I matter to you. Maybe more. I was floundering before I moved here, and when I met you, it felt like I'd finally swum to shore. I could breathe. I had something to hold on to, this friendship, our connection, and because I do not want to wreck it, this precious thing, I can't let myself explore anything bigger." Brynn looked up at the ceiling and back again. "I'm not in good enough emotional standing to do that. My last relationship ended in the worst way imaginable, and not only that but you're leaving."

"Should I not leave? Tell me not to go."

"And resent me forever? What? No. You're absolutely going. This is your dream, Aster, and I will not stand in the way." She took Aster's palm and placed it against hers, threading their fingers. "As much as it will crush me to lose you to Boston, it's where you need to be. I'm going to be here for the handful of months I have left, cheering you on, and missing you like crazy." Something unexpected happened. Brynn's eyes were filled with tears, which was just about the most upsetting thing Aster could see.

"Please don't cry. I get it." She reached for her, and Brynn's arms went around her neck automatically. "Is there anything I can do?"

She heard Brynn sniffle and laugh against her shoulder. "You can ignore my blubbering and be my friend. The one I need more than any other friend."

Resolve. She could do this. Her heart hurt because this put a full stop to the kernel of hope she'd gone into the conversation cradling. But this was what Brynn needed. "The best part is that's something I think I know how to do."

Brynn pulled back and took Aster's face in her hands. "If someone had told me, when I met you months ago, that the shy and kind of curious girl back at Larry's was going to become this person in my life, this important fixture, I would have laughed you off."

Aster's mouth fell open. "I think that was a compliment, but I'm not clear."

"I should strive for better delivery." Brynn placed a hand on Aster's shoulder, and with their physical connection plugged back in, she sank into warmth and comfort. "The cosmos knew we'd be good together even if I never would have guessed."

Aster grabbed Brynn's hand and sat back, taking that hand with her. "The cosmos makes me feel noteworthy. I accept this characterization, shy and curious girl that I am."

So there would be nothing more between them than what they had. But for Aster? It was already pretty great. Her relationship with Brynn was unique in its closeness. She could shoot a look across a room at Brynn and have her know exactly what it meant. They were special, and Aster vowed to treasure and protect their bond, making sure Brynn wouldn't lose her and she wouldn't lose Brynn.

Because that simply wasn't an option.

❖

"Happy birthday, dear Violet. Happy birthday to you." The entire Lavender family broke into happy applause, and the rest of the patrons dining at Kimble's joined in. Violet, celebrating her thirty-fourth birthday, beamed from her spot next to Tad at the long table. It was tradition for the Lavenders to all go out for a big dinner to celebrate the birthday of each family member, a tradition that dated back to their childhoods when they got to choose any restaurant they wanted. Violet, a fan of the finer things in life, had selected Kimble's Surf and Turf, the only relatively upscale restaurant within ten miles of Homer's Bluff, for her celebration. The family had dutifully assembled on not only her behalf, but also to celebrate Aster on the brink of her move. While it was nice of her family to include her, she tried not to steal any thunder from Violet.

"What do you have in store for your next year on earth?" their father asked the birthday girl. He'd cleaned up impressively for the dinner. His beard had been trimmed close, and he wore the nicer of his two sport coats, receiving compliments from the entire family.

Violet stared dreamily at Tad and his coiffed dark hair. Aster imagined he owned a hundred sport jackets. "Oh, I don't know. Maybe finding a way to make my life feel a little more permanent. That might be nice."

Tad touched his rocks glass to Violet's glass of red wine. "One never knows what the future holds." The two of them made puppy-dog eyes at each other while the rest of them watched. Speaking of puppies, Aster checked her watch and wondered how little Dill was doing back at home. She'd had him for a little over two months, and so far, he'd shown himself to be semitrustworthy when she left the house, having only chewed one of her shoes to smithereens and the corner of one blue couch cushion.

"I probably should have had Brynn check in on Dill," Aster said to Sage. "I'm sure he's fine. He's just in that puppy stage still where every object is a toy to be tossed or destroyed."

"You could always send her to your place now." He nodded his head somewhere behind Aster. "She's been at the bar for the past twenty minutes."

"What?" Aster had passed by the bar earlier and had seen only a couple of football watchers nursing tall beers. How had she missed this? Aster swiveled, and sure enough, there she was, nursing something in a rocks glass, wearing jeans, a white blouse, and heels. Heels? No. That was new, and it did things to Aster. Like clockwork, almost as if she felt Aster's gaze on her, Brynn turned. When her eyes landed on Aster, she relaxed into a smile and raised her glass. They held for a moment, their connection snapping into place like a seat belt. Aster raised her very boring glass of iced water. She inclined her head to their table. Brynn shot back a look of question. Aster nodded vehemently.

"You guys, Brynn Garrett's on her way over," Marigold said. Aster watched her straighten as if preparing for some kind of mission. She remembered her sister's plan for Sage and Brynn when Brynn first arrived in town, but surely, she'd moved on, right?

"Hi, everyone!" Brynn said, grinning warmly at the table. "I heard there's a birthday?" Aster swallowed. She really looked fantastic, and Aster couldn't wipe the smile off her face. Was this just a casual night out? Aster hadn't mentioned where she was going, so the coincidence was fun.

"Violet is celebrating," her mother said and introduced her father to Brynn. "Brynn, we've met a couple of times in town, but this is Tom. He mostly sticks to the farm."

Her father nodded, cheeks pink as always. "Heard so much about you, Dr. Garrett." He was always friendly, polite, but shy, too. Aster loved that about him.

"Well, I'm a big fan of your whole brood, so it's my pleasure to finally meet you in person."

Marigold leaned in with her chin in her hand. "Brynn, we have a spot down here at the end of the table near Sage. Please join us." It was also next to Aster, so that would work fine. She only had two nights left in town, and she wanted to squeeze in as much time with Brynn as possible.

"Are you sure that's okay? I don't want to crash dessert." She looked genuinely embarrassed.

"More than okay," Violet said, "and as birthday girl I demand you join us for a slice of strawberry vanilla swirl cake. Is that all right with you, Aster, as my co-guest of honor tonight?"

Aster nodded conservatively. "I approve."

Brynn flashed her a smile and sat between her and Sage. Marigold immediately launched into host of their side of the table. "Brynn, I'm not sure how well you know Sage, but he's a whiz on a tractor." *And here we go.* Aster smothered an eye roll at Marigold's misplaced efforts.

"Is that so?" Brynn asked.

"Just doing my job," Sage said and took a sip of his draft beer. He wasn't interested in Brynn. She knew that complacent face anywhere.

"And he's adorable. I don't know if he's flashed his proprietary dimples yet, but they're something." Marigold was nothing if not a determined woman.

"You have to stop making me sound better than I am," Sage said and raised his eyebrows at his sister. He was a little drunk. He'd been drinking more these days, probably missing Tyler, who Brynn said was living it up with her classmates in Chicago.

"I've seen the dimples," Brynn said, "and they are as magical as you describe."

"Thank you," Sage said and flashed a killer smile anyway. He simply couldn't resist, could he?

"I want to hear about Aster's plans in Boston," Brynn said, already knowing most all of them. All eyes swiveled to her expectantly. She was caught off guard, happy to give all the attention to Violet tonight. Brynn had other ideas.

"Okay," Aster said. "Well, I'm arriving a little early because I want to get my ducks in a row. Visit campus. Unpack before classes start."

"I still can't believe we won't see you every day," her mother said. She'd been a mixture of proud and crestfallen when Aster had broken the news about Boston.

"I'll call. Send smoke signals," Aster said, pulling a direct smile from her mom. She was going to miss having her biggest cheerleader just a few minutes up the road. In fact, she didn't allow herself to think about that part too often, because she'd never been separated from her mother before and couldn't stand the thought.

"And what classes will they have you attending in the first semester?" her father asked.

That part got her excited. Just perusing the list of coursework was the very thing that made her take the leap and apply, all those months ago. She sat taller. "Well, they have a whole class just about ingredients. I'm really looking forward to that one. I'll also be taking artisan breads, culinary techniques, and world cuisine. Sixteen courses over two years." She could feel the smile take over her face as she spoke. She was *drowning* in anticipation of all that lay ahead. This was the biggest thing that had ever happened to Aster, and she planned to take full advantage of every moment in school, refining the techniques she did have, and adding to her knowledge base. She was confident that there were many gaps to fill.

Underneath the table, Brynn took her hand and gave it a squeeze. When she began to pull it back, Aster tugged, and Brynn left it right where it was, meeting Aster's gaze and offering a private smile. Her heart kicked. Brynn made her feel in ways she wasn't familiar, and her touch, the simple brushing of their fingertips beneath a table, pulled a response from her body that she didn't quite know how to channel. Instead, it tended to just take over, like now. The table was lively and loud, with folks a couple drinks in and talking over each other. In the midst of the commotion, Aster only saw Brynn. She'd never been more beautiful, and this was quite possibly the last time they'd see each other before Aster left. She dreaded that part, especially when everything in her wanted to spend more time together, either away from the world or smack dab in it. She wasn't picky.

"Aster, cake?" She looked up to see Tad offering her a piece of the birthday cake.

"I'd love a slice," she said, accepting the plate.

Moments later, Brynn set down her fork and inclined her head. "It's fun to watch you eat."

"Me? Don't do that," Aster said, horrified.

"Too late. It's not the first time either. You go slow with each bite and then pause for a short, thoughtful break before going on to the next one. I just race through the whole thing."

Oh, this was a compliment. "I think it's because I like to think about each ingredient that goes into a dish. I play a little game where I make a list and try to guess each one. Sometimes the quantities, too."

"Your brain is always busy, isn't it?"

She exhaled, because Brynn was right. She understood her in these little but important ways that people who had known Aster her entire life did not. She nodded. "A blessing and a curse."

"I can imagine," Brynn said, her knee brushing Aster's. Not an accident. Not the way it lingered. She saw that much on Brynn's face. She brushed Brynn's right back. All the while, down the table, the check was paid, her parents' treat as always, and everyone was assembling themselves to leave in the midst of their customary overlapping chatter. What everyone was doing the next day. How amazing the steak had been! When Tad was going on his next business trip for his father's firm.

"Need a ride home?" Brynn asked quietly. "I know where you live."

That sent a shiver. Aster had walked to the restaurant and was now glad she had. "Yes, please. And you're coming over." They held eye contact until Aster was pulled away by social norms.

She hugged Violet, who took Aster's face in her hands. "You are going to do amazing things in Boston. And we will be eating all the doughnuts while you're gone."

"You better. Happy birthday, Vi. I'll come by the shop tomorrow for a proper farewell."

Marigold swallowed. "I refuse to think about saying good-bye to you, so I will not think about it until the moment comes. Then I will crumble like a sandcastle kicked by a toddler."

"That's fair," Aster said and watched her sisters link arms as they rounded the table, always the pair. She said good-bye to the rest of her family and turned to Brynn. "I guess I'm ready." She really was. She wanted to be alone so they could exhale into *them* and relax away from it all.

"Me, too. Let's go."

She slid into Brynn's white SUV and smiled because the very clean car smelled so much like Brynn, faint oranges with vanilla like those Creamsicles they used to eat as kids on warm summer days. Only so much better. "Brynn."

"Yes, Aster."

"You always smell so nice."

Brynn glanced over at her as she drove. They shared a smile. Each exchange carried so much more weight now that their time was short. "Thank you. So do you."

"Just soap."

"Like fresh cotton. That's what I always think when I'm around you. And maybe a little cucumber."

Aster nodded. "Not bad. My shampoo. You're apparently good at identifying ingredients yourself."

"Or I just get lucky when it comes to you."

"Don't sell yourself short." A pause. "And I mean that in the larger sense, too, Brynn. Don't."

Brynn frowned as they turned into their neighborhood. "What do you mean, the larger sense?"

"I guess I meant with your ex. You've not said too much about her, but the little bits you've dropped make me think that she didn't treat you as nicely as she should have, and you're still paying for it now. I see that much. It's a shame."

"Oh." Brynn nodded. "I won't lie. She chose someone else over me. After cheating. Then tried to come back. Then chose the other woman again. Until she didn't."

Aster sighed. "I was afraid it was something like that." The idea infuriated her. What an idiot that ex-girlfriend was. Didn't she know what she had? "You deserve someone better than that, and I need you to know it. You deserve the world."

Brynn rolled her lips in. "Wow."

"What?"

She shook her head. "I think on a fundamental level, I do know that. Hell, I say it to myself every day. But hearing it from someone else who articulates the idea with such…sincerity. Well, it resonates. Maybe one day."

"Good. It's true." She took her time with this next part. "You should know that you're more important to me than anyone ever has been."

She saw Brynn adjust her grip on the steering wheel, affected.

"Don't you make me mist up. I'm not going to cry. I'm not. I'm already dreading you not being twelve big steps from my driveway." She looked over at Aster. "I feel the same. Okay?" But the tears pooled in her eyes anyway, sending a lump to Aster's throat. "I'm keeping you."

They drove on for a bit of silence, approaching Baker Street.

"Don't go back to her, okay?" It was bold of Aster to make such a request, but it felt like there was nothing to lose at this point. She didn't know how closely they would stay in touch once she left, and the next time she'd be back to Homer's Bluff, Brynn would be back in Chicago. This was it. So she wasn't holding back.

"I don't plan on it. I don't take her calls."

"Keep that up. And if you need someone to call in her place, you can call me. We can read books on the phone."

Brynn pulled into her driveway. "Thank you for that." Her voice was soft like the satin of a glove. She'd miss that voice soon. "Shall we go in?"

"Yeah," Aster said, hopping out into the quiet night. In fact, she couldn't remember another night being as quiet. No movement on the street. No crickets to underscore them. Just the stars keeping watch as an evening chill moved across her skin. She walked alongside Brynn as they covered the short distance to Aster's door. She opened it and turned back. "Come in?"

"If you want." Aster led them inside, and they both smiled as tiny footsteps raced toward them in a furious pitter-patter. "There's the best little guy. Hi, Dill!" She scooped up the clumsy puppy and kissed the side of his face as he wiggled gleefully in celebration of his person's homecoming. When Aster set him back down again, he did that thing where he ran in place until he found traction on the kitchen floor. He grabbed his stuffed carrot and, after dancing around Aster's feet for her official greeting, raced to the back door.

"I'll let him out. He's gonna toss that carrot around for half an hour before ever asking to come back in."

"Sign of a smart dog when they invent games for themselves."

"He's amazing. So cute, but also already learning everything I try to teach him."

"You look really happy together. I love watching you with him."

Aster nodded, her heart full. "It was a really good thing that happened to me, running into him." She met Brynn's gaze. "A lot of good has happened lately." She took a moment. Brynn let her. "I'm happy we met."

"Aster." The word on Brynn's lips gave her goose bumps. The way Brynn whispered it brought on more.

"What do we do?" Aster asked. It was an all-encompassing question.

Brynn's answer was upon her. As if she simply had to, Brynn was moving toward Aster with a look in her eyes Aster had never seen before. The world slowed down until it was just the two of them in her kitchen, face-to-face, sharing air in maybe the most intense moment of her life. Brynn took Aster's face in her hands, her gaze on Aster's lips and her lips alone, transfixed and not in any hurry. She closed the small distance, angled her head, and pressed her mouth to Aster's, whose eyes slammed shut at the onslaught of heat and everything good in this world. Her hands went to Brynn's waist automatically, and she pulled her closer, but it would never be enough. Their mouths began to move together slowly, as if memorizing, savoring, keeping. She deepened the kiss and pushed her tongue into Brynn's mouth just as her back met the wall. Every nerve ending in Aster's body shot to life like a symphony approaching a crescendo. She'd never felt so much when kissing another person before, but this was not just any woman.

"God, your mouth is amazing," Brynn said, pulling back. "How is this so damn good? Why couldn't you fall short of my expectations just for once?" She traced Aster's bottom lip with her fingertip, as Aster found air. Just in time, too, because Brynn came back for more, thank God. This time, she kissed Aster with welcome authority. The air around them scorched her skin, and she reveled in unfamiliar lust. They weren't frantic or hurried, but they were thorough and good at it. Very good. Too good. God. Her center ached.

Brynn went back down on her heels and took her fantastic lips with her. "Is it bad that we did that?"

"No," Aster answered honestly. "I really, really liked it."

"Me, too."

A pause.

"But I'm leaving."

Brynn nodded. "And then I am."

They stared at each other, the understanding of their dilemma strung between them.

"So we leave it here," Brynn said.

"Yeah. I suppose we do."

"It's the smartest thing. Aster, I can't offer more. My head. My heart."

"I know. It's okay. I promise."

Yet Brynn didn't turn to go, and Aster hadn't moved a muscle. It was as if they were holding on to a moment that was slowly slipping away into the history books. That one time they kissed after dinner in Aster's kitchen. "Don't forget me, *this*, okay?"

"Not a chance. Our dogs are related, remember?"

"That's right. Maybe we'll reunite them someday."

"Would be cruel not to."

Brynn took her by the hand and gave her a playful yank, pulling her in for a good-bye hug. "You take Boston by storm. I'll never forgive you if you don't."

"How about I just work on not upsetting anything there? I plan to walk in and keep my hands to myself."

Brynn backed up. "Speaking of hands, I had lots of thoughts of what it would be like to touch you, Aster, and though we never got past first base, let me tell you. Your body? Sigh. Yeah."

Aster's eyebrows rose automatically. Her midsection went soft, and shocking arousal showed up again, replacing the sentimentality of a moment before. Because after that comment, what she wanted more than anything was to take Brynn by the hand and lead her straight back to the bedroom where they would pick up where they left off. She would kiss Brynn reverently, passionately, and take every stitch of clothing off her slowly until she could worship her body properly. She imagined Brynn naked on top and then beneath. She swallowed. "I can easily say that nothing about you disappoints either. I mean that in every sense."

"Take care of yourself, Aster Lavender." Brynn nodded, offered one last regretful smile, and opened the door. "Good-bye for now."

"Bye, Brynn. You take care."

PART TWO

CHAPTER SEVEN

I need two pork chops, a risotto, and a beef Wellington," Ed Talbott, their head chef, called to the kitchen.

"Yes, Chef," Aster yelled back and went to work on the chops, while her fellow chefs on the line handled the rest of the order. When a ticket came in, she didn't delay, preparing her meats promptly, paying close attention to temperature and efficiency with simply the touch of a finger to the outside. She spooned the citrus sauce over the tops of the chops as they cooked. When her meat sizzled and she achieved the perfect sear, she slid them onto the plate and garnished with more sauce, an orange slice, and patch of fresh slaw.

"Pork chops up."

"Nice work, Aster," Ed said, inspecting her work. He was also her instructor and taught two of her classes at the institute. As executive chef, he oversaw the ticket as a whole, making sure each dish was of quality and worthy to serve.

Aster nodded and called back dutifully. "Thank you, Chef."

No time to dawdle. She prepped her station for the next ticket, adjusting the blue bandana she wore around her forehead. She'd been on her feet for six hours now but loved every second of working at Stone Top, the restaurant owned by the culinary school. Not only was it used to showcase what the school brought to the city by way of fantastic food, but it served as a training ground for the second-year students. Aster could hardly believe how far she'd come since arriving in Boston just fifteen months ago. While she'd carved out a great niche for herself with doughnuts, she had no idea how much she didn't know about food, its makeup, and its preparation. Until now. Her time as a student had proved invaluable, and she'd lost herself in a haze of bookwork, quick-fire labs, and hands-on training from enthusiastic instructors. While her passion remained pastry work, her skill set had grown and flourished, and she'd finished first in most of her classes. A badge of pride.

"You killed it tonight," Nora said, pulling her toque off as they walked through the parking lot after a long night of service. They'd worked side by side that night, Aster on meats and Nora on seafood, which she excelled at. "You didn't have a single dish sent back by Ed and were constantly on pace."

"Thanks. I found a good rhythm," Aster said, leaning against Nora's car. They'd gotten in the habit of riding to work and school together as classmates who also lived in the same building.

"Oh, don't tease me with talk of your rhythm," Nora said. Her eyes shone playfully, and her eyebrows bounced. The streetlight illuminated her face, and Aster was reminded that Nora Delgado was not just a lot of fun, but also very pretty. Jet-black hair, curls when she wanted them, big brown eyes, and a freckle to the side of her right eye that Aster liked.

"Stop that," Aster said through her own laugh. But she didn't move out of the small space they occupied together. It felt nice. Why not? They'd flirted here and there. It was fun and kept the long days interesting. Though, Nora was making it increasingly obvious that she'd be interested in taking things farther with Aster. Little touches here and there that were growing longer as time went on. Prolonged stares and then, of course, the innuendoes. Nora was good at those.

But Aster had found the whole thing tricky to navigate. Not that she hadn't tried to get there, mentally. Nora was playful and light. She valued her work just as much as Aster did, which made them kindred spirits in a lot of ways. Nora was outgoing and ambitious in any given social situation, which was a nice complement to Aster's more reserved demeanor. Plus, Aster liked her. Nora pulled her out of her shell. There was no good reason for her not to seize this opportunity with Nora and see what might develop between them. The only problem was that whenever she'd decide to give things a try, something got in her way. She could play dumb and pretend to not know what was holding her back, but that would be false. The reality was that there was a woman she'd spent time with once upon a time that she simply couldn't get out of her head.

She dreamed about Brynn. Reminisced a lot, especially on the harder days. She missed her smile and easygoing company. The care she took with the animals she treated. The way she smelled. The way she kissed. All of it.

They hadn't talked except for a few early text exchanges after the move. Perhaps some unspoken agreement that it was easier that way. A clean parting. While Aster wasn't on social media, she'd heard from her family that Brynn hadn't left Homer's Bluff when it had been time for Tyler to return. Instead, the two had gone into practice together. Formed a partnership. And though Aster wasn't a huge fan of the slower pace of Homer's Bluff, the idea of two of her favorite people working side-by-side there made her really happy.

"Look at you," Nora said, joining Aster as she leaned against the car. She poked Aster in the ribs. "You've got that faraway look in your eye again."

"Just thinking about next week when I head home."

"It's been a while for you, hasn't it?"

Aster nodded. "Over a year. I miss my family. My mom. It'll be good to see them in person and not on a screen." She exhaled. "It will also be strange." She pulled her shoulders to her ears. "I don't feel like the same person who left that town. So much has happened for me."

"Well, you're a rock star now. Everyone who encounters you thinks so."

That made her feel good. "I feel like I've changed a lot."

Nora nodded. "I've seen it. You're more confident now. More talkative, too."

Aster shrugged. "I think that's it. This place makes me feel like I'm, I don't know, somebody."

Nora's eyes met hers. "Trust me when I say that you are. Your family is going to love all the new parts of you if that's what you're worried about. And after fall break, you'll be back here with me, refreshed and good as new." Nora took Aster's hand and laced their fingers together. Aster smiled down at the gesture, a little surprised, a little not.

"That's new."

Nora grinned proudly. "I'm taking a few liberties these days. You don't seem like the type who makes moves." Aster inclined her head from side to side, only halfway agreeing with the declaration.

Nora straightened and faced her. "Another liberty coming at ya. I was thinking that maybe when we get back from the break, we could steal a weekend off and head to Provincetown. Spend some time together alone."

"Friend time?" Aster raised an eyebrow, trying to understand the nature of the trip. "Or…"

"Any kind of time. We can play it by ear. We'll eat some really great lobster in butter, stare out at the water, and do a little window-shopping. No requirements, only options."

Aster had never been to Provincetown, but she'd been dying to check it out. "Yeah. Okay. That could be a worthwhile getaway."

"Only you would categorize it with those words." Nora shook her head with affection.

"But I have to be honest, I don't know where my head is at in terms of romance. I have some things to sort out in that department."

Nora nodded, pensive. "Some things or some*one*?"

Aster covered her eyes with both hands and held them in silence for a beat. Finally, she let them drop. "Both."

Nora wasn't deterred. "Tell you what. I'll book it. A two-bedroom. Totally platonic." She squeezed Aster's hand and hopped in the car. Aster hesitated a moment, feeling light and heavy at the same time. Nora had made it clear that there were no expectations, and that should have relieved some of the pressure. And it did. But was she being a complete idiot about a woman she hadn't spoken to in a year? She could fall into bed with a beautiful woman in a quaint little town and just enjoy. That wasn't a bad thing at all.

If only her heart wasn't anchored to another back home. She had to wonder *What if?* And she had to find out. If for no other reason than what happened *then* was affecting her life *now*. And it was time to be brave and go after what she wanted.

As they drove back to their shared apartment building, Aster watched the lights of downtown Boston race past in a blur of color and concrete. Quietly, she remembered a pair of green eyes. She'd likely see them soon and had to figure out what she was going to say to Brynn because she couldn't just sit on what she'd been holding on to for all of these months—her very real feelings and a small kernel of hope that something just might come of them. Brynn hadn't been in a place to reciprocate, last they'd met. But what about now? Time had passed.

She was heading back to Homer's Bluff the next day for a week, and in that time, she had an important goal. Tell Brynn Garrett that she missed her, thought about her more than she should, and longed more than anything to kiss her again and for a long time after that. She also had to find out if there was any kind of chance that possibly, maybe just a little, Brynn felt the same.

Aster braced against the nervous motion of her stomach at what was ahead. The stakes felt incredibly high. For now, she could take out thoughts of Brynn and turn them over in her mind, relive the little moments between them that had resonated so intensely, and quietly wonder about more. But if Brynn hadn't thought about Aster since she'd left, if she didn't feel the same, not only would Aster lose the chance of a future with Brynn, but she'd lose the purity of those memories, too. And she treasured them more than anything. Then what?

"Aster?"

"Yeah?"

Nora stood in front of their building, door open in her hand. "Um, we're here. You coming? I hear there's a dog up there waiting for a walk."

"Yeah. I am." She shelved her fears, hanging them back up until tomorrow when she'd make the big trek back home, feeling like a different person than the one who'd left. It would be an important day. It would be a good day. She just had a feeling.

❖

In the quiet of Tuesday morning, Brynn woke slowly to the *tuk-tuk* of a robin in the tree just beyond her bedroom window. She stretched, enjoying the feeling of her muscles pulling pleasantly. A hand on her bare back reminded her that she wasn't alone this morning. Micah had stayed over, that's right, and was making herself known.

"Good morning," Brynn said, turning onto her back.

Micah's short red hair stood straight up like it did every morning after a good sleep, and she held the sheet to her chest. "I slept like the dead. Hi."

"Hi there."

Micah placed a quick kiss on Brynn's lips and fell onto her back. "I have three client meetings this morning and lunch with the partners."

Micah was a corporate attorney in Wichita, who had a love-hate thing happening with her job. Brynn didn't mind being her escape but did feel bad that the time they spent together forced Micah to commute the eighty minutes into the city, sometimes round trip in one day if they had plans.

"I have a schnauzer, a kitten, a cockatiel, and a Shetland pony, if my memory serves correctly. All before noon."

Micah stared at the wall. "Your day sounds so much more interesting."

"Well, none of them are merging or acquiring anything, so I don't know. They need to get it together."

"They might surprise you." Micah was up and out of bed, off to shower and hit the road. She really wasn't one to snuggle or chat too much on those mornings after, which actually suited Brynn fine. In fact, it was probably better that way. It kept everything in the neat and orderly column Brynn very much needed. Micah liked to be at her desk by eight thirty, which was going to be a lofty task today, given their slight sleep-in.

Brynn watched her walk naked through the room. Micah was tall with small breasts and a willowy body. She also looked incredibly powerful in a business suit. Brynn wouldn't want to mess with her in court, that was for damn sure. The two of them had been seeing each other for going on three months now. It was an easy relationship. Low on drama and conflict, and worked well with their schedules. They could enjoy each other's company but were also great at retreating to their respective lives when they needed to. Micah had just recently started referring to Brynn as her girlfriend, and honestly, that part felt pretty good. Like she was back in the saddle at last. Albeit, a modified saddle, fitted to what Brynn needed. Simple. Low angst. No big overarching feelings. Micah didn't make her feel vulnerable, heartsick, or love-drunk. She liked that very much. She liked Micah, too.

"I'll make coffee. Want some for your drive?" Brynn called.

"Yes. Yes. Yes!" Micah called back over the already running shower. She always made herself at home, assuming what was Brynn's was hers. And it was. Well, in a way. That kind of assumption was the reason their relationship had progressed at the pace it had. Micah had decided that it should, and when she decided something, it generally happened. Part of Brynn really liked that. Another part wished for more of a partnership, and perhaps that was something they'd discuss at some point down the road. No relationship was perfect without work, right?

When Micah emerged exactly twenty-five minutes later with her red hair tamed, Brynn poured the coffee into two travel mugs and slid one to Micah. "That Autumn Harvest Festival is tonight. Do you remember me telling you about it?"

Micah closed her eyes, her hand going flat on her forehead. "Vaguely. You wanted to go? I'd need to drive back."

"I did." Brynn winced. "But I'll cut you a rain check. Small towns have festivals for everything. You can catch the next one." Though in her experience, the Autumn Harvest was the best one, hands down. They held it out at the old fairgrounds, a beautiful spot surrounded by dogwood trees. The festival hosted pumpkin carving, warm beverages of all kinds, a hay maze, and live music. Don't even get her started on the vendors with all the artisan items for sale. Even that stale-doughnut lady impressed with her array of quilts, one of which Brynn now owned.

"I'll take you up on it," Micah said, downing a swallow of coffee that had to have burned her throat. She didn't flinch. That was Micah. "Killer afternoon to get through, but I'll call you after. Deal?"

"Deal."

"I'm off. Knock 'em dead." Micah kissed her quickly and was out the door in a typical Micah dash.

Brynn had a little time before heading into the clinic, less of a dasher. They'd agreed early on in their partnership that Tyler would handle the early mornings and she would pick up by nine and stay until six or whenever the last patient needed her to. Now that the clinic could accommodate more clientele and with the addition of Tyler's dentistry certification, they were seeing more and more patients coming in from neighboring cities. The clinic was in great shape as a result. Plus, Brynn had helped streamline a few of their processes and procedures, saving them all money and operating more efficiently.

As for Brynn, she had fallen in love with the slower pace of small-town living, which was one of the reasons she'd opted to stay put and make Tyler the offer to go half in on the business. She'd slowly begun to make a life for herself in Homer's Bluff and now felt like a true resident after close to two years. She knew most everyone's name, was invited to the homes of her clients for dinner, made cookies for bake sales, and donated to the firefighters' silent auction. She even applauded their shirtless pancake breakfasts because abs needed fanfare, too. She was happy these days. Well, *happier,* at least. Life was simple. Easy enough. She floated along.

"Brynn."

It was like a loud scratch on a record player. She stood on the east side of the fairgrounds, frozen in place with the scarf from Ming Humphrey's vendor table in her hand. She knew the voice. The Autumn Harvest Fest was in full and lively force all around. People everywhere. Conversations overlapping. Had she heard correctly? She turned, clutching the green and red plaid scarf she'd just been considering purchasing. And there, staring back at her, was none other than Aster Lavender. The world slowed down, and the action around her dimmed, leaving a spotlight on the woman she hadn't seen or talked to in over a year now. After a moment of shock, happiness flooded. She grinned and returned the scarf to the portable rack immediately. "Aster. You're here." It was Aster all right, but there were changes. Her dark hair was longer and had layers. She looked super put together, wearing navy jeans and brown ankle boots with a matching brown sweater. Sophisticated and…wow. Fantastic. In the amount of time that she'd been away, the youthful version of Aster had been noticeably replaced. Brynn swallowed her surprise at the newer, hipper, more grown-up version of Aster and allowed her joy to come through instead. "It's great to see you." It really was. Once it got going, she couldn't wipe the smile from her face. It almost felt like a part of this town had gone missing and had now snapped back into place.

"You, too," Aster said, moving to her without hesitation. She pulled Brynn to her for a warm hug, which she happily returned. "I wasn't sure if I'd run into you tonight. I'm glad I did." She exhaled, her eyes searching Brynn's face like she was a sight for sore eyes. Aster sure was. She just wanted to drink in the sight of her. It had been too long.

"Are you here for a visit? Are you staying? What's the story?"

She nodded. "We're in the middle of fall break. Last year, I kept my nose to the grindstone and stayed in Boston working during my time off, but this year, well, I'm taking back a little of my own life."

"Your family must be thrilled. I just had lunch with Violet yesterday." It had become their new tradition. A newer friendship that she enjoyed. Maybe because through Violet she was reminded of Aster. She hadn't analyzed it too much. "She should have told me."

"It was kind of last-minute. I made the leap and booked the ticket just a few days ago. My parents knew. Not sure if Violet did."

Brynn wondered distantly if Aster knew about Violet's personal struggles but decided this was maybe not the time. "Have you seen them yet? Your siblings?"

Aster nodded. "I have. My sisters are just through there. They insisted we do the festival together. Sage is running around with his guy friends like middle school. But we'll meet up with them later."

"If I remember correctly, you were a huge fan of the large town gatherings." A joke.

"I'm better at them now. When you give yourself a chance to miss something, you likely do. Speaking of long distance, Brynn, you should see Dill. I'm not kidding. He's eighteen pounds of fun now. Loves Boston. Can't eat enough hot dogs." She slid her hands into her back pockets and something about that very casual gesture made Brynn's middle section dip, which startled her. It had been a while, but Aster still managed to affect her in the physical sense, apparently. She found that interesting and, quite frankly, jarring. She wasn't starved for physical affection the way she had been a year ago. Yet Aster still checked that box in a big way. "You have no idea how happy that makes me. He used to be all paws."

"He's a tank who longs to be a gazelle." Aster laughed, and Brynn's gaze skipped from Aster's eyes to her lips and back again. *Do not stare at her mouth, no matter how good a mouth it is.* Just because they'd kissed, once upon a time, did not give Brynn permission to go there now. Aster rolled her lips in, right on cue. Could she sense the trajectory of Brynn's thoughts? Did she have them right back? *What? Stop it. No.*

"You okay?" Aster asked with an easy smile. Since when did she have an *easy* smile, and why was it now affecting Brynn's knees? Aster had moves now?

"Yeah. Yes. Sorry, I got lost in the flurry of activity around us." She gave her head a shake to clear it.

"Right," Aster said. "I was actually wondering if we could steal some quiet time to talk. Just us."

Brynn didn't hesitate because in this moment, she wanted nothing more in the world than to talk to Aster, catch up, and hear all about her time in Boston. In fact, she couldn't wait. "I have time now. We could—"

"There you are." Arms were around her waist from behind, and a kiss was placed on her neck. She watched as Aster's eyes went briefly wide. *Micah.* What was Micah doing here? And why did this exchange leave her a little mortified. She shoved it aside. Questions for later.

"Hi," Brynn said, turning in Micah's arms. She frowned and searched her face. "I don't understand. I thought you were staying in the city."

"I thought so, too, until my four o'clock canceled and I packed a bag." Several inches taller than Brynn, Micah stood behind her, her arms still around Brynn's waist in what felt like an obtrusive grip. "Happy to see me?"

"Yes, yes. Of course I am." She remembered to brighten. Because she was *happy.*

"Now we can do the shopping and the strolling that you like. Want to?"

"Yes. But first, I want you to meet someone, okay?" She gestured to Aster, who stood waiting, her face noticeably blank. "Micah Henderson, meet my good friend, Aster Lavender."

"Oh, you're one of the Lavenders. I've met several of those. Violet's one of them, right? You have lunch with her." Brynn nodded.

"I'm the last in the sibling lineup," Aster said.

Brynn jumped in. "She's been studying culinary arts in Boston. Her food is out of this world. I'm telling you—"

"Amazing. It's so fantastic to meet you. I think we're going to stroll. You enjoy yourself." Micah laced her fingers through Brynn's and gave her hand a squeeze. Brynn watched as Aster's gaze fell to their hands. Why did Brynn feel a little sick? "Shall we?"

That was Micah. Never one to dawdle when there was something on the to-do list. She briefly tried to imagine Micah reading a book on a bench in the town square, but the image was near impossible to conjure. She couldn't shake the feeling that Micah's competitive side had fueled their abrupt departure. She didn't love that. But Micah wasn't in her life for great big bursts of love. Micah brought other very valuable qualities to the table. She couldn't forget that.

Brynn turned to Aster, who immediately raised a conciliatory hand. "Oh. Hey, it's okay. We can catch up later, right?" But the spark behind her eyes was gone, and the confidence she'd arrived with was, too. Brynn felt that loss all over.

"Okay, because I need to hear all about little Dill and how he's doing. And Boston. And you. And the food. The books."

"You will." Aster stayed right where she was and watched them walk away. While Brynn was aware of Aster's eyes on her, she resisted the urge to look back.

As she and Micah walked the festival hand in hand, she tried for glimpses of Aster. She didn't like the way their encounter had ended, unfinished, dangling, if that was possible. She saw Aster once at the cider stand, Marigold's arm slung around her shoulders, and Aster laughing at something her sister said. A pang of jealousy struck. She wished for a moment she was there laughing with them. She wondered now what had been said. But the sight of Aster laughing made her smile. She'd missed it.

"What's got you all lit up?" Micah asked, rubbing her shoulders from behind. "Is it because I surprised you? It is, isn't it. I knew you'd like that. You should have seen your face when you saw me. I don't think I've ever seen you so surprised."

"It was a huge shock. Yeah," Brynn said, meeting Micah's bright blue eyes. Behind them, Sage and Tyler walked together, heads down in what looked like a serious conversation. Uh-oh. Tyler, upon returning to town, had vowed to keep Sage at arm's length. After being home two months, she'd let the truth come falling from her lips.

"We slept together that first week I was home from Chicago."

"The first week? You two are like magnets." They had been sitting on the floor of Tyler's living room late one night after binging a couple of Jennifer Lopez movies because Tyler thought she took on kickass characters they could all look up to, and Brynn harbored a longtime crush. Equal-opportunity viewing.

"I couldn't explain it if I wanted to," Tyler said. "But you're right. There's this undeniable pull. He's my person who happens to be so hot that it makes me angry."

"But I thought you were done with the complications of your will-they won't-they status?"

"Because I'm weak, and because he's Sage Lavender, sent to Earth to torture me with all I can't have."

"Oh no." Brynn frowned, already nervous for her friend, who she knew to have the kindest heart.

"I was humiliated and hurt after that first time when he ghosted me, but this time was different. The sex was something out of a novel, and Brynn, he didn't run." Taylor touched her head, eyes wide. "I'm not sure what to do with that."

Brynn exhaled in relief. Maybe Aster wasn't the only one who'd done some growing up. "Well, that's something."

Tyler went for a handful of popcorn, a hint of confusion and misery on her face. "I've known Sage my whole life, and he's a good person. I think he just didn't know how to reject me properly, so he dropped me instead."

"And now?"

She seemed lost. "He wants to give things a try. For us to actually date."

"You deserve the world, Tyler." Brynn squinted, wanting to wrap Tyler in a protective bubble. "Are you sure he's the one to give it to you?"

"I honestly don't know. He's too afraid of his own damn shadow." Tyler wiped away a tear that had made its way to her cheeks. "I'd refused to give it any more of my energy. Planned to let him live his life, date several hundred women if he wanted to, and I'd live mine. I'd made peace."

"And now the door is open," Brynn said.

"That damn door. I hate the way it swings."

Seeing them now at the festival, it looked like the door had yet to settle one way or the other. She took out her phone and sent Tyler a text. *Let me know if you need backup.* She sent another one. *Or encouragement.*

A few minutes later, a reply came. *I'm okay. Just hearing him out. Lots of promises.*

She imagined it was a difficult leap for someone like Tyler to make. She'd been hurt, yet she still wanted what she wanted. Tricky. Brynn decided that instead of stalking Aster, or watching out for Tyler, she should focus on the here and now, enjoy her night with Micah.

She made a point to brighten, giving their hands a swing. "Do you want to grab some spiced wine? Maybe sit and people watch?"

"Nah. I think I need to move around, take it all in awhile. Can we people watch later?"

"We can." Brynn showed Micah her favorite parts of the festival over the next hour, and when they headed back to her place, she did something awful. When Micah's lips found their way to her neck, she feigned a headache she didn't actually have. "I probably didn't drink enough water. I'll grab a glass now, but go on ahead to bed. I'll be there in just a minute."

"All right, babe. I hope you feel better."

She smiled and waited as Micah retreated to the bedroom. So different from Aster. And she only made the comparison because Aster was fresh in her mind from their run-in. Where Micah was straight and long, Aster was soft with perfect curves. Micah had pursed lips much of the time, thin but very expressive. Aster's mouth was full and a little pouty. She had that thick dark hair you just wanted to shove your fingers into, while Micah's was short, red, and generally coiffed to an inch of its life.

In her darkened kitchen, she brought the glass to her lips, the cool water refreshing as it went down. She closed her eyes, touched the sweating glass to her neck, the cold helping bring her down from the heat just that simple train of thought had inspired. She hadn't had a chance to talk any more with Aster that night, but she was home for a week, and Brynn would make the time. It was that same feeling that came when she couldn't put down a really good book even though other areas of life called. She placed the glass on the counter and allowed her hand to skim her breast on the outside of her T-shirt. *Oh wow*. Then she slipped her hand underneath the fabric and caressed the skin from her neck to her breast. She murmured quietly at the powerful sensation and realized it was because of *who* she imagined touching her that way. A woman she knew really well, but didn't at the same time. She wanted to know more of Aster. Intimate details. What was her deepest fear? What did she sound like when she came? That realization struck her hard. She straightened, stepped back, and dropped her hand.

This was not at all the way things were supposed to go.

There was a wonderful woman in her bed right now, and her mind was inexplicably pulled in another direction. Why? She took a deep breath and let it out slowly. She was tired. It had been a long week, and that was likely why her thoughts were all over the place, overlapping into areas they had no business.

She stalked back to her bedroom and slid beneath the sheets next to Micah. Aster Lavender, sexy and sweet and intriguing as hell, could not just waltz into town and disrupt all that with an easy smile. She was best left on the shelf, and that was where she would stay.

Decided. She slammed her eyes closed and banished all thoughts. That didn't mean she was successful...

CHAPTER EIGHT

Aster hadn't anticipated Brynn would have a girlfriend. She should have.

She sat there numb. It had been so naive of her, she realized in retrospect, because Brynn was universally loved, beautiful, and ambitious. Of course she'd be out there dating, not pining away for someone with whom she once spent time. And what did that say about Aster, still hung up on a phantom relationship, holding Brynn to who she was when Aster left town, when she had every right to grow and change along with the rest of the world.

Her green eyes were the same, though. Aster had lost herself in them all over again in just their short exchange. For a few short moments, the world had felt wonderful again as she stood face-to-face with the one person who'd populated her thoughts on an ongoing basis. When the girlfriend had shown up, Aster had plummeted to reality with a thud. Fantasy over. Her stomach had curled up in the most uncomfortable knot, and her chest had seized as if trapped in a painful vise. Anguish had pulsed through her blood as she watched the woman with the short red hair kiss the side of Brynn's neck with such ownership. Ah, so that's how things were now. It had been good that Brynn and Micah were talking to each other because Aster's words were a jumble of black and white nonsense, inaccessible, as she worked overtime to comprehend the scene playing out in front of her.

"When did Brynn get a girlfriend?" she'd asked her sisters a short time later as they watched Ray Summers attempt to shoot ten baskets in sixty seconds in exchange for a giant stuffed whale.

"Oh, right. Micah," Violet said. Ray missed the first four attempts before finally sinking one. "I meant to tell you. It's been a few months that they've been an item."

Aster nodded because that would have been helpful information. Not that her sisters knew anything about her feelings or their romantic connection. She'd kept that information to herself. "Good for Brynn." She didn't mean it. In fact, her very being loathed the words she'd just spoken, but she minimized her reaction to save a little face. She preferred to nurse her heart quietly.

Marigold nodded in between cheers for Ray, who seemed especially vested in winning that damned whale. Hell, he could buy it for much cheaper at this point. This had to be his fourth turn. "Micah is from Wichita and comes to town to see Brynn several times a week." Leave it to Marigold to have all the gossip. "They're quite the couple. Oh, she's gay. Brynn. Did you know that? Faster, Ray!"

"I did know. Cool." Bolstering any sort of positive emotion was an uphill battle, so she committed to nonchalance.

They walked on, Aster with her hands shoved into the pockets of her black jacket. She made a point to focus on her sisters and spending time with then, soaking up every second. Together, they shared a few laughs and even grabbed an apple beer to celebrate the season.

But something was off, and it wasn't just Brynn's new girlfriend. As hard as she tried, Aster couldn't shake the hunch that Violet was not at all Violet. Where was her zest for fashion? Her energy. Her playful sense of humor. Aster was confused and pulled Marigold aside the next day for more information.

It wasn't what she wanted to hear. In fact, it was awful.

Homer's Bluff hadn't changed a whole lot in the fifteen months Aster had been away. Small things. The awnings in the center of town were now navy instead of green. Her brother's blue ball cap had been traded out for a new favorite red one, given to him at Christmas, apparently. But the most awful of all news was that Violet wasn't being treated the way she should by her new husband and father of her child.

Marigold shook her head sadly. "It's been pretty bad. Tad changed once they were married. It got even worse when Ethan was born. I feel like it's maybe time we *all* start talking with her about leaving. She'll listen if it's not just me spouting off again."

"You should have told me, Marigold," Aster sputtered, seeing red,

THE LAST LAVENDER SISTER

given the information she'd just learned. She and Marigold stood on the curb in front of their childhood home after the festival.

"She didn't want me to. She's adamant that everyone thinks she has the perfect life, the perfect family. She was already embarrassed that they didn't have the big wedding she'd always dreamed of."

"God. Who cares about that?" A lot can happen in a short amount of time, apparently. Fifteen months and Aster was out of the loop on a lot. What she didn't understand was why her family hadn't sent up a red flag, but if what Marigold was saying was true, maybe they didn't have the full picture. Leave it to Violet to put a fine finish on what sounded like control and abuse. But even in the midst of the lively festival, Aster could see, plain as day, that Violet was not herself. Something was wrong. Her smiles were dim, less confident, and sucked away almost as quickly as they appeared. She'd clearly had a good time out with Aster and Marigold and let loose a little more at a time. Aster was blown away by how someone usually in charge, so full of life, had shifted to a shell of her former self.

Aster tapped her bottom lip, searching for what to say, what to do to make it all go away. She'd not attended the wedding, which had been announced just days before it happened. She would have, only there had not actually been one. While Violet had always dreamed of a white fairy-tale wedding, complete with a train as long as she'd ever seen, it hadn't worked out that way. Unbeknownst to them all, Violet had been pregnant the night Aster left town, and baby Ethan had been born to Violet and Tad just seven months later. They'd married at the courthouse on a Tuesday afternoon and planned to have a lavish reception one day. Only that hadn't happened either.

Marigold blinked, and Aster realized it was because she was attempting to hold back tears. "They're not happy, Aster. He yells. Throws things. I think he smacked her in the mouth, though I couldn't get her to admit it. It's been hard to watch." Marigold placed her hands on the small of her back and looked up at the stars. "She doesn't take my calls as much. That's hard, too. We used to be close, you know?"

"I never would have guessed. How did it come to this?"

Marigold rolled her lips in. "He seems to resent her and the baby for tying him down. I don't think he would have even married her if his father hadn't forced him for appearances. I just kept hoping things would get better."

She was crying now, and Aster was at a loss. "Come here." She pulled her sister into a hug and held on, not sure how she could help, and hating so much that they were even here. "She's going to be okay. We'll make sure of it."

She would, too. This entire situation was out of her depth, but Aster didn't care. Violet was too wonderful a person to live under the thumb of a rich, entitled narcissist. She knew exactly who to go to first.

❖

"Good morning, baby girl," her mother said, as Aster descended the stairs still in her shorts and sleep shirt, her dog at her heels as always. It hadn't been the most restful night given all she had to think about, but morning had come all the same. It was still dark outside, and the silhouetted trees peeking in from the backyard offered a nice greeting. She'd never really shaken the habit of getting up in the wee hours of the morning to get started on the doughnuts. Perhaps she'd always be an early riser.

"Morning, Mama," she said and accepted a kiss on the cheek. Being back home again, staying in her parents' house near the farm, was like being wrapped in the warmest of security blankets. She'd had no idea how much she needed this. She let Dill out and joined her mother in the kitchen, relishing the quiet period before the sun came up and the world got started. To Aster, these were sacred minutes.

"Your face is telling stories. Want to fill me in?"

Aster slid a strand of hair behind her ear and helped herself to coffee. "You doing that mother's intuition thing again?"

"Always. I know when you're upset about something, and you are. Just look at those little lines on your sweet forehead." She held out an arm and Aster automatically slipped beneath it for one of those hugs only a mother could bestow. In the warmth of her mom's arms, Aster felt safe, like maybe everything was going to be okay. "Are you going to tell me about it?" her mother asked.

She sighed and slid onto one of the counter stools that used to be so tall that her feet would swing back and forth. She had a couple of things on her mind, so she went with the order in which they'd happened. "I found out last night that Brynn has a girlfriend."

Her mother was quiet for a moment, which was a little excruciating because she was now the first person Aster had even hinted to about her feelings for Brynn. Finally, her features softened. "And you were hoping she was single for personal reasons?"

Aster nodded. "I was too passive. I see that now. I could have called or kept in contact. Told her about my feelings."

Her mother sipped her Earl Grey tea. Her favorite. "And what held you back?"

It was a great question. "She wanted to protect our friendship. But looking back, I also think I wasn't ready. I was low on confidence and thought there was no way she'd be truly interested."

"And now?"

"I was ready to find out." She shook her head. "And I guess I have."

"Do you know what I think? There's still hope."

"I don't know about that."

"Brynn Garrett is not married and sitting on her front porch yet, Aster. And I think your plan for honesty is a good one. Don't abandon it quite yet." She smiled. "I speak from experience."

"I'll think it over," she said glumly, still not entirely convinced.

"For your heartbreak, you get a brownie for breakfast," her mom said and slid the plate of chocolate frosted brownies her way. She'd baked them fresh the day before to celebrate Aster's arrival home. Little things like that, small touches to let others know she cared, were one of the best things about her mom. Being out in the world had been life-changing for Aster, but there was nothing more comforting than having a mom like Marilyn.

"I accept this brownie. I've earned it." She snagged one with lots of frosting and took a bite. "I'm heading over to Hole in One in a bit to meet with Tori."

Her mom nodded. "She's done well with the place. I think you'll be pleased."

"Word is she's offering six flavors a day. Ambitious. I think she's going to make me an offer on the business."

"And how do you feel about that? Ready to give it all up?" Her mom's forehead creased with concern. "You put a lot into that shop."

She had. Her lifeblood. But it had always felt like the beginning of something much bigger. A stepping stone. "It's touchy. I love that place, but maybe I've outgrown it to a certain extent." She chewed her brownie for a moment, still unsure. "And I'd love it to go to someone who has the same kind of passion for it that I did. Tori has been there since the beginning."

"Still. It must be hard."

"Still." She met her mother's gaze, unsure how to segue into a discussion about Violet, knowing from Marigold that it was likely her mother didn't know all that had been going on. "How are things at The Lavender House?" She'd ease into it slowly. Back the car into the garage with finesse.

"Business is up seven percent this year, and our margins are improving on the infused dish towels, too." She tossed a celebratory fist in the air for the project she'd been working on for a while.

"And Violet and Marigold are killing it in sales?"

"They're a powerhouse team. Marigold has really taken control over there."

"Does that mean Violet has faded a bit, because I'm worried some."

Her mother put the lid back on the creamer. "She's quieter these days."

"Mom." She held eye contact, communicating silently.

That's when her mother's entire tone changed. "Tell me what's going on." She moved to Aster in mama bear mode and paused, one hand on her hip, waiting.

She bit the bullet. "I don't think Tad treats her all that great, Mom. In fact, he sounds awful behind closed doors. Controlling. Mean."

"I know they've argued lately."

"Marigold says it's all Tad. That he yells. That he's hit her at least once."

Her mother straightened, and Aster knew there was no undoing this now. Her mother wouldn't sit idly by. She wasn't the type, especially where her children were involved. "Marigold said this to you. Why hasn't she said this to me? This is unacceptable."

"Sister code is different than parent code. We tell each other things that don't always get back to you and Dad. And I just pretty much broke that code, but I'll take the heat. Worthy cause."

"Damn right it is," her mother said, getting loud, which she never did. "If he hit her, so help me, Aster, that boy will see stars. I'll send your father over there, and he'll see how it is." She seemed to be looking for her purse.

Aster held up a hand, wanting to slow everything down. They needed to be smart about this, and that meant thinking clearly. "I think we press pause on Dad slamming Tad's face into the wall until we can get a handle on this thing."

"Well, I'm going over there today."

"Okay, I think that's good, but maybe as the warm, concerned mom that you are and not woman on a warpath? I mean, this isn't my area, but I'm thinking we should stay calm. And maybe go over when Tad's not home, so you can speak to Violet privately. If there's anyone's opinion she values, it's yours, Mom. That's a compliment."

Her mother took a deep cleansing breath, and Aster could see that she was getting through. This was good. "I hear you. And I will internalize your advice." She took Aster's cheeks between her fingers. "But no one hurts any one of you. Do you hear me? Not my babies."

"Yes, ma'am. I do."

Relief infused everything. Her mom had the information now and would help. Violet was going to be okay.

She had to be.

CHAPTER NINE

Larry's Last Stop was more crowded than it had any business being on a Wednesday. It felt like the whole town had filled up the wooden tables that surrounded a small dance floor in front of what had to be the tiniest stage in history, used tonight for bad karaoke. Brynn scanned the room and finally found her date, Tyler, nursing her beer at a high-top table along the wall. With Micah in Wichita for the next few days, she and Tyler decided to burn a girl's night and blow off a little steam. Brynn was particularly looking forward to getting her buzz on and moving past the wayward thoughts that had her off balance and preoccupied with glasses of ice water in her damn kitchen.

"You are holding this side of the room down like a champ," she told Tyler as she slid onto the stool across from her.

"I feel compelled to do my part. You look hot. Why are you all hot? I should have come hotter."

"What are you talking about?" she asked Tyler. "You're the hottest chick in this bar, and I'd do you."

"Bless your heart, but you lie. After the four dachshund siblings slobbered all over me, I decided to embrace today's mediocrity and merely changed my shoes for our outing. Good thing the pups were adorable and now vaccinated."

"You're a champ. I've met the dachshund four, and they don't do anything halfway." Brynn sat back. "How many drinks so far?"

"Just the one."

"Is that enough for you to spill your guts about what was going on between you and a particular Lavender at the festival two days ago?"

Tyler deflated, and Brynn felt bad for killing the fun vibe. "I've been talking to that guy I told you about from school. Casual. Seeing where it might go. Sage asked about it, and when I told him, everything changed. He doubled down on his big feelings for me. He not only wants us to give it a go, he wants a relationship. Full-on. I'm floored and terrified."

"Is that awful?"

"It's not fair. He's Sage. He's my person. Always has been, but he uses it when he needs to, you know? In this case, he turned on the attention because I'm interested in someone else. And so of course, I'm pulled right back in, wanting him, wanting us."

"Give it a go, Tyler. I think it's what you want. Don't let your fear get in your way."

"I'm working on it." She sighed. "It would be really nice to not feel this weight on my chest."

"I think it's time to put it down. Let yourself go after what you want."

Tyler stared at the table. "It's also a subject we should move on from because his little sister just took a seat three tables to our right."

Brynn turned automatically and saw Aster in a leather bomber jacket seated across from Tori. They were smiling as if in celebration of something, and Brynn couldn't tear her stare away. In that moment, Aster turned and their gazes hit. Man, she had a way of changing the room for Brynn. It seemed quieter in there now, slower. Aster's smile dimmed, but not in a less-than-happy way. Softer now, personal. Brynn rolled her lips in and nodded. They each returned to their conversations, though now Brynn was only half able to concentrate on Tyler's story about Eve and the argument she'd had with the delivery driver over a torn package. It sounded colorful, but all Brynn was aware of was that Violet and Marigold had joined Aster and Tori, and shortly after that, Tad Jourdan arrived at their table and made his presence known. Oh, this wasn't good at all. He looked mad, and from what Brynn understood from her last lunch date with Violet, his bite could be as bad as his bark. She went on high alert. Even Tyler paused her story when she heard his voice rise above the others in the bar.

"Did you hear me? Did I stutter? Get your stuff. We're going." He wasn't asking. He was telling.

"I'm staying with my parents, and so is Ethan. I told you," Violet said, her eyes downcast.

"And I'm telling you that your mom needs to stay the hell out of it." His eyes were dark and narrow. It was a sight. Brynn had never seen Tad look anything other than overly confident and smiley in his five-hundred-dollar suits. This public anger was new, but exactly what Violet had described to her in supreme confidence. She'd begged Brynn not to say a word to anyone until Violet could figure out a strategy for handling the situation. Things seemed beyond that now, and Brynn was close to getting out of her chair. She saw two men exchange a look across the room that told her they were about to intervene. Thank God.

"Please leave us alone," Aster said in a low tone. Tori looked wildly uncomfortable, and Violet had yet to lift her gaze. "My mother cares about Violet. She's trying to help. Let her."

"Your mother can go fuck herself," Tad said. Aster lunged for Tad and used the sheer force of that action to slam his back against the nearby bar, catching him off guard. Brynn, too. She didn't realize Aster had that in her. Tad's eyes went wide and his face red as he took her by the shoulders, clearly intent on retaliation as he moved forward, taking Aster with him, shaking with anger.

"Let her go!" Violet screamed.

The two men Brynn had seen earlier were instantly on the scene, grabbing Tad and holding him back until he released Aster. Violet choked back a sob, and Brynn was on her feet. She caught Aster from behind and whispered quietly in her ear. "Let them take it from here. You're good. Okay?" Aster nodded, saying nothing, but she allowed Brynn to pull her away.

"I've never wanted to punch someone in the face in my entire life, but I do right now," Aster bit out, as she watched Marigold comfort Violet. Her eyes flew back to Tad, and Brynn knew it was probably best to get Aster out of that situation.

"I think we're going to go," Marigold told them, her arm around Violet, who reached out and squeezed Aster's hand. "Come with us, Aster. Come on. You don't need to be here."

Aster squeezed back, but her gaze didn't waver from Tad.

Time to act before the tension boiled over and someone got hurt or thrown in jail. "We'll go for a walk," Brynn told them. They nodded, grateful. "Take a walk with me?" Brynn asked Aster. She gestured to Tyler, who nodded and indicated she was joining a nearby table of friends. Tyler would be okay. It was Aster who needed her now.

"Yeah, okay. We can walk," Aster said and grabbed her jacket. It was cold out even for November, and Brynn distantly wished she'd worn one that night. She shrugged into her turquoise sweater, allowing the sleeves to pull over her hands as they headed down the sidewalk, Aster walking slightly ahead, still hopped up on adrenaline.

"You gonna wait for me or work this out on your own up there?"

Aster paused. "Sorry. I just…" She waited for Brynn to catch up. "Thank you. For back there."

"Anytime." She touched Aster's shoulder, turning her so they faced each other. They stood beneath a blinking streetlamp. Someone had forgotten to change the bulb. "You okay?"

"I will be."

"Violet will, too, you know. After that display, there are going to be a lot of people looking into what's going on between them."

Aster shoved her hands into the pockets of her jacket. "It sucks that she got mixed up with a guy like that. She was so excited when they first started dating."

"We all fell for it. Some people are good at wearing a mask." They walked on. "Not showing you who they really are."

Aster looked over at her. "You sound like you speak from experience. The ex?" She still had the wild look in her eye.

Brynn nodded. "It's been over two years, and I can still feel all the damage she did. Again, the mask is a powerful thing. If only I'd known then who she really was."

"You and Violet both."

They walked in silence for an extended time. Brynn let Aster choose their route, hoping the control would help return her to a calmer state. She'd never seen Aster angry before and got the impression it was a rare display. As if reading her thoughts, Aster tossed her a sheepish glance. "I don't have a temper. I'm surprised he got that out of me. For what it's worth, I'm sorry I lost my cool."

"You have nothing to apologize for." Brynn took Aster's hand in a move that felt so natural it startled her. God, she was gorgeous beneath the moonlight. She'd always found Aster attractive, but tonight was off the charts. And it had nothing to do with the way she'd valiantly stood up for her sister. Well, maybe a little. "Tad was out of line. I just didn't want you getting hurt. The idea of that…" Brynn trailed off.

"What were you going to say?" Aster asked and looked down at their hands.

"I just don't think I could stand that."

They stared at each other. A gust of wind hit, and Brynn braced against the intrusive chill.

"You're cold," Aster said, immediately shrugging out of her bomber jacket. "Here. Wear this."

"No, no. Then you'll be cold. I'm the thoughtless one who forgot a coat."

"The cold doesn't bother me. In fact, I need it right now." Aster took her hand back, cupped it with the other one, and blew into them, her gaze fixed on the path ahead. Brynn snuggled into the jacket that fit her perfectly. It smelled like Aster, fresh cucumber and clean laundry. A unique combination she would never get used to or tired of. "Why'd you take my hand?" she asked finally, eyes still forward.

Brynn had forgotten how straightforward Aster was. She asked what she needed to know, and said what she thought.

"What?" Brynn absorbed the question, searching for its motivation. "Oh. Well. I guess I just wanted to show you that I was here with you. Supportive."

"That's all?" Aster stopped walking. So did Brynn.

"Are you upset? Did my taking your hand upset you?"

"That would never upset me. Can we keep walking?"

"Yes."

They did so, entering the heart of Homer's Bluff where most of the businesses had gone dark. That had been an interesting discovery upon moving to town. After seven p.m., the citizens scattered like ants, closing up shop for the night. Larry's stayed open, the diner, and the two-screen movie theater had showings until ten. The rest of the place? Tumbleweeds beneath the stars. They had the place to themselves.

And there it was. They approached the bench, Aster's bench, that had become their bench. Reading at lunchtime was still a favorite pastime of Brynn's. She touched the back of the bench. "Read any good science fiction lately?"

"Actually, yes. Two books this week." The moonlight created a soft halo around Aster's hair and face. She looked angel-touched, her big brown eyes so expressive.

"You still tear through those things, don't you."

"I've always been fascinated with words and their arrangement. When you add in outer space, I'm a goner."

Aster's bottom lip was a thing of beauty. Brynn wanted to run her thumb across it. "Can aliens be sexy, though?" Why had she just said the word *sexy*? Simply introducing it into their conversation inspired forbidden thoughts. It had nothing to do with this conversation. She was off the rails now, but also riding the exhilaration.

"Anything can be sexy in the right context." Aster watched Brynn, studying her as if she was a rare find. "Some things just happen to be sexy all on their own. All the time."

"Like what?"

"Well, you."

Brynn paused and dodged. "Let's keep walking."

"If you want." Aster obliged, and a short while later they found themselves at the entrance of the community park.

"Closed," Brynn said, eying the sign.

Aster turned, walking backward right past it. "That has never stopped me, and since I'm already behaving recklessly tonight, why not?" She bounced her eyebrows to Brynn, challenging her to follow. Brynn couldn't come up with a reason not to break laws with sexy Aster Lavender tonight. That's right. She'd said it. How many chances did she get to do that?

She laughed as she picked up her pace. "You're corrupting me now."

"You'll thank me one day," Aster called.

Her heart thudded at the sentiment. Exhilaration coursed through her bloodstream. "And where are we off to?"

"Swings."

Brynn laughed because what a night. Aster went toe-to-toe with her angry brother-in-law and then searched out a playground for a session on the swings. Not that she was opposed. Brynn just hadn't been on a swing since she was maybe ten. Aster seemed right at home, however. With dark hair bouncing on her back, she jogged over to the nearby swings and hopped on. Brynn watched as she pumped her legs, established a good pace, and smiled. That did it. The smile was everything and affected Brynn more than anyone else's smile ever could. She knew why. Because nothing about Aster was manufactured or put on. She simply wasn't capable of false emotion, and that made everything she communicated important. These swings clearly made her happy, carefree, and that lifted something in Brynn, as well.

"Coming?" Aster called from midswing.

"I think I have to." Brynn hopped onto the swing next to Aster's, and in under thirty seconds, she joined her, slicing high through the air, bursting toward the sky full of stars. Their timing was opposite, with Aster swinging forward as Brynn swung back. They passed each other looks and fleeting smiles in what felt like private moments in time, set aside for just them. No one else.

"How's it feel?" Aster asked.

"Exhilarating," Brynn admitted. "But I'm a doctor on a swing set, so also a little bit like I'm breaking the adulting rules." She passed Aster on her way back down. She pumped her legs to sync them up and did in a matter of moments. The joint rhythm, swinging in time with each other, linked her to Aster. In that moment, it felt like the fog cleared. Her stresses all fell away, and it was just them and the night.

"Doctors, probably even more than other people, need to let off a little steam. A good swing set could probably take a decent chunk off a stressed person's therapy bills."

"I wouldn't have believed you until tonight."

Aster leapt off, impressing Brynn with her ability to gracefully stick the landing like a cat. "But we are breaking rules tonight. This park is closed, remember? And you're not supposed to be out with me."

Brynn let her swing slow, having no business attempting Aster's youthful landing. When her feet touched the ground, she met Aster's gaze. "True about the park. But why can't I be out with you?"

"You tell me."

Oh, that was bait, and Brynn would be smart not to take it. Play dumb. Because the back of her neck was prickling, and her cheeks were warm at the suggestion that she and Aster were forbidden. They were. Her emotions were a hurricane of unexplained feelings anytime she was in Aster's presence, and time had only amplified that effect. How?

Boston Aster came with a new skill set to unnerve her, turn her the hell on, and make her long for things unnamed. Some sort of voice calling to her in the night. Tempting, but dangerous.

And there was Micah.

Her real life. Her sturdy life. The one she depended on for sanity and safety. The risk was low, and wasn't that just what Brynn craved?

It was not something to be ruined for a sexually tense romp on a playground with a woman she was infatuated with. She closed her eyes, knowing that was an understatement, and brushed the sentiment to the side. What she felt for Aster was not lust alone. Their friendship was deep, and that was the scary part, the component that had her holding Aster at arm's length. "I don't think there's anything to tell. Being with you is not breaking a single rule that I know of." She boldly walked to Aster, closing the distance between them, prepared to show that she wasn't afraid of proximity. See? No crazy chemistry here. She swallowed against the energy that swarmed now that they were face-to-face. She shoved her hands into the pockets of her jacket. Correction, Aster's jacket, that smelled like her and hugged Brynn like the most wonderful glove. "Tell me about your time in Boston."

Aster's eyes lit up. "It took a while for me to feel settled and relax, but once classes started, I was so enthralled and focused that I forgot to be nervous. I made a couple of friends, which was really cool." She nodded as if approving of the memory. "I was surprised to learn how much I didn't know about food."

"You seem like you'd enjoy studying."

"If I admit that, am I a complete nerd? I'm okay with maybe ninety-five percent nerd, but I might be approaching the full one hundred."

"Join the club. I love to study and learn new things. I miss school."

Aster seemed enthralled. "Yes. That's exactly it." She began to walk in the direction of the playscape, and Brynn followed. "How is it that I've lived on this earth three decades and know so little? I want more. I want to know all I can about the things I love. I want to cook for you."

"What?" That pulled Brynn up short, the non sequitur.

"One day. I want to make you an entire meal made up of things you love."

"Oh." She imagined such a night, and her stomach tightened. The image of Aster focused on a series of pans, tossing in ingredients, and passing her that sideways smile, the one she was known for in Brynn's mind. She then flashed on the night she had Aster up against the wall of her kitchen as she kissed her face off with their breasts pressed against each other through their clothes, and oh, it was something.

"You okay?" Aster asked.

"Yeah, yeah," Brynn said, recovering. "Just remembered something I forgot to do. Grocery list."

"Now?" Aster rolled her lips in.

"When do you go back?" Brynn asked, dodging.

"I have five more days."

Brynn didn't know whether to cling to each of those remaining hours, or wish they'd hurry the hell up so her life could right itself again.

Aster studied her phone. "Marigold says Violet is good. She's at our parents' house and settled in with a hot toddy. Mom will take care of her tonight. She's great at that."

"And Tad?"

"Dad and Sage are moving her and Ethan's stuff out of his house tomorrow. He's going to rage but only temporarily. His ego is bruised. That's all this is. My prediction? Once he gets a taste of freedom, he's gonna back off."

"And then you head back to Boston. For how long?"

Aster climbed to the top of the slide. "I don't know. A while. I like it there. I could really see sticking around. Get a job at a nice restaurant."

"Or open your own place."

Aster whistled. "Not in Boston."

Brynn watched her slide down, enjoying the burst of adrenaline that hit. "Why not? Let me tell you, Hole in One is amazing in how unique it is. Not just the doughnuts, but the feel of the entire shop. You opened that business. You gave it the flair it's now known for. I went in the other day at eleven, and Tori was sold out."

Aster paused, seated on the base of the slide. "But that's here, in a small pond. I've found that people in the bigger city are harder to impress."

Brynn took a seat in a patch of grass nearby, feeling the chill of the ground through her jeans. She hugged her knees. "You need to find the confidence that I have in you. You do that, and you're going to accomplish great things."

For what felt like an eternity, Aster stared at her, almost as if she'd heard a set of words she wanted to memorize and hold on to. "You always have a way of propping me up with your words when I need it most."

"Good," Brynn said, hearing the quiet quality her voice had taken on. "Then maybe on those days when it feels like you can't do something, or shouldn't attempt the impossible, you'll hear my voice in your head and you will."

"I don't know how to look at you like a friend anymore," Aster said, her eyes searching Brynn's from where she sat on the slide. "I don't think I have it within me."

"Try," Brynn said, finding it hard to breathe. "Because..."

"I know. You're not available." Aster pushed herself to a standing position. "But here, tonight, we're alone in this park."

"We are."

"Just you and me. And I need to know if you feel half of what I do when we're together."

"I don't think I can have that conversation."

"I'm not going to ambush you. I'm not going to move from where I'm standing. I'm just trying to assemble all the pieces." Her eyes said so much, brimming with emotion that Brynn could literally feel in her bones.

Hell, Brynn wanted to understand, too. They'd shared a kiss, once upon a time. More than just that. She could see the same intensity in Aster when she looked at her now. This was perilous. She wasn't in a position to act on any of these swirling and confusing feelings. She had Micah and the life they were slowly building. Everything was in place, and after what she'd finally recovered from, neat and tidy was exactly what she required. Even *boring* was fine with her. She couldn't let Aster flit into town and disrupt that because nothing about them felt orderly. They were big and jagged and a jumble of overflowing everything. Their connection overwhelmed, and nothing about the way they moved when in each other's orbits felt predictable. In fact, her head felt like it was spinning in a wonderful, uncomfortable, confusing way in this very second. Half of her loved it. The other half wanted to get off the damn ride before it threw her.

"There's nothing to understand," she said too defensively. A lie.

But Aster could likely tell she was avoiding the question. She was not only brilliant, but very intuitive. The look she leveled Brynn said she didn't buy the pushback. That made Brynn relent. This was not someone in her life she could hide from. Aster saw her, plain as day.

Instead of looking at Aster, she hung her focus on a nearby fire hydrant that was in desperate need of a paint job. "I'm involved with someone. I'm with Micah. It's what I want. It's that simple."

Aster wasn't deterred. "I know that part. I saw, up close and personal. That's not what I'm asking. Do you feel anything for me?"

Aster got right to the point again, unblinking in the things she'd say in either innocence or sincerity. Subtlety be damned. It was a quality Brynn had found refreshing in their past interactions. Now, it terrified her. "Of course I *feel* something for you. We crystalized from the beginning."

"I think about you a lot in Boston." Aster shook her head, a ball of frustration and longing. "I think about kissing you again, and talking to you in person or on the phone, and seeing if there's maybe more here between us to explore. I think there is." She hadn't moved. She'd kept her promise.

"No. There can't be," Brynn said automatically. This was not a path she wanted to go down. She wasn't capable.

"It doesn't sound like you fully believe that, but what I am hearing is that I'm not what you want for yourself."

"I didn't say I didn't *want* you. God. Why do we have to do this?" She pressed her hands to her eyes and pulled her knees in to her chest tightly. "I do. I want to walk to you right now and pull you in and..." She couldn't finish the sentence.

"What?"

"No." She stood, using the action to gather her courage to resist. It didn't work.

"What, Brynn? You want to what? Why can't you just tell me?"

"To what end?"

"My sanity. My understanding. Just say the words. What is it that you want, Brynn?"

The words tumbled out in a burst. "To kiss you and not stop. To be with you. To not be afraid of us, of you and what I feel."

Silence. The night held them tightly.

"So I'm not crazy."

"No." Brynn paused. "But that doesn't change anything. My life is still my life."

Finally, Aster spoke, resigned. "And since that's the case, maybe I should walk you home. Put myself out of my misery."

Brynn shivered and ached, torn in two directions, hating both her heart and her head. "Aster."

"It's okay. You want me, but you don't."

"I can't."

"Right. You have someone. You must love her, and that's good for me to know. I'm happy for you."

Nothing about Aster's posture or disposition said she was. She'd put herself out there, she'd pushed for a chance, and Brynn had put up a roadblock. It wasn't comfortable or desirable, but it's what was best for everyone. She'd learned to look five steps ahead to keep her life from ever becoming the messy saga it once was. Self-preservation. Hell, she was finally in a spot where she could breathe.

"That doesn't mean I don't care about you."

Aster nodded from where she walked along Brynn's elbow. "I care about you, too." They walked in silence the handful of blocks to Baker Street, where Aster stared at the grouping of houses. "Mr. Anderson painted his mailbox."

"He did. I miss the dusty blue."

"Me, too," Aster said wistfully. "A lot." It felt like maybe they were talking about something else.

"Want to come in and see Pickles?" Brynn asked. Her dog would likely be snoozing in her doughnut bed, cuddling her stuffed ear of corn.

"Badly. But no. I don't think I should."

"Aster, please." She reached for her hand and intertwined their fingers. "You have to be my friend. I'm not going to be able to take it if you're not." Desperation huddled in her chest, burning a hole.

Aster swallowed, and Brynn pulled her gaze away from the smooth column of her neck. Aster seemed to make a decision. "I can try and do that. Again."

"Let's not lose touch this time. I don't want to go a year without hearing from you."

Aster nodded. "I'll send you my address. You know, for the

wedding invitation." She punctuated the comment with the sideways smile, but the tense undercurrent remained.

"No. For my words." Brynn felt her smile fade.

"You want to exchange words with me in the mail? Don't people use text messages and socials for that?"

"Not us. We're different."

"I can't argue with that part," Aster said.

Suddenly, Brynn wanted nothing more than to write letters to Aster. The idea of telling Aster about her world and hearing about hers in return sounded like the best kind of salve. A consolation prize. She needed this.

"Okay." Aster toed the grass. "Pen pals it is."

"Walk me to my door?"

"Anytime." With their fingers still interwoven, they made their way up Brynn's sidewalk, the impending farewell looming, an unwelcome interloper on an evening full of what-could-have-beens.

"Will I see you before you go?" Brynn asked, clinging to time.

Aster shook her head. She was pulling away. "Maybe not. Family stuff." Brynn didn't buy it, but she accepted Aster's decision. This was hard. All of it, and why drag it out?

"You take care of yourself," she said, scanning Aster's features one last time. "And visit soon, okay? Hole in One needs its fearless leader to look in on it. Not that Tori doesn't do a fantastic job."

"Hers now. I sold it."

Brynn's lips parted as she absorbed that news. It meant Aster was really moving on, officially. She'd grown up and found her wings. Bittersweet in many ways. Her heart tugged unpleasantly. "The end of an era. I'm glad I got to experience it."

"Me, too. It helps to know the shop is in good hands."

They lingered, watching each other. "It feels wrong to say good-bye to you."

"Then don't." Aster smiled. "Can we hug? Is that allowed?"

"Yes," Brynn said and practically launched herself into Aster's arms. *Oh wow.* She buried her face in Aster's neck, stealing a minute to simply absorb. "It was really good to see you, Aster," she whispered, holding her tight. When Aster let her go, she looked down into Brynn's eyes, touched her cheek, and took a step back.

"I'll see you someday." She didn't wait for Brynn to answer and headed off down the sidewalk until Brynn could only make out her silhouette beneath the streetlight. That's when she realized she was still wearing the jacket.

"Aster! Wait. You forgot your jacket."

"Keep it," Aster said. "It looks better on you. Remember me when you wear it, okay?"

As she stood alone in her doorway, Brynn ran her thumbs over the lapels, wondering about all the different ways they could have taken the night. Pickles appeared at her side and gave her shin a nudge. "We went to the playground," she told her dog. "I was on the swings." She grinned and tapped her lips, knowing it would be one of those nights that stood out in her memory for the rest of her life.

PART THREE

CHAPTER TEN

While wearing a butterscotch-stained chef's coat at eleven p.m., Aster unlocked mailbox 12D with a thudding heart, hoping she'd find what she'd been waiting for. It had been a long week of restaurant service, and if there was a letter waiting for her, it would go a long way toward soothing her tired mind and body. She allowed herself to hope, holding her breath as she shuffled through the pile of envelopes.

There, peeking out from a stack of advertisements and bills, was the pale stationery she recognized immediately. She smiled and exhaled, her heart squeezing. A letter from Brynn. It had been a week since she'd mailed her letter and two since she'd heard from Brynn, which felt like a lifetime. They'd been writing back and forth for a year now, and in spite of all she'd felt that last night back in Homer's Bluff, they'd finally done the impossible and transitioned into a solid friendship that Aster had come to truly treasure. She looked forward to each new letter from Brynn, accounts of veterinary life, updates from home, and the everyday thoughts of someone so important to her.

She tucked the rest of her mail under her arm as she walked to her fourth-floor apartment, holding the unopened envelope reverently, like the most delicate treasure. Once she reached the top of the stairs, she set down her things, took a seat on a concrete step, and tore into the envelope, ready to devour the four small handwritten pages. She smiled at the swoopy *S* in her name, a Brynn Garrett handwriting signature.

Dear Aster,
Pomeranians are scarier than they look. I should know
after going toe to toe with Sheila, a three-year-old Pom,

who swallowed three ibuprofen and needed intervention. Did I mention they're loud? Sheila and her mournful yaps to escape her kennel echoed through the town. They thought I was holding her hostage. Luckily, Sheila the Sad Pom recovered and is home yapping to her owner, Bill from the garage, and not me. Until next time, Sheila!

How are you? Tell me everything. How is little Dill, and has he yet to master the great art of sleeping till noon? If I remember correctly, he had eleven a.m. down to a science. I do love a lazy little dog as cute as he is.

Did I ask how you were? I think about that a lot and worry sometimes. I feel like your last letter was you minimizing how much you're working, but I also know how much you love it. I read the write-up on the restaurant's food in Boston Magazine. *Aster. They mentioned you by name. You're a big deal now, and I'm not sure you'll even want to write to me anymore. I still hope to make it up there sometime and try a dessert of yours firsthand.*

Micah's good. She's been around a little bit less simply because her schedule's riddled with court dates. It's nice when we get a chance to sit down and have a meal together, really catch up. I wonder what she thinks about my job sometimes. She glazes over if I go on too long about a complicated case. Do I ever bore you with those? I'm sorry if I do.

Violet is fantastic, flourishing even. Now that Tad has a new girlfriend that none of us envy, he seems to have lost interest just as you once predicted. Money will buy you companionship. That's for damn sure. Little Ethan is growing like crazy. He has his mother's smile, which is not that far off from yours.

You take care of yourself, okay? Have you seen the moon this week? Full and big. I feel like it's one you would appreciate. In fact, I think of you when I look up at it. Bye for now.

Sincerely yours,
Brynn

Aster let herself into the apartment and smiled at the aroma of fresh cut rosemary. "You're cooking," she said. "I could tackle you with joy."

"You're welcome to, but watch the sauce. It's fucking awesome, and I don't want to lose a drop." Nora turned around from her spot at the stove and smiled, hand on her hip. Her dark as night hair was on top of her head in a mess of curls, and she wore a white apron with the words *I'll feed all you fuckers* across her chest. They'd been living together as roommates for two months now, working killer hours at separate restaurants, trying to make ends meet. The living arrangement afforded each of them a bigger, nicer two-bedroom since they shared the rent. Plus, it was nice to have a roommate, a friend, someone to hang out with after work, shoot the breeze. Not that they weren't without a little gray area. They'd hooked up twice since moving in. Once after killing two bottles of wine together—most of that was Nora—and another after a party with their chef friends where they'd laughed half the night and headed home on a life high. Nora hadn't pressed for more, but it was probably coming, and honestly, Aster was feeling like maybe she'd put this off long enough, the two of them. She'd never taken that trip to Provincetown that Nora had offered. But things felt easier now. She liked Nora. Nora liked her. The sex was good. No, it didn't make her blood run hot. She wasn't desperate for it. Nora didn't make Aster breathless or spur an urgent need to be close to her, touch her skin, or stare endlessly at her face. But Nora was a ton of fun, and the older Aster got, the more she valued life's little enjoyments. "Try this." Nora held out a spoon, and Aster tasted the sauce as she passed by.

She closed her eyes and took in the layering of flavors. Spot on. "I love the red pepper."

"That was a last-minute addition."

Aster nodded her approval. "A good one."

"Now I have your attention." Nora winked, swatted Aster's ass, and went back to her prep. That's how it was with them these days, flirty and light until someone's clothes came off. "Don't disappear in there for too long. Dinner in twenty minutes."

"I'll be there. I hope the sauce is, too."

"Count on it. How was dinner service?"

Aster ran a hand through her hair. "We were crushed but somehow managed to dig our way out of the weeds. I stepped away from desserts and hopped on the line for a bit just to help out."

"Always a team player."

"I try. Gonna change."

But she had a letter to write first, and her fingers were itching to pick up a pen and get started right away. She pulled out a white sheet of paper with her initials at the top. A Christmas gift from Marigold, who never could have anticipated her letter writing needs, but somehow had known she could use her own stationery.

Dear Brynn,

I saw the moon and not surprisingly thought of you, too. Not a lot of people appreciate those things, but for me, they are the reason life is good. I remember undervaluing a good thunderstorm when I lived in Homer's Bluff. I appreciated their beauty, but not enough. I don't do that anymore. I relish them. Dancing lightning is my favorite of all. You never can guess its pattern. That's the stuff of life. Do you enjoy the sound of rain on the roof, especially when it's not too hard and not too soft? It's become a new favorite of mine. Isn't it interesting how we grow and change? Find value in new things as we age?

My brother said Violet isn't interested in dating at all. If I were her, I'd be opposed as well. She has time, though. Fuck Tad, and forgive my language. Let him ride off into the sunset, drink expensive champagne, and wear a lobster bib with whoever the hell he wants, as long as he's far away from my family.

Sorry. That was harsh, but it's actually an accurate representation of my feelings. I've been paying more attention to those recently, giving them space to breathe and expand.

Say hello to Micah for me. My parents used to watch Law & Order *when I was younger and I think of her in the courtroom, whittling away at a hostile witnesses. If that's not accurate, please don't ruin my delusion. Dill sends his love and apologies for the Pomeranians of the world. He's asleep at the feet of my roommate while she cooks, but I did get a tail wag when I arrived home.*

I'm gonna go steal another look at that moon before

dinner. This is likely the last night. Maybe you'll be looking, too.

> *Take care,*
> *Aster*

PS I'll never look at a Pomeranian the same way again.

PPS Please come try one of my desserts soon. Please?

She sealed her words, found a stamp, and walked straight to the mailbox. That's what was so great about her written relationship with Brynn. They wrote back promptly, keeping the exchange alive. The letters were never overly long, and that kept the pressure low. But Aster had come to depend on those letters, looking forward to each one as a bright spot in her day. She didn't know if it was the same for Brynn, but she did write back just as quickly.

Six days later, Aster had a reply in her hands.

The blue envelope sat on the seat next to her as she drove to work, beckoning her to open it and absorb Brynn's words. She parked her car near the back entrance to the restaurant and checked the clock. She had a few minutes before she needed to start her dough for lunch service and used them. She eased open the envelope and read the words slowly so as to not finish too soon.

Dear Aster,

I like that as a culture we begin salutations with the word dear. It communicates a certain fondness that kicks the correspondence off to a warm start. I smile when you write Dear Brynn, and it keeps going for the rest of your letter.

I hope you're sitting down. The saga of Tyler and Sage continues. As much as Tyler doesn't want to shout it from the rooftops just yet, she's hard-core in love with your brother. She's stopped all correspondence with her classmate from school and makes gaga eyes at Sage all over town. They hold hands, Aster. They kiss in public. They're the new supercouple of Homer's Bluff. I've never seen Sage look so happy. He's really come around, leaving his playboy days in the dust. You'd be proud.

You never answered me about working too many hours?

Are you? If you are and you're loving it, then I'm thrilled, but if you come home each night dead and sad, then I'm going to keep pushing. It's impossible for me not to care. You get that, right?
Sending you moonlight,
Brynn

Aster placed the letter back in the envelope, her heart full, her energy replenished, sending her to work in the best possible mood. She rolled out the dough for her pistachio shortbread crust for the goat cheese cheesecake, the dessert on special that day. She smiled at her executive chef, who quirked her head at Aster. "You seem happy."

She nodded. "I am. I really am."

❖

Herbert, the giant orange cat, eyed Brynn, and she eyed him right back. "I'm your friend, Herbert. I don't know how many times I can explain that to you."

Herbert offered a meow and looked at the wall, refusing her affection.

"I just want to feel that little mass you have under your arm." He still refused to look at her. "Pretty sure it's just a fatty tumor, but let's check it out to be safe. You know, if I haven't told you so, you're very handsome."

"You're great with him," Tessa from the boutique said. "I always think so. It's the time you take to let him warm up to you. No rush at all to get us in or out." Brynn smiled inside because that very skill was something she'd been working on. *Match the speed of the town.* And people moved slow in Homer's Bluff. Molasses style.

Brynn scratched behind his ears. "Well, he prefers we take it slow is all, and I can do that for him. How's the shop?" Brynn had stopped into Yay Clothes! the week prior and picked herself out a heavier jacket for the change in seasons. Fall was on the way out. Winter was crashing in.

"Business isn't what it could be, but we're hanging in there." As Tessa talked, Brynn slowly shifted her ear scratching to a veiled examination of Herbert's mass, pleased to feel that his tumor was exactly as suspected, harmless, unless it one day got in the way of his mobility. "Oh! I meant to tell you. I saw your girlfriend a few weeks back. She did a stroll through the shop. Didn't buy anything, but was nice enough."

Brynn winced. "We broke up." She released Herbert, who decided it was okay to look at her again.

"Oh, that's too bad." Tessa's eyes were the size of saucers. "I've gone and made it awkward in exam two. I thought maybe we'd have wedding bells for you, Dr. Brynn."

"Sadly, no." She smiled, feeling a little melancholy about the whole thing. It was a shame to say good-bye to Micah because what they'd had had been nice. But over time, she couldn't lie to herself anymore. She watched Sage and Tyler and how happy they were once they finally faced their fears. She wanted that for herself in one way or another, and no matter how she organized her thoughts, it became clear that it wasn't going to happen with Micah. A segment from Aster's last letter had resonated and tossed her brain into evaluation mode.

Dear Brynn,

I'm proud of Sage for finally owning up to what he feels for Tyler and of Tyler for giving him the chance, no matter how terrified she must have been. I know we all wanted to knock him upside his head, but it's scary, declaring yourself and going after what you want. In so many ways, those two are meant to be. I'm happy they're finally getting their shot. I think maybe we can all take a page from that book. We're only here once.

No matter what Brynn did to distract herself, Aster's words followed her. She was content with Micah, but content wasn't happy. And as time moved on, as her heart healed and found strength, she had to face the truth. Micah didn't bring her that kind of happiness you grow up imagining you'll find. She didn't give Brynn goose bumps or make her race home because she simply had to see Micah and tell her all about her day. She'd had a taste of that happiness with Tiffany back in the day before her heart had been ripped out.

But there was someone else standing off to the side who was capable of toppling all others.

And she couldn't stop thinking about her, no matter what she did.

For Brynn, the time had finally come to step out onto that very scary ledge and see what this life was all about. It might deliver big, overwhelming, disorganized feelings, but it might also be the best thing that ever happened to her.

"Well, now that you're single, do you have any big plans for yourself?" Tessa asked, trying to smooth things over. "I know when my marriage ended to Karl the creep and a half, I was sad, but also amazed at the freedom I had to explore life on my own terms. I went to waffle shops. Karl always hated waffles, so he can suck it."

"I like that idea. Not the sucking it or the waffles specifically, but the freedom to explore what you haven't before." Brynn placed a hand on top of Herbert's head and he pressed back, purring quietly. She was forgiven. "I'm actually headed to Boston later this week to do just that."

"Beautiful city. On business or pleasure?" Tessa asked.

"I'm hoping pleasure. Time will tell."

"Dr. Brynn, this sounds saucy. Are you getting saucy on me? With who?"

Brynn smiled, her stomach wrapped into a nervous knot because this was a pretty big deal. "I'll let you know."

Brynn hadn't told Aster she was coming simply because she was afraid she'd chicken out and at the last minute get cold feet. But when the time came to get on that plane, her head was clear, her heart was open, and for the first time in a very long while, she knew exactly what she wanted.

After the plane reached cruising altitude, the flight attendant placed a glass of white wine on her tray.

"Thank you," Brynn said. "I'm not a big plane drinker, but I'm celebrating."

"What's the occasion?" the attendant asked.

"I think I'm ready to start a brand new chapter and hoping the other person might feel the same."

"Congratulations. That's fantastic. Are you nervous?"

"A little," Brynn said. She sipped her wine and stared out at the clouds. "But I'm ready."

CHAPTER ELEVEN

Aster couldn't remember a time when her shoulders hurt more than they did in this moment. She'd been going hard at work all week, skipping her day off to truly focus on the holiday menu. She'd been told she was turning out the best desserts the restaurant had ever seen. As lead pastry chef at Omniscient, she had free rein to create and build the dessert menu of the high-end eatery, which was a true score for someone not long out of school. Apparently, her professor had recommended her personally, and after a week on the job as her interview, she'd been hired full-time. She'd been in the position for a handful of months now, and the reviews had been stellar, farther catapulting her star, at least on a local level. She smiled to herself as she slid a caramel apple tart into the oven for table twelve.

"Table two is requesting the bourbon butter cake made specifically by the famous chef slash puppy rescuer," Delia, one of the servers, reported with an amused grin. "Something we should know? Do you rescue puppies—because if you do, I like you even more. Score one for the quiet pastry chef."

"One time I did." Aster froze with her hand on the oven door. "What does table two look like?"

"Blond. Very pretty. And alone."

It couldn't be. Could it? Her heart must have thought itself in a thumping contest. Her mind raced and her skin prickled. "Got it. I will deliver this one personally."

Delia was enjoying this. "Well, well, Aster's getting her groove on. Look at you."

"I'm merely slinging desserts over here." She tossed in her winsome smile because she was already on a high at just the chance that it was Brynn in that dining room. She prepared the butter cake and added her signature warm bourbon caramel sauce and took a deep breath to steady herself. "Gabriella, can you take over for a few minutes? I think I might have a VIP guest."

The restaurant's second-in-command, a friend of hers, nodded, hopping over to her station. "No problem, Chef. I've got you."

Aster smoothed her chef's jacket and, with the plate in hand, made her way to table two.

She didn't have to get very far into the dining room before she saw Brynn's profile and knew. The world slowed to that wonderful, comfortable, exciting hum. She was *here*. Her friend. Her person. Since their letter writing had kicked into high gear, Brynn's importance in her life had skyrocketed. She had become someone Aster confided in, trusted. She had never had that in someone before on this level.

Brynn sat alone, just as Delia had reported, surveying the sleek restaurant with its black tables and cream-colored linens with what looked to be a glass of water in front of her and a whiskey to her side. Aster took a moment to digest the sight. Brynn put the rocks glass to her lips, and Aster wished she had a camera or a paintbrush. Either would do to capture the perfection of the moment.

"Butter cake for table two?" Aster asked, unable to play it cool the way she'd planned, and grinned, embracing the thrill she could no longer tamp down.

Brynn was immediately on her feet. As soon as Aster placed the plate on the table, her arms were around Aster's neck in the kind of hug that felt all encompassing, when you blew past formalities and really clung to the other person without inhibition.

"I'm more than a little surprised right now," Aster said, inhaling every inch of Brynn and that familiar scent that was all her. "Thrilled. What? How? Tell me the details of your appearance in this restaurant."

"I think it was the *please* in one of your more recent letters that did it. I've always been a sucker for manners."

"I can appreciate that." Aster gestured for Brynn to please sit and stole a moment, settling into the chair across from her, still not quite believing this was happening. "So, hi. Surreal."

"Hi. It is." She looked down at the cake. "This was recommended to me, not just by the maître d', but by my server as well. They said I simply had to try the butter cake, and whenever anyone says *simply*, I'm compelled to obey."

Aster sat back, folded her arms, and waited as Brynn picked up her fork. With a medium-sized bite of cake loaded up, sauce plentiful, Brynn slid the fork into her mouth and closed her eyes. It felt like an eternity passed, but Aster sat patiently and waited for the verdict. She was not about to complain about the extra seconds because watching Brynn enjoy the flavors she'd created was just about the most satisfying experience ever. She was proud of that cake, having developed the recipe in school. She'd added to it over time since, finding the perfect balance of sweet and savory. It was the dish that got her the most attention, but it was Brynn's opinion that mattered to her more than any write-up.

"I'm stumbling for words," Brynn said, making a circular gesture with her hand near her mouth. "I also don't want to stop eating to tell you my thoughts."

Aster laughed and rested her chin in her hand. "Then keep going. I can wait."

Brynn didn't hesitate and scooped up another bite and then another. Finally, "It's rich, but not so rich you can't keep eating. How do you do that?"

"Magic. And a lot of work."

"I thought it was unfortunate that you walked away from doughnuts, given how amazing they were, but now that I see you're spreading your gift to other areas of enjoyment, I'm all in favor." She slid another bite into her mouth before Aster could say a word, which made her laugh.

"How was your trip?" Aster asked.

"Busy with this cake…" Brynn said, mimicking her inflection. She let Brynn enjoy in silence, watching as she used the side of her fork to scoop up any remaining sauce on the plate. "Do you sell this by the liter?" Brynn gestured to the last drop of sauce with her fork. "No? Big mistake. I should be your business manager. You'd be rich."

Aster nodded. "You know finances?"

"I don't. I just want a way to be closer to this sauce." She set the fork on the plate and sat back. "Now it's over, and I'm hovering near heaven." She sipped from her rocks glass. Aster spotted the small smile behind the rim.

"I'm really happy to see you. Words don't do the sentiment justice."

"I hope I didn't show up, crash the party, and you're completely unavailable. But if you are, I get it. It will be enough just to get to taste one of your desserts."

"How long are you in town?" Aster asked.

"Four days."

She exhaled slowly because it was the best news. Four whole days. Four *long* days. So much time. "I work tomorrow. Saturday. I'm off Sunday, but I can take Monday off if I can convince one of my two assistants to cover."

"Please don't go out of your way. I'm the one who just dropped in on you." Brynn placed a hand over her heart. "I'll take whatever time you can give me and explore Boston on my own when you're busy."

Aster glanced behind her, knowing that she was likely needed in the kitchen. Gabriella was great but only had two hands. She'd be hard-pressed doing double-duty. "We close at ten tonight, and if I hurry, I can be out of here by ten thirty. Thoughts?"

"Maybe we can meet for a drink in the lobby of my hotel. I'm at the Newbury."

"I've met their head chef. I love that place."

"Meet me at the bar."

"You're on," Aster said. She stood, bumped into the chair, and made a gesture aimed at comedy, but surely missing the mark. "I better get back. Or whatever."

"Just do so carefully. Precious cargo."

She felt the blush hit on her walk back to the kitchen. This was shaping up to be quite the Friday night. She placed a hand on her chest and closed her eyes. "You have to slow down now," she told her heart.

"You talking to yourself again, Chef?" Gabriella asked with a grin as she plated a key lime pie while wearing a Santa hat.

"The desserts like it," she said and passed her an I-do-what-I-want look.

"Just be careful out there," Gabriella said with a nod to Brynn's table. Aster understood. Gabriella had recently come off a breakup with her girlfriend, Madison, and was still licking her wounds. It made sense that she'd look out for Aster.

"No worries. We're just friends."

Gabriella raised an eyebrow. "Really? Wow. Wouldn't have called that."

Aster shrugged and got back to work but found it hard to concentrate. Brynn Garrett had just busted in on her life, her everyday world, and made it all sparkle with magic dust. What was she supposed to do with that? And more importantly, what was Brynn doing here?

❖

The hotel bar was surprisingly quiet for a Friday night. Brynn found a table off to the side with two blue velvet wing chairs facing each other. The walls of the bar were lined with tall library shelves and what had to be hundreds of books. She loved it here. The place wasn't too busy, but she knew it would pick up soon.

She swirled her drink as she waited. The whiskey she hadn't finished back at the restaurant was for courage, but the Brandy Alexander she cradled now was purely for pleasure. It felt like the kind of establishment for drinking a Brandy Alexander and declaring yourself. When Aster appeared ten minutes later, she felt downright sophisticated. Until she got a better look at Aster, and then she felt nothing but appreciation with a sidecar of lust. *Look at this outfit.* Jeans and a black T-shirt that hugged her...everything. The V-neck offered a glimpse of a line leading to cleavage. She had her dark hair pulled back in a ponytail with long wisps falling out in the front. Her eyes were as soulful as always. Her lashes went on for days. She saw glimpses of the younger version of Aster from several years prior, but the woman in front of her was different, steady, and in control, a change even from the last time they'd seen each other. Aster Lavender absorbed knowledge like a sponge and learned from every day she spent on the planet.

"Aster, hi. Sit down and talk to me."

She did. "I was watching the clock like a kid in school."

Brynn sipped her drink. "You're so not a kid anymore. I can't get over it."

Aster's eyes widened slightly when the server approached. "Anything for you, ma'am?"

"Dogfish Head?"

"Coming up."

Aster drinking a beer after a long night on her feet was simple. Fitting.

Aster eyed her. "What are you smiling about? Share with the class."

"I like the idea of you drinking a beer."

"You're easy to please then. That show repeats almost every day. We usually open a cold one at the restaurant after closing. Mini-tradition." She nodded a few times. She was nervous. Brynn could identify.

"It's a really impressive restaurant. The dining room made me feel a little out of my element."

"It is a nice place, but I was just thinking how great you looked there." A pause. "I want to hear about you. Were you just suddenly interested in a little sightseeing? What brings you to Boston?"

Brynn understood that there wasn't going to be too much preliminary conversation. Her presence begged some questions. "Oh. Well, Micah and I broke up, and I wanted to see you." There. Like a Band-Aid.

Aster sat back in her chair. Her mouth formed the shape of an *O*. Her thumb moved across the pint glass the server had placed in front of her moments before. "Ah. Hell, I'm sorry. So you were looking for a way to distract yourself. Get away. Well, I'm glad you came. It's—"

"No. I broke up with her knowing I was coming here. Because I was."

Aster's thumb went still. "She didn't want you to visit."

"I didn't ask. I'm here for me. Us."

The table went silent for what felt like far too long. It was enough time to make Brynn nervous, crawl around in her chair unsettled, and feel like maybe she'd stepped out onto a limb that was about to break beneath her feet. But she didn't crawl out of her chair or demand a response. She simply waited. Aster deserved time to think and absorb what she'd said.

"Okay, I think I'm following, but I want to be sure." Aster circled the rim of her glass with one finger. She did that thing that Aster did where she bit the inside of her cheek when she was working out a complex thought. "When you say you had to see me. What do you mean?"

Brynn nodded. Aster needed words, clarification, and a clear reason for her visit. Aster worked with logic and truth. Brynn needed to give her just that. "The plain answer is this. From that night in the park on, I've questioned a lot about what it is that I want out of life. I had a chance that night. You—and correct me if I'm wrong—extended your hand."

"You aren't wrong."

"But I wasn't strong enough to join you there. I think I was still figuring out how to live my own life, that I couldn't fathom taking on someone else."

Aster frowned. "But you took on Micah."

"Micah's not you." Aster raised her gaze. Brynn had her attention. "You're a lot for me, Aster." She stared at her drink trying to slow the words that continued to spill out. "You make me feel things in a new way. It's overwhelming and all-encompassing. I can't describe it if I wanted to." Brynn marveled. "It started so slow. Crept up on me, really, until it got to the point where your words on a page, the image of your face, your lips, the way you see the world rose above everything else." She raised her shoulders. "I couldn't look away anymore. And so here I am."

Aster's hands went to her knees beneath the table. She met Brynn's eyes with a direct stare she never could have executed when they first met. It did things to Brynn now, Aster in control. Her breath caught. Her hands trembled. She set the glass down to make it less obvious.

"I don't want you to look away," Aster said. She blinked, and Brynn swooned a little at the long dark lashes. "All I want to do is kiss you in the middle of this damn bar."

Okay, the swoon had been premature because those words brought a heat that Brynn was not used to. She crumbled beneath it, imagining Aster doing just that. She still remembered what her lips felt like, the way she tasted. She'd shoved it all aside back then, but the memory had come roaring back with a vengeance recently.

Brynn nodded, but no words emerged. She sipped her drink, her eyes never leaving Aster's. "I don't know about this bar, but I do have a key and a room."

Aster watched her, remaining very still. "Are you inviting me up?"

"Mm-hmm." The level of eye contact was surely something someone should document. They were locked in. "I am."

Aster took a swallow of her beer, raised her hand for the check, and Brynn smothered a smile. The anticipation of being alone with Aster, whether they talked for hours, kissed, touched, or just watched each other from across the room, was slowly undoing her. Her legs felt shaky in a really good way.

The ride on the elevator was silent. They stood at opposite ends. The tension in the small space was like a guitar string pulled tight. When the doors opened, she took Aster's hand in hers, placed them both behind her back, and led down the hallway to her room, scanning the key, and allowing them entry.

She released Aster's hand and walked farther into the room. "Pretty standard setup. There's a couch if you want to sit and talk. I have a bottle of wine we could open."

"Brynn," Aster said quietly from just inside the door. "No wine. I don't want to talk right now. Do you?"

Brynn shook her head, her heart thudding. She walked back down the hallway to Aster and placed her palms on Aster's shoulders and slid them down her chest. She could hear Aster's breathing change and registered the effect her touch had. She went onto her toes, evening out the height disparity, and encircled Aster's neck with her arms. Delicious unravel. Their lips were close, and for a moment they simply breathed in the same air, hovering in that heady spot right before something important happened. Brynn made the move she'd been waiting to make for a long time now. She parted her lips and brushed them against Aster's. She went slow for a reason because this rollout of sensations was too good to rush through, no matter how much more she wanted to do. She kissed Aster more fully, parting her lips, sinking deep into the kiss. Their mouths fit to perfection and now moved in what was quickly becoming hungry tandem. She didn't know why it startled her, how much she loved kissing Aster. She didn't want to compare it to Micah or anyone else she'd been with out of respect, but kissing Aster felt like another activity entirely. She was drunk, and it wasn't from the alcohol.

Aster's hands were firmly on her waist and walking her backward into the main room. She'd sprung for a suite because she wanted this weekend to be special. She hadn't had to wait long for that to happen. With her arms around Aster's neck, she could feel the outline of her breasts as they moved. A slight sway. She wanted to see them, lick them, devour them. She wanted to experience all of Aster, and the more they kissed, the less control she had over thoughts like those. "I want to do so many things to you," she murmured against Aster's mouth. "And I want your hands on my skin."

"I'm yours. I've always been yours," Aster said, and the quality of her voice said that was true. Brynn had heard the term *heart soaring* in the past, but in that hotel room hers really did soar.

This felt right. Scary. But right.

They didn't make it to bed. How could they? The dresser stopped them cold when the back of Brynn's legs pressed against it. More kissing. With Aster's tongue in her mouth, she struggled to think clearly. But she *felt*. Oh, she felt. Most notably the aching between her legs that began to eclipse everything else. But she had urges, too. The first one required Aster's clothes on the floor so she could finally see all that she'd imagined for so long. Her fingers trembled as they touched the hem of Aster's black shirt. She lifted it with purpose, dropped it on the floor, and pulled her face back to look at Aster in just a bra. Oh, my. Her hands moved to the breasts she knew would not disappoint. Aster's style of clothing rarely gave much away, but her body amazed Brynn. The navy bra offered a generous glimpse of the tops of her round breasts, larger than Brynn had visualized, and she'd done a lot of that. Through the satin fabric, Brynn cupped Aster's breasts and pressed them back against her body. Aster's breathing shifted drastically then. She helped things along by unclasping the bra for Brynn and dropping it to the floor, granting her unobstructed access.

"Unreal," Brynn breathed, overcome with lust and relishing every second. She bent down, placed a heated open-mouthed kiss on Aster's right nipple, flooding her own body with yet another hit of arousal. Her underwear was wet, and her legs shook noticeably now. The low moan Aster offered encouraged her as she continued to kiss, lick, and suck every inch of her breast, maybe even too hard, but she'd waited so long and didn't hold back now. She raised her head, kissed Aster's neck, lingering, inhaling her scent, kissing up her jaw to her lips where she stopped just shy. "I want you naked while I do this." Aster's eyes fluttered, and she offered a nod, unbuttoned her jeans, and lowered the zipper. She stepped out of them and the show was a good one. Long legs were revealed to Brynn, smooth and elegant. She wore a pair of black bikinis. The sight of Aster in nothing but a thin piece of fabric made her mouth go dry. It was a good look. "Take them off," Brynn said, unable to tear her eyes away. Aster hooked her thumbs through the waistband of the bikinis, lowered them to the floor, and stepped out. Brynn didn't wait. Her hands were dancing across that skin and following the outline of her waist down the curve of her hips. She wanted to touch her everywhere. She caught Aster in a searing kiss as she slid her hands around to her backside, cupping her cheeks and pulling Aster firmly against her. The pressure ignited a burst of sensation at her center. She heard herself respond audibly in a murmured cry.

"Let's go to the bed," Aster said.

"You first," Brynn said, barely recognizing her own voice. She watched as Aster lay on the bed. With Aster's eyes on her, Brynn removed her clothing, down to her matching raspberry lingerie set that she rarely wore, but did tonight. She watched as Aster's eyes went wide. She sat up, enraptured.

"Come here." Aster held out her hand and pulled Brynn to her lap. Straddling Aster, skin to skin, the position took them to a new level of hot. With her center pressed to Aster's stomach, they began to kiss slowly until their need took over, leaving them breathless. Brynn rocked her hips against Aster, seeking release, desperate to be undone. Her raspberry bra hit the floor and Aster's hands covered both breasts as they rocked, pressing themselves together then apart. Then Aster's mouth was on her breast, sucking, taking Brynn to a height that left her quite close to the edge of oblivion.

As if reading her thoughts, Aster helped her along. She reached a hand between them and moved the raspberry square of fabric to the side. "Go ahead," she whispered in Brynn's ear and ran a thumb across her intimately as Brynn rolled her hips. Then again. God. Brynn closed her eyes and held on to Aster's shoulders. With each stroke Aster took her higher and higher until a warmth cascaded down her face to her breasts, her hips, until her whole body shook. "Aster." The only word she had. She dug her fingers into Aster's shoulders. Hard. "Aster." Seconds later she was overcome with the most intense wash of pleasure she'd ever known and pressed firmly against Aster's hand, riding it until she practically burst.

"You're so beautiful," Aster said quietly. "Sexy." She touched Brynn's cheek. "Brynn. I've never known anything like you."

Brynn's cheeks were hot, and she was still shaken by the intensity of that experience. "I didn't mean for that to get so out of control."

"I did," Aster said, running her fingertips lightly up and down Brynn's bare back. She placed a kiss on Brynn's shoulder that inspired goose bumps. She kissed her breast, palming the other one. She was still exploring, acquainting herself with Brynn's body. "And where did this lingerie come from? I'm going to daydream about it every day for the rest of my life. How am I supposed to hold a job?"

"You like it?" Brynn asked, still rocking softly against Aster as the tiny shockwaves continued to wane.

"I like everything about tonight," Aster said, her brown eyes so much darker than usual. This was her turned-on face, and Brynn loved it. She took such satisfaction in getting to see this whole new private side of Aster. This was her at her most vulnerable. "I have a confession. I've been imagining us like this for a long time. But you're even better than what my brain came up with."

"What your brain came up with?" Brynn asked. "I love the way you think. The way you talk. I also very much like the way you look." She swept a thick strand of hair off Aster's shoulder and kissed the exposed skin. Aster trembled, and Brynn got a heady shot of power. "Do you like it when I touch you?" she whispered in her ear, grinning. Aster nodded. "When I kiss your body?" She placed a passionate kiss along the column of Aster's neck.

Aster nodded again and swallowed, her heartbeat visible through the pulse on her throat. Brynn's hands slid up Aster's ribcage to her breasts where she played, watching as Aster's eyes slammed shut. "Does this turn you on?" Aster bit the corner of her lip as Brynn continued to lavish her breasts with attention. "Because it turns me on." She watched just what action seemed to affect Aster most. It was most definitely when she let her teeth skate across Aster's nipples. She really did have the best breasts, and while Brynn could have lingered for much longer, the sounds Aster was making, the squirming beneath her touch, said she was ready for more.

And God in heaven, so was Brynn.

❖

Aster wasn't often amazed, but tonight took the definition of the word to a whole new level. Not only was Brynn naked in her arms, but she was talkative during sex. Asking Aster questions, tickling her ear with the quiet of her voice, saying things she'd never thought she'd hear Brynn Garrett say. The matching fuchsia lingerie and the way it hugged and displayed Brynn's body had also nearly blown her mind. But it was the way Brynn was touching her now that was the icing on the already alluring cake. She could hear her own heart thudding out of control as her arousal grew, but it didn't matter because the rest of her body pulled focus. She had needs she didn't know were possible.

"You want a little more?" Brynn asked, circling Aster's nipple with her forefinger. She lifted onto her knees in front of Aster, bringing her breasts to Aster's eyeline.

"Now that's a view," Aster managed, mesmerized.

"Mm-hmm. For you." Brynn climbed off Aster's lap and moved down her body on all fours, kissing Aster's breasts, her stomach, and then paid extra attention to the tops of her thighs. The proximity to her center, to the longing that had overtaken everything, was almost too much. She trembled. As if reading her thoughts, Brynn parted her legs and placed a gentle kiss between them, sending a hit of white-hot pleasure that caused Aster to buck her hips.

"Don't you go anywhere," Brynn said and began to trace lazy circles with her tongue. Aster covered her eyes, and her hips started to move in rhythm with Brynn's pattern, trying for release. Yearning. Brynn wrapped an arm around each leg and held her in place like an anchor. She kissed her intimately, pulling her more firmly into her mouth. This would be her undoing, and Aster was rarely undone. It was when Brynn began to gently suck her most sensitive spot that Aster thought she might actually lose her mind. No, that sentiment was premature. Because Brynn pushed inside her and began to move, causing the world to crack open. Pleasure rained down, immeasurable and intense. She felt Brynn everywhere. Throughout her body, coursing through her blood, and in every breath she took. Their unique connection climbed to a whole new category, and everything else dissolved for Aster, leaving only them. Not only was her heart whole, but the physical payoff was better than anything she'd ever experienced.

"Brynn." A pause. "Oh God." She only managed the words after several long moments of recovery. Her eyes latched on to the patterns on the hotel room's ceiling, and her hands had somehow made their way into thick blond hair. She began to stroke it as her faculties clicked back into place at their own meandering pace. She was aware of Brynn's fingertips softly grazing her stomach, then her breasts. "Where are you?" Aster asked with a smile. She lifted her head and looked down. Brynn had her cheek pressed to Aster's midsection, looking rather pleased with herself.

She smiled. "I really like it here."

"You can stay as long as you like."

She lifted her head, laughing. "Dangerous. Here I come." Brynn crawled up the bed, looking like a masterful seductress. She was. Aster lifted her arm, and Brynn slid beneath it. Perfect fit.

"We should have done this sooner," Aster said, feeling happy and accomplished. "Think of all the wasted time. We could have been having a lot of fun."

"We did in my imagination. A lot, actually."

Aster was dumbfounded. "No. You did not fantasize about us." The idea of Brynn thinking those thoughts about *her* was a concept Aster couldn't quite digest. It was too preposterous but also the most amazing idea.

"Oh, you're going to have to trust me on this one. It's been you in my head for quite a while now. Even when I tried to get you the hell out."

Aster gave Brynn a squeeze. "My mom always said I was stubborn." She felt the corners of her mouth tug just at the thought of telling her parents that she and Brynn were involved. "Are we a couple?" she asked.

Brynn propped her head up on her hand. "There's no nuance with you, is there?"

"Is it cooler to just play it by ear? Act aloof? I don't want to be those things. I want to be with you, so I just say so. I want to be yours."

Brynn's voice went soft. "Well, that's why I flew all the way to Boston."

Aster melted, playing the declaration over a second time. "You want us to be an *us*?"

Brynn nodded. "Ripping your clothes off was fun. Don't get me wrong. But I came for more than just that." She slid a strand of Aster's hair behind her ear. "I've never been with anyone like you. No one compares."

She pursed her lips. "I can't tell if that's a good thing."

Brynn laughed. "It is. But it certainly got in the way of me recognizing what this was. I didn't see you coming."

Aster laughed. "Story of my life. That last Lavender. A little forgettable. A lot different. What's her name again?"

"Pretty sure I called it out a couple of times tonight."

That pulled a laugh. "My kingdom for a replay of those moments."

"Sold." Brynn rolled them over, leaving Aster on top, a position Aster liked very much. Oh, but she also coveted the reverse.

"Remember when you came into Hole in One for the first time?"

"After encountering you on your reading bench."

Aster nodded, staggering their thighs. "I remember peering around my stacking cart, seeing you standing there surveying the menu and thinking to myself, this is the most beautiful woman I've ever seen in my life."

"You really thought that?"

Aster nodded and kissed Brynn. "I was a little faster in noticing you, I'm afraid. As in seconds."

"Well, some of us weren't near perfect on our SATs."

Aster's jaw dropped and her eyes went wide. She grinned. "Who told you about my SAT score?" A kiss. "Give me their name."

"I'll never say."

"SAT scores are protected by the government."

"They are not." Another kiss. A deeper one. And then the kissing got even hotter. "Oh, hello," Brynn said, parting her legs and letting Aster's hips settle between.

If there had ever been a night to remember, it would be this one. How had Aster been preparing desserts in a restaurant like any other day just three hours ago? Not a clue what was coming.

"Is that a yes?" Aster asked, before taking a single liberty.

"That's a hell yes," Brynn said, pulling Aster's face to hers for an open-mouthed kiss. "I plan to last a little longer this time. Just watch."

"You want slow? I can deliver slow."

Brynn closed her eyes and her cheeks flushed with warmth, something Aster now knew happened when she was turned on. She pocketed that information and pressed her lips to Brynn's neck, already wet again herself, and ready for anything and everything that lay ahead.

CHAPTER TWELVE

"I want to show you Boston."

Brynn blinked. Her hotel room. It was Saturday morning. Aster. They'd made love the night before. Finally.

She smiled and gazed up at the one and only Aster Lavender, who was propped up on one arm and tracing the underside of Brynn's breasts with a thoughtful look on her face. Ah, that's why every part of her body tingled. That, and the lingering effects of what they'd done to each other the night before.

"It's a great city," Aster said, continuing, "and I've found some really cool spots. Maybe we could have lunch at one of them? I'm sorry that everything I'm excited about has to do with food, but there's this little Italian place. It has a chicken scallopini you won't forget. Do you like scallopini? I can't believe I don't know this about you."

Brynn smiled. So, this was Aster in the morning. Talkative and ready to get going. "Good morning."

"Oh. Yes." A pause. A blush. "Good morning. I didn't mean to forget that part. That's something most people say."

"That's okay," Brynn said, reaching up and touching Aster's cheek with affection. She was still naked, and that made the morning so much better. "And I would love to be taken to lunch and shown around this city you've grown to love."

Aster lay down next to Brynn, staying close. "Is that how you feel about Homer's Bluff? Has it become a city you love?"

Brynn didn't have to think. "I never in a million years would have predicted it, but yes. I'm a sucker for the meandering speed of daily life there. I didn't realize it until it was almost time to leave and I didn't want to." She adjusted the sheet across her waist. "I know you hate it."

"There's a big part of me that misses it, though. I wouldn't have ever predicted *that*."

"No, me neither. You were so anti–small town."

"I'm not even sure it was the town's fault. I felt stuck and like something was missing." Aster linked their hands. "Everything got better once you showed up. I just wasn't expecting you to stay."

Brynn slid down her pillow, so they were face-to-face on their sides. "Is Boston where you want to end up?"

"I want to end up where you end up."

She hadn't been expecting that. Not so soon. But it made her entire body go still, and she was forced to crawl on top of Aster, who grinned in surprise. "Do you mean that?" Brynn asked excitedly, nestling her hips between Aster's legs. "Even if it was Homer's Bluff? Not that it has to be."

"My family lives there. Lots of reasons to go home someday. Maybe even soon. Where would we live?"

"Oh, okay. We're playing house right now, huh?"

"I love this game." Aster's eyes flashed the way they did when she talked about one of her books. "I'd make the breakfast and coffee each day after watching you get dressed out of the corner of my eye as I brushed my teeth."

"Oh, early morning objectification. I can always leave my robe open."

"See? Best game ever. Then you'd go to the clinic for work. I'd commute to a really cool restaurant with amazing butter cake."

"Your own, maybe."

"A whole restaurant?" Aster grinned wider. "I'm fancy in this daydream."

"I'm serious. The place would be packed. You're not only an amazing chef, but you bring so much personality to an establishment. I still can't get past how cool Hole in One is. And Tori has changed very little because it was turnkey awesome."

Aster's smile faded, and Brynn could tell her words resonated. She pulled Brynn's face down and kissed her with precision.

"I should say I'm serious a little more often. Do you have any-where to be?" Brynn asked, already a little breathless.

"Not anymore. I'm free all weekend. I made the arrangements."

After a leisurely morning of exploration in bed, they headed out into the world. Aster took Brynn for lunch at Nico's Trattoria where they luxuriated in that amazing scallopini and even allowed the chef to send over a complimentary wine pairing after recognizing Aster from the cooking school.

"Do all chefs know each other? Is that a thing?"

"Yes," Aster said seriously. "Because the more chefs you know, the more food you get to eat."

Brynn smiled around a fork loaded with pasta. "I didn't realize your appreciation for food fully until you sent me an entire letter that served as an ode to homemade garlic croutons."

"Don't you dare buy the boxed ones."

"Well, I won't after that impassioned letter. The guilt."

"My work is done."

They sat at that small table well past the meal, sipping the glass of wine, and then a cup of coffee, and then more than a few glasses of water just talking. Brynn held tightly to every moment. She loved hearing Aster express herself, give her take on things. And this time, she rejoiced in the knowledge that she didn't have to police herself around Aster, turn off her attraction, or chastise herself for her feelings. At long last, she could celebrate what had been building steadily. No regret involved.

"Speaking of chefs, some of my old classmates are getting together tonight after the kitchens close down, something we do regularly to keep in touch. It's at my friend Mitchell's apartment."

"The one you wrote has the obsession with heirloom tomatoes in food."

Aster laughed. "You have a good memory."

"I pay attention to what you say is all. I would love to meet your chef friends."

"Really?" Aster inflated. "Should be good food. Lots of leftovers from the best kitchens across Boston."

Brynn sat back, still full from lunch. "In that case, we should skip dinner."

"That's not in my DNA."

"Oh. You're really cute in your staunch defense of mealtime."

She glanced at the table and back up at Brynn. "Yeah, well, when I find something to love, I don't let go."

Brynn felt drunk on those words, picking up on Aster's insinuation but playing it cool.

"I'm really happy you're here." Aster placed her hand on Brynn's knee beneath the table, just like she'd done at the hotel bar the night before. The weight of that hand grounded her. She exhaled. She could get used to this. Good conversation. Fantastic sex. Kindness.

"I'm happy I got on that plane." She paused. "It wasn't easy. You're more than a little scary for me."

Aster nodded. "I wondered about that part."

"The last time I went all in, it about destroyed me. And you? Well, you inspire a lot in here." She touched her chest. "It overtakes me sometimes."

"Which is why it took a while for you to succumb to my mad game."

Brynn laughed. "I will say, your game has come a long way from the first day we met and you could barely look me in the eye."

"You were out of my league. You still are. You should go. Ditch me."

She covered Aster's hand on her knee. "Nope. I still haven't seen Dill."

"Want to?"

"Yes."

The afternoon was a languid one, mostly spent on the floor of Aster's apartment with the dog they'd once stayed up all night to save. Playful and still showing his youth, Dill danced around them, darting forward and then back again. "You never get tired, do you?" Brynn asked the adorable dog.

"He can run fifty laps around the perimeter of the dog park and then passes out in the car." Dill offered Aster's face a lick in agreement as if to stay, *Yep. I do that.* He ran circles around them, tossing his stuffed bone in the air and chasing it. A happy guy, content to just play and love and be a silly dog. The best kind, really. All because Aster had taken a bike ride that day.

"What are you thinking about?" Aster asked, looking up at Brynn from where she lay on the floor. Her dark hair was fanned out around her. She had her flirtatious eyes on. That was the thing about them—a mundane activity was still laced with an undercurrent of heat. She wondered now if it had always been that way between them. She was pretty sure it had. With other relationships, the feelings were a lot more even-keeled. She and Aster hummed. Always. Life would never be uninteresting. Who knew how satisfying this level of affection could be? Why had she run from it?

"I'm thinking about the past. You. Dill. Us."

"I feel like he knows you helped save him." Dill placed two paws on Brynn's shoulders, stared into her face, and offered a tail wag before he was on his way again.

"I think we don't give pets enough credit. Pickles is similar. There's a level of gratitude whenever she looks up at me with those great big eyes. She's a sweet girl. Calm and just interested in snuggling."

"Which you're good at. I now know." She glanced behind her at the room. "What do you think of my little place here?"

"I like it. Your room is neat and tidy but also really welcoming in its decor." Aster had decorated her space in the apartment with blues and yellows. She'd remembered the little things that really make a room pop, like curtains that pulled in the colors of the artwork on the walls. She'd always had an artistic eye, above and beyond Brynn's own.

"Have you seen Nora's room? Like a cyclone," Aster said, laughing. She'd not met the famous Nora, but she'd heard about all the ways she contrasted Aster. Loud, messy, and energetic. It sounded like she'd been instrumental in pulling Aster out of her shell once she moved to Boston. Their friendship seemed like a helpful one. Brynn was grateful.

"Will I meet her tonight? I want to."

"She's usually around. You guys are very different, but I think you'll like her."

"She's more fun than me."

"No," Aster said, leaning over casually and kissing her. "But you would definitely feel like the grown-up in the room, Dr. Garrett."

"I like it when you call me that."

Aster's cheeks colored in pink and her eyes darkened. "I mean, maybe we can use it. And I'm kinda embarrassed I said that."

Brynn rested on both her forearms, meeting Aster face-to-face.

"Don't be. I like your adventurous side. And the bedroom is the perfect place for it."

"You were so sexy last night." Aster covered her eyes, falling head first into the memory. "I didn't quite know what to expect."

"You thought I'd be reserved in the sack, like a proper science-minded person."

"Maybe. And that alone was still mind-boggling hot, but the reality, the determination..." She let the words die. "Your tenacity was very much appreciated."

It was fun to see Aster embarrassed. It carried shades of the early Aster, shy and tentative. "Oh, you mean when I took your clothes off and straddled you in my lingerie."

Aster nodded, swallowed. "Yes. That."

"Are you thinking about it now?"

She nodded.

"Maybe we can come up with more things to think about tonight."

"Or right now," Aster said, glancing at her bedroom. It was an offer. Brynn couldn't remember the last time she'd had daytime sex, but she instantly couldn't think of anything she wanted more.

With Dill busy tearing into a stuffie at the foot of the couch, Brynn crawled over to Aster and slipped a hand under her shirt and pulled the cup of her bra down, freeing her breast. She watched Aster's face, the way her lips parted when she circled her nipple with one finger. "I'm in," Brynn said, closing her eyes to the way her own body was beginning to respond to touching Aster. "Take me to your room and do decadent things to me."

Aster crushed her lips to Brynn's. "You don't have to ask me twice."

❖

The get-together with Aster's friends that night was laid-back and comfortable. People trickled into Mitchell's decent-sized apartment until there was a group of about ten divided into two to three different conversations at any one point. Brynn enjoyed the vibe and this peek into their culture. Wine had been opened, and fantastic food that had been cooked that very night at various restaurants lined Mitchell's countertops, deposited there by the handful of chefs who'd hung up their chef's jackets for the evening. She got the feeling that this was a standing gathering where the friends talked about the culinary scene and life. They all seemed to run in the same circles and know the same people. The Boston food community was smaller than she would have guessed.

Brynn had herself a glass of white while she sat back and took in the overlapping conversations. She smiled as each person made a point of introducing themselves and saying hello. Aster moved about, chatting with this friend or that one before returning to Brynn and checking in.

"I'm doing great. Please have fun," Brynn said, encouraging Aster not to worry about her.

Staying the entire weekend had been the right call because it afforded Brynn the opportunity to see Aster around the people who mattered to her. Similar to how she was in Homer's Bluff, Aster wasn't the loudest one in the room. She would never be that, but she was very much at home with this group who liked to reminisce and tease each other. Aster took everything in first before chiming in with a thoughtful contribution. Less was more for Aster, and it worked. People seemed to value her opinion as much as Brynn did.

Nora, the roommate she'd heard about, arrived after about half an hour. She was friendly enough and flashed a smile every time they made eye contact, but she also hadn't taken her eyes off Brynn for a second since the moment she'd arrived. That was curious. Brynn felt the need to assure her she had no intention of pocketing Mitchell's silverware and she could relax.

"How was your flight?" Nora asked, joining Brynn in the kitchen.

"Faster than I thought it would be and uneventful." It was mundane conversation. The kind of thing you asked someone to check a box.

"So, interesting, you two," Nora said, reaching across Brynn for the bottle of cabernet. Brynn topped off her pinot gris.

She took a moment to catch on. "Oh. You mean Aster and me?"

"Yep. I saw you holding hands a few minutes ago, so I imagine your cute letter-writing has blossomed." She said it with a smile, but there was an undercurrent attached. The word *cute* had a pointed edge. It didn't sit well in Brynn's chest.

"We're seeing where things go." She sipped her wine and turned to rejoin the group.

"She told you that? Interesting update. Good to know." Nora bit her lower lip. What was she driving at? She was baiting Brynn. But why? While she should have walked away and left Nora unsuccessful, something made her take a swipe at what Nora was trying to offer up.

Brynn shifted her weight, unsettled. "Is it? Interesting, I mean."

"Well, to me. Given our history. Mine and Aster's."

"Right." Confusion. "History." Maybe she meant their roommate status. Brynn decided to leave it alone. She followed Nora's gaze to Aster and shifted the trajectory of the conversation. "She's pretty great."

Nora folded her arms, still holding her glass. "No one like Aster. Unique in her talent and the way she approaches the world. Wouldn't you say?"

"Yes." Brynn agreed very much with that sentiment. "And I'm really happy we've reconnected. It's so great to see her." She was staying vague on purpose. She didn't know Nora and decided to keep her cards close to her chest. Something told her that was wise.

"Hey, I get it." Nora turned to Brynn fully. "As someone who has been there with Aster in the will-they, won't-they romantic sense, I certainly understand the appeal. She's hot as fuck and doesn't seem to know it." She fanned herself. "That adds to the whole thing. Right?"

All of this felt weird. Romantic sense? She was lost and struggling. Alarm bells were beginning to sound. "She is that."

The moment felt like one of those tsunami movies where the wave rumbled in the distance while the people on the shoreline had an inkling that *something* was off but weren't quite sure what.

"But also incredibly intelligent." Nora laughed to herself. "How many people are that smart and look so good naked?"

Every part of Brynn went cold. She nodded and sipped, downshifting. Her brain went to half capacity. Her defenses flared. But the awful thread was loose now, and she couldn't keep her fingers off it. "What do you mean? You guys were together in some way?"

"Oh yeah."

"I didn't realize." She stayed as casual as her body would allow. She needed to hear what Nora had to say. She and Aster told each other everything. No details were spared. Certainly, not relationship ones. Or so she thought.

"We have a thing. Or maybe the word is *had* now that you're here. My door was open to her, and well, she used it." Nora bopped her head to the music and stared off at the others, who were lost in their own conversations.

"Oh." In her brain, Brynn heard the sound of brakes screeching to a halt. Across the apartment, Aster nodded along with something one of the guys was explaining with vivid gestures. She seemed like an entirely different person now. How was that possible? She pulled her gaze away, still stunned. "Friends with benefits or...?"

"That's just it. We've never really assigned it a name. We just really enjoy each other in a lot of ways." She shrugged. "Have you ever just really clicked with a person? That's us. From the first day of classes, really. Everyone said we were inseparable. It was kind of sweet."

Brynn's breathing went shallow, and nausea swirled like poison in her midsection. "You said *recently*."

Nora met Brynn's gaze in half apology, half victory. "I did say that." She went up on tiptoe and shouted across the room. "Janice, I know you're not about to do that shot without me.' I've had a night." Back to Brynn. "Excuse me." And she was gone, leaving a whole lot of destruction in her wake. Brynn was numb, and her brain was about two beats behind, stuttering with new information that simply did not make sense with anything that she'd known to be true. They weren't in a relationship. Aster didn't owe her that kind of loyalty. She was free to sleep with whoever she wanted to. The problem was something else entirely. She'd offered Brynn the illusion of transparency when that hadn't been the case. They'd written letters and seemingly held nothing back. Aster never mentioned *any of this*. Not an inkling of a physical connection to her roommate. Why? And what else didn't Brynn know? More alarm bells.

Almost as if their brain waves connected, Aster turned midconversation, searching the space for Brynn. When she saw her face, her brows came together in concern. She immediately set down her drink and made her way across the room. "Are you okay? You look like something might be wrong."

"I don't know. Maybe. Just a weird night."

Aster interlaced their fingers and gave Brynn's hand a squeeze. "Okay. I hear you. Tell me what's going on."

"I just talked to your roommate and am a little confused. So...you and Nora?"

Aster's eyes darted across the room and then back to Brynn. She blinked a moment, still yet to say a word.

"Aster. You can just tell me. It's me."

But Aster was busy doing the math, and that didn't bode well. "Yes. We've been…It was never anything serious or formal. It's not something to worry about. I promise."

None of this felt right. Almost like they'd slipped into a parallel universe Brynn didn't know existed. "Right. I hear you. But how come I didn't know?"

"Would you have wanted to know?"

Brynn opened her mouth and closed it. "Yes. It's important in the scheme of your life. Wouldn't you have wanted to know if I was with someone?"

"Well, you were," Aster said quietly, tossing a glance at her friends across the room, making sure they were speaking privately.

"Exactly. And I told you all about Micah."

"Because you had actual feelings for her. That's the part that mattered."

"I'm not sure I agree. I'm still figuring this out." She took a moment to just breathe. "And you don't have feelings for Nora? Be honest."

"Not like that. No." Her eyes were so sincerely filled with confusion that part of Brynn wanted to wrap Aster up in her arms while the other part wanted to throttle her for hiding this part of her life. Causing Brynn to question so much. Why were all of her Aster feelings always so big? For the good or the bad, they overwhelmed her, full-on consumed. Everything was Aster.

"But you slept together." It was a statement. Brynn was piecing together the details, so she could assess the larger picture. She could already tell she didn't like it.

Aster touched her hair and then let her arm drop. She was uncomfortable and didn't know what to do with her hands. "Yeah. We did."

"Okay. Once?"

She hesitated. Great. Fabulous. Brynn's face rushed hot, and the room ran oppressive in its lack of oxygen. She felt the urge to tug the neck of her sweater away from her body because she was drowning in discomfort. This whole thing was sickeningly familiar, and her past came roaring back to her. The details of Tiffany's betrayal settled all over her. She couldn't let something like that happen again. Was Aster capable of something like that? Two days ago, the answer would have been positively no. Now, she wasn't sure. She hated that she was here again, blindsided by someone she cared about. "It's too hot in here for this conversation. Can we go?"

Aster didn't hesitate. "I'll get our coats."

They spilled into the parking lot of the apartment complex, and the blast of cold air was a helpful slap in the face. Brynn could breathe now, and that meant she could think.

"I'm sorry about not bringing up Nora," Aster said. "We were friends first who pushed that boundary."

"You were sleeping with her." To Brynn, that wasn't even the part that mattered most. "But that part I understand. You were single. You weren't cheating on anyone. But you framed your life and relationship with Nora with tons of details. I knew what you guys watched on TV together. Why leave out such a major one unless your goal was to purposefully withhold or mislead? I don't even know which."

Aster looked back, confused. "I just...couldn't."

Brynn closed her eyes, wishing for a clearer explanation. They were on different pages in this conversation. "Can you drive me back to the hotel? I don't feel well." The total truth. Her stomach lurched uncomfortably. How had so much changed in the span of ten minutes?

They drove in silence for the first half of the trip, which was too long. It gave Brynn time to simmer in bewilderment and distrust as she examined this thing from every angle.

Finally, the incredulity exploded. "None of this adds up. You told me what time you finished work. Jokes your friends cracked. Conversations with your boss. Even the quiet parts of your thoughts. You were never dishonest, but you also weren't forthcoming."

"I know." Aster opened her mouth and closed it.

That was a big problem for Brynn, who'd tied herself to an emotional train the moment she decided to profess her feelings to Aster. Now, here she sat, speeding toward a brick wall all over again against her fucking will. How?

Aster seemed to regroup. "I hear all that you're saying." She squeezed the steering wheel. "It didn't feel like the kind of thing you'd put in a letter to someone who...was you. You're Brynn. The person

I think about a lot. Almost every minute of the day since we started writing. And, well, maybe it was more that I didn't want you to think of me in this other light. With someone else."

"The light you were actually living in?"

Aster closed her eyes. "It sounds awful when you put it in those terms. What if hearing about me with Nora scared you away? You're too important, Brynn. You're the most important. You have no idea what you mean to me."

Brynn pushed that last part aside. She had to. "Okay, letters aside. How about when I showed up in Boston and professed my stupid feelings?"

"Your feelings aren't stupid. Please never say that."

"Don't you think at some point you offer up that there's been someone? Come clean. Cards on the table. It matters at that point. I thought I knew everything because you made me think I did. You should have corrected that."

"If it had been more, I would have said something. Nora and I are *friends*."

"Who have sex with each other. In secret."

"No. It's never been a secret, it's just—"

"Something you purposefully *omitted*. Look I get that there are tons of people who would not see this as a big deal, but given the nature of my past, the wounds I still carry, I'm not one of them."

Aster pulled into the parking lot of the hotel and pressed her forehead to the steering wheel. "Please. I get it now. I can see that this has hurt you, and I hate it. I mishandled this whole thing. What you have to understand is that I don't have a lot of experience in this area. And I clearly misjudged Nora and what kind of person she is. I'm sorry you heard this from her when it should have been me."

"I know." Brynn opened the car door and stepped out. "I don't think you purposefully set out to hurt me, Aster, but you really did, and all of this is feeling like it was just a big mistake."

"No, no, no. Can we start over?"

Brynn wanted to. She wanted to rewind, go back to an hour ago, or find a way to move past all of this. She'd had the best two days of her life and had been thrilled for what was ahead, the plans they'd started to make, the memories just waiting for them create. Aster was hers, and together they were better than she'd even imagined. But she couldn't undo this turn in the road because it wasn't just a mistake. And yes, she was aware that her own hang-ups were part of the problem. If Aster would knowingly hold that kind of information back, what could Brynn expect from her in the future? She was doubting herself now, too. Her own judgment and assessment of character. It was humbling and unnerving. If she didn't know Aster, of all people, maybe she didn't know anyone.

"Stop for a second." Aster was out of the car and came around the back. "Let me come up with you. We can talk this through. I'm really sorry. I can keep saying that. In fact, I will."

She took Aster's hand and kissed the back of it. "I don't think I can do anymore tonight, okay? Good night, Aster. My request is that you don't follow me."

"Brynn," she said quietly. She loved the sound of her name on Aster's lips. If only it was enough. "Please?" The word broke her heart. And maybe it wasn't fair, how hard she was taking this, but she couldn't change who she was and what she needed. Taking this leap was wildly out of character for her and now seemed like a huge mistake.

"I'm so sorry," Brynn called back, but she made sure not to turn around. Because if she saw Aster's face, those beautiful brown eyes, she just might give in, invite her up, and set herself up for disaster down the road. She simply wasn't equipped for any of this, and her heart was too important to her these days. She had to protect it at all costs. Even if that meant against Aster.

She walked slowly down the long hallway to her room. The same square footage that had delivered so many wonderful moments that weekend now felt barren and sad. She climbed into bed with her clothes on and asked herself how she'd ended up here. Part of it was her fault. Part of it was Aster's. She tried to be angry, but it died in her throat.

Sleep didn't come that night. Instead, her mind played cruel tricks, showing her all the mistakes she'd made, most notably, letting herself leap into something with both feet, heart wide open for the breaking.

There were things in life that a person longed for, craved, and actively wanted for themselves. None of that changed what they were capable of. After believing with all her might that Tiffany was the person she'd spend the rest of her days with, her life had been upended, and it had taken *years* for her heart to recover. She couldn't go down a similar road again, and this whole thing with Aster felt like a giant red flag waving right in front of her face. She wanted Aster. She wanted a them. But maybe her head should win out this time.

By the time the sky showed signs of light, Brynn had solemnly packed her things.

She didn't know where this path would have led, but it was best she get off it now.

"Where are you going?" The voice was tired. Weak.

Brynn raised her eyes as she wheeled her luggage through the lobby. Aster stood from a bench along the wall, wearing the same clothes she'd last seen her in. Brynn's shoulders sagged and she exhaled. "There you are. I was going to call you before I left."

Aster eyed the bag. She pointed to it half-heartedly. "From the airport."

"Yes." She let her head fall to the side. "Were you here all night?" Aster nodded. "Oh, Aster, no."

"It's okay." She glanced at the luggage. "Why are you leaving?"

"I have to do what feels right. For both of us. I'm not sure we're the best match." She rushed to explain. "It doesn't take anything away from either of us. I know that you're a good person, Aster. And I still think the world of you."

"So that's it? It's over?"

"I think I need to sort through everything until I find myself again. I don't even trust my reflection in the mirror right now, and that's on me."

Aster nodded, accepting. Too accepting actually, and that tugged at Brynn's heart. "Can I say one thing before you go?"

"Yeah. Please do."

"I will never hurt you the way Tiffany did, and I will swear off any and all secrets if you decide to give me a second chance at some point."

"I appreciate that." There was a key difference between what happened with Tiffany and this weekend. Aster seemed truly sorry and wanted to make it right immediately. She'd screwed up and was owning it. That mattered. But was it enough? Brynn was exhausted and needed her own bed and her dog and her life. The rest would figure itself out. "For now, I better go."

"Will you write?" Aster asked.

She couldn't imagine losing that part of her relationship with

Aster, but at the same time, maybe she'd let it go too far. After all, she'd wound up here. "Yes. At some point I will."

The look of defeat on Aster's face was hard to process. Guilt struck. What was wrong with her? Why was she still broken? Suddenly all Brynn wanted to do was get the hell out of there. She couldn't make it through some dramatic good-bye in a hotel lobby on no sleep and a wounded heart. "Take care of yourself, Aster, okay?" With that, she hurried outside to meet her waiting Uber. It would take her back to the safe haven she'd carved out for herself on Baker Street in Homer's Bluff, Kansas, where scary things rarely happened.

PART FOUR

CHAPTER THIRTEEN

Two years later

Aster's hands shook as she stood in the aisle waiting to deplane. She hadn't been back home in far too long, and now this visit could be under better circumstances. Sage was waiting for her in baggage claim when she exited through the big automatic doors. He looked tired, which was to be expected. He likely hadn't slept. Who had?

"Come here," he said as she approached. He opened his arms, and she walked into them, tears already filling her eyes. Just seeing her big brother brought them on, and when his arms went around her, the emotion bubbled over full and strong. For several moments, they stood just like that, holding on to each other, willing the news not to be true.

"How is she?"

He hesitated. "It depends on the moment. She's in and out of consciousness. Sometimes her head is clearer than others."

"Can we go straight there?" she asked.

"Of course."

They'd have a couple hour drive from the airport to Homer's Bluff, but Aster knew there wasn't time to waste. Her mother had been admitted to hospice the day before. It was happening too fast, and Aster couldn't believe they were already here. The doctors had thought there'd be more time. Aster had planned using every bit of it. Her mother's diagnosis had come as a shock six weeks earlier. She'd been tired. Aster had noticed herself when her parents had visited her in Boston recently. Her mom had smiled her way through the sightseeing, stealing hugs from Aster along the way, and going on about how amazing Aster's food was and how proud they all were of her success. It had been the absolute perfect visit. But when her mother's health had continued to deteriorate, they began to run tests and learned the worst.

Sage grabbed her bag, and in a short amount of time they were on the road. Sitting in that truck, her mind had too much space. The closer they got to town, the more anxious she became. Memories of her family, her room, the old days back at the doughnut shop, Brynn. They swirled and circled until it felt like they swallowed her whole.

Sage kept his eyes on the road. "You're quiet."

"I am. Can we talk about something? Anything. I don't care what."

"Tyler's pregnant."

That woke her the hell up. "Did you say pregnant? Who is she having a baby with?"

His brows dropped. He passed her a look. "What kind of question is that?"

Aster held up her hands. "Just checking." Tyler and Sage had been an official couple for over two years now, reveling in all things love and friendship. "Sage, you're going to be a dad? You're gonna need a miniature tractor."

"I was thinking the same thing."

"Wow. I'm going to have a new niece or nephew. Ethan's getting a cousin."

"In a little over six months."

"Mom and Dad must be over the moon." She hadn't thought the sentence through. It was so automatic to imagine their future with the Lavender family the way it had always been. Things got quiet in the truck because they both understood that their mother wouldn't be with them when the baby arrived. She'd not see Sage become a father, or Aster's future journeys. Any of it. It was unbelievable and awful.

Her sisters were waiting at their parents' house when Aster arrived. They pulled her onto the couch with them wordlessly. Violet kissed her hair, and Marigold held her face. "Hi, you guys," she said, happy to see them, and sharing their pain.

"You can go in and see her if you want," Violet said.

"I do. Is she…?"

"She's sleeping, but she would want you to wake her," Marigold said.

Aster nodded and headed to the back bedroom. As she passed the sliding glass door, she saw Ethan on the swing set, playing quietly in the very backyard the four of them used to tumble through, playing freeze tag or the grass is lava before their mom called them inside to wash their hands and set the table for dinner. She wanted to go back to those moments and relive them. Anything to escape the suffocating reality of this one.

The room was dark and quiet when she entered. She remembered pushing that very door open as a kid when she couldn't sleep or she heard a scary noise. Her mother would raise the blanket, and she would scamper into the big bed with her parents. Her mom would snuggle her tight, taking away all of her fear. Today, the sound of her feet shuffling on the tile floor must have woken her mother, who raised her head. "Violet?"

"It's Aster, Mom."

"You're here." When she got closer, her mother smiled. "You came to see me. My baby." She was so much thinner than the last time they'd seen each other. That had happened so quickly.

Aster turned on the small lamp next to the bed and placed a kiss on her mother's cheek. "You think I was going to miss the opportunity to hang out with you when you have all this free time?" She tried to smile. "You're always on the go, keeping this place afloat."

"Violet has got it now. She knows how to do my job."

"Exactly. So, me and you? We can relax."

"How are you?" her mother asked. "You've been sad. So sad."

She frowned. "What do you mean?"

"Since Brynn."

"Ah. Well, I haven't seen her in a long time. She's busy with the clinic, I imagine. I'm good."

"No, you're not. She's sad, too." Her mother closed her eyes, and Aster could tell that even this little bit of conversation took a lot of her energy. "We had her over for dinner with Sage and Tyler one night. Her spark is gone. Probably ran off with your spark. Can you hand me that water?"

Aster picked up the glass of water and placed the straw in her mother's mouth. "Well, I wouldn't know anything about that. She stopped writing me not long after she came to Boston. It's been, what, close to two years."

She swallowed and nodded. Aster returned the glass to the table. "She misses you."

"Well, she knows where to find me and hasn't." Yes, there was a hard kernel of bitterness nestled in her chest. She'd screwed things up for them that weekend, but for Brynn to pull her friendship back entirely? Aster didn't understand or sympathize. It had felt cruel and unusual. In her mind, they'd been so much more than just romantically involved. They'd been friends, confidants, therapists, everything. And Brynn had left it all by the wayside simply because she couldn't forgive? "I think that's a chapter in my life that's now closed."

"No. Don't do that." Her mother closed her eyes as she continued, gathering what energy she had to impart her advice. "People always bumble along. As humans, it's what we do. Some find their meant-to-be person early. Some take the more scenic route. But you don't close doors, do you hear me?"

Aster didn't have it in her to argue. "I do. I will remember that."

"You're not convincing me, and I don't have much time to make my points to you."

She swallowed. Her throat hurt with emotion. She didn't like that sentence at all, but it certainly got her attention. "I'm listening. I promise, I am."

"You've always been my quiet child, Aster. It's because you're thoughtful. You like to hang out in your own head and stay out of other people's way."

She smiled through her tears, reflecting on how empty her life felt these days. She loved her job, her dog, but that was pretty much it. "Lot of good that did me. I really miss you guys."

"Then maybe it's time you come back home."

She exhaled. She'd learned so much about the world since leaving this town. She was richer for it. But there had been a time to leave. Was there also a time to return? That tug was starting to pick up momentum. As she sat here now with her mom, Aster wondered about all that lost time with her family and friends. She'd missed the birth of Tori's kids and Sage's transformation from playboy to dedicated partner. The Lavender House had undergone a major renovation that her sisters had shouldered themselves. Ethan had sprouted like a weed. And now her mom was sick, and she'd never get that time back. The idea that they'd always have the future to look forward to was now a somber lie.

"I do miss this place. Never in a million years thought I would say that. So much of me is here."

"I don't know where this life might take you, Aster, because you have so many wonderful possibilities. But let this place be your anchor. It will be here waiting for you when you're ready for it. But above all, I want you to seize life by the throat, and don't for one second let go. Do you hear me? If I have to leave this world, I'm not doing it without telling my kids what I know. Life is precious. It's a joy if you find the things that are important to you."

"I'm trying. It's been hard lately."

"I can tell just by looking at you." There weren't many people in Aster's life who could do that. How was she supposed to do this on her own now? Her mom was her rock, the person she could always count on for a smile, or a warm hug, or a kind ear. She was a cheerleader for Aster, who very much needed her. "You've lost the spark in your eye. You've lost your hope. Get that back. And when you do, I want you to eat all the best tasting foods, and take walks in the rain without caring if you get wet." She paused to cough, and Aster squeezed her hand. "You can always change clothes after. It takes five minutes." That pulled a smile from Aster, who was memorizing every word. "See all the best movies, too. Lose yourself in a wonderful unravel of story. And not just science fiction, young lady. Expose yourself to all genres of storytelling."

"I will. I promise."

"And take care of your dad for me. He's a good soul, but I've always been his navigator. He'll need you kids now. He can cook but might need pointers. You can help with that."

"I'm all over it."

"And don't leave old wounds with Brynn Garrett festering. I don't know every detail of what went on between you two, but it feels like you've each lost something important, and maybe life would be better if those fences were mended."

Aster exhaled slowly. That was a taller order. "Yes, ma'am."

"You're going to need someone to walk in the rain with. When you take that walk, know that I'm smiling."

The tears filled her mother's eyes, and that was Aster's emotional dismantling. She laid her head on her mother's shoulder and clung to her, crying without restraint. None of this was fair, and yet there was nothing to do but treasure this last little bit of time.

❖

They lost her two days later on a rainy Monday.

Aster drove through town over and over again, shouldering the grief. She couldn't sit still. She couldn't read a book or focus on a dish. Driving made her feel like she was doing something in a world where she felt entirely helpless. Homer's Bluff, while comforting, was also haunted. She passed the fire hydrant that had busted the summer of fourth grade. They'd put on their bathing suits and had the best sprinkler party while her mom had looked on, laughing and snapping photos. Larry's Last Stop and the night Sage had won the dart throwing competition and had his photo in the paper. Her bench in the center of town. The Lavender farm where her father had worked his hands raw and her mother had stayed up all night making the budget work for a business and raising four kids. Hole in One with her mural still on display. Baker Street and her old house. The vet clinic where she'd held baby Dill and nursed him back to health. Aster could scarcely breathe, reliving those moments in snatches.

But everywhere she drove, she felt Brynn all over. She had from the moment she'd set foot in town. They'd not shared the same space since that day in the hotel lobby. There had been a few letters, surface level at best. Brynn had pulled herself back emotionally, and that had hurt. But when the response time between letters had grown longer and longer, Aster got the message. When they'd stopped altogether, it had felt like her heart had been ripped from her chest. She'd lost her person. And now she'd lost another.

As she drove, Aster heard her mother's words in her head. *You're going to need someone to walk in the rain with. Life would be better if those fences were mended.*

She didn't allow herself to think. She drove automatically to Brynn's house, got out of her car, and stood there in the driveway. Lost. Seeking. Wounded.

Within sixty seconds, Brynn opened the door, stepped out, and stared. She nodded and made her way to Aster steadily. "Come here." And Aster did. Brynn wrapped her up and held her. The world slowed down, and a sense of peace descended. Temporary or not, Aster needed this. She reveled in it, the first true comfort she'd felt in days. Brynn's arms around her, the way she smelled, the softness of her skin, the tickle of her hair. Aster was right back to everything good and memorable in life.

But she couldn't stay here.

She let go, aching deeply at the loss.

"I'm so sorry, Aster," Brynn said, her eyes sad. "There are certainly no words."

"Thank you," she mumbled before sliding back behind the wheel of her car. "I just wanted to…"

"I know," Brynn said. She stood in the driveway as Aster pulled away looking like there was so much more to say. If there was a time, this wasn't it. They both knew that.

The funeral was a blur. People. Food. But mostly heartbreak and a true confusion about how life proceeded from here. Nothing felt quite the same without Marilyn Lavender in the world to lead them. Brynn hung in the background, attending every event but giving Aster space. The siblings were there for each other with little touches, squeezes, or hugs. None had many words as they existed in the aftermath. Their father cried but not much in front of them. He'd retreat to his bedroom, and they'd hear him in there, sniffling and trying to muffle the sounds. They'd cry themselves, listening.

"Can you stay a little longer?" Marigold asked. Aster lay with her head in her sister's lap as she stroked her hair softly on their parents' couch. It had become their gathering spot all over again, echoing their early years. It had been over a week since the funeral, and the family was slowly returning to normal activities. Aster was needed in Boston, even if her executive chef had been incredibly understanding about the time off. They'd covered for her, but the kitchen was stretched thin.

"I have to be back in Boston by tomorrow night for dinner service."

"Damn."

"I'll be back."

"Yeah," Marigold said quietly, and everything about the tone of her voice said she didn't fully buy it. Of the four of them, Marigold was the sweet and soft one, no matter how robust her bravado could seem, and she was holding tightly now to each one of them. Her family. Aster identified.

She sat up. "I want to come home. I don't know how soon I can make that happen. It might take a while. But I need to be here. I want to be."

"Really? I thought your wandering spirit had finally found adventure." She said it with a smile, reluctant but proud at the same time.

"I can still wander. But there's no reason I can't home-base here."

Marigold cupped her cheek with one hand. "I would love to see your very cute face every day, you know."

"I'm not cute. I'm in my thirties."

"You will always be five," Marigold said and placed a hand on top of Aster's head.

"MG?" she said. "You doing okay?" Marigold was great about worrying about everyone else, but Aster wondered who worried about her.

"You know me. I'm always okay." Aster wondered how honest she was being. Marigold loved to play matchmaker, but where were her own prospects? She was beautiful, vivacious, and full of life. Aster wondered what exactly held her back. Maybe one day, she'd find the love of her life and settle down. Hopefully, she wouldn't blow it like Aster had.

She flew back to Boston a different person than the one who'd landed in Kansas. She'd lost part of her and gained a new appreciation for what she had left. She could still experience the world and keep those she loved close to her. New goal? Beat Sage's baby to Homer's Bluff.

CHAPTER FOURTEEN

There was a rumor of a new restaurant going in halfway between Homer's Bluff and Wichita. There wasn't a ton along that route, so this place would require a deliberate trip. The last place that had occupied the space hadn't fared so well, and the building had sat empty for years.

The rumor mill was busy with what kind of place it would be and, namely, who was opening it. A big corporation was one idea. Or a national chain was installing a new location. Maybe Aster Lavender was giving entrepreneurship another go. Obviously, that was the theory Brynn couldn't get out of her head. She resisted the urge to track down a Lavender that very moment to find out for certain. With the loss of Marilyn less than half a year ago, the group had had a rough time of it. Tyler would know, and she hadn't said anything. But Tyler also knew what a sensitive subject Aster was and would choose her moment. It was possible that moment hadn't arrived yet.

But when Sage Lavender showed up at her practice with his sidekick Buster who was in need of his annual vaccinations, she seized the opportunity for some casual fishing. "How are you guys doing lately? Your family."

"Breathing again, but it's been a process," Sage said, scratching behind Buster's ears.

"Glad to hear it." A pause as she gave the dog a once-over, checking his teeth, his ears. "And your sisters?"

He eyed her knowingly. Dammit. "Marigold is looking forward to the baby finally getting here. She can't wait to be an aunt again. Violet has her hands full with Ethan but is talking about dating again. And

Aster"—he met her gaze pointedly—"has been in town for a couple of days now. Getting everything ready for the big restaurant opening. But you likely knew that part. I think word is starting to leak out."

"I didn't. No." She blinked, realizing she'd stopped her exam. "Sorry," she said, giving her head a shake. The room felt weird, and her face was hot.

Sage nodded. "I've been where you're at. No need to apologize." It looked like he made a decision. "Tyler told me to stay out of it because I always say the wrong damn thing, but trust me when I tell you that it's so much better when you're honest with yourself." He offered a supportive wink, which she ignored.

She went through the rest of her day feeling like an automaton, numb to the world and splitting her focus between strict work concentration and stealing moments for her brain to absorb the information about Aster. Her world felt rocked. The idea of Aster Lavender back in her sphere made her dizzy.

She went home to her sweet dog, who promptly curled up in the crook of her knee on the couch. Brynn considered picking up the thriller she'd been reading. Maybe it would help take her mind off things. But that only catapulted her back in time to the nights she'd spent at Aster's place, reading side by side, touching every chance they got, behaving themselves while aching to take things further. Sexual tension oozed from those walls. That, of course, had her remembering the weekend they had in Boston. Flashes from that night overwhelmed. Skin, lips, touches, the sensation of their bodies coming together in a tremble after waiting so long. She tossed the book back onto the coffee table and took a lap around the kitchen, and then another, because what was she supposed to do now?

She was the one who'd pulled away. That part was on her. She had no right to feel anything right now. She had allowed the letters to trail off, always imagining the safe distance between them would act as a buffer. But she had no claim to Homer's Bluff, and certainly not over Aster who had grown up here. The day she'd held Aster as she cried for the loss of her mother had been a startling wake-up call. She'd spent every day since missing Aster brutally, wondering how she was, and having no right to ask.

"You're about to find out," she said quietly and tapped her lips.

If only she wasn't completely terrified.

❖

Marilyn's. Aster stood in the parking lot, watching as the sign in black script was placed by a crane and a team of workers above the building still under renovation.

"Yeah. Perfect," she said to herself, placing a hand over her heart. She could feel her mother's presence wash over her in the moment. The restaurant still had a way to go until opening, but slow and steady was the pace Aster preferred. No rushing to meet a lofty deadline. She wanted to do this thing right, and that meant taking her time.

She took a deep breath and let the emotion settle. This was where she was meant to be, and this was what she was meant to be doing. She could feel it in her every inch.

At her lunch with Tyler later that day, she finally found a way to articulate it. "Do you know when you're really sleeping hard, and the smoke detector starts going off?"

Tyler pointed at her with her fork. She'd ordered a very plain looking salad because her morning sickness wouldn't allow much flavor in her meals. "That's my nightmare. When the beeping starts it's always middle of the night. Satan takes his revenge in small ways."

"It started going off for me when we lost Mom. It didn't stop until I was back here. The strangest thing."

Tyler's brown eyes softened. "That's not strange. It's meant to be. I think we all have moments like that where the fates grab us by the collar and drag us over to our ordained orbit."

Aster shrugged. "I guess that's it." She set down her club sandwich and regarded her friend. "You look great, by the way. Pregnancy is your friend."

That made Tyler glow all the more. "Thank you. I think I'm one of those rare women who really loves to be pregnant. Also, I have news."

"Twins?" Aster asked, half serious. She imagined Sage and Tyler miniatures, toddling through Homer's Bluff.

"Bite your tongue. No. We're getting married. Did your brother tell you?"

Aster went soft like a puddle of vanilla ice cream. This was a big deal and a long time coming. "You are?" she managed to squeak out.

"Yes." She shook her head. "I can't believe we're actually here, but he stopped being a knuckleheaded man-child, and I dropped my stubbornness-just-for-the-sake-of-punishment, and we'd like both you and Brynn to be in the wedding. You on Sage's side and Brynn on mine. Is that okay?" She let out a long breath because that was a lot.

Aster tensed and released, imagining that scenario. Her. Brynn. Vows. No. "We'll be fine." She'd known coming back to town meant that she'd be tossed into the mix with Brynn, and they'd find a way to muddle through.

"Good. I was really only asking as a gesture because we're having you both up there no matter what. Are you still in love with her?"

Aster didn't hesitate. She was past the point of lying to herself. "I've probably always been in love with Brynn Garrett, and I likely always will be."

Tyler's lips parted. "I was expecting a bigger protest."

"Why? Because she gives you one when you ask about me?" Tyler closed her mouth and Aster had her answer. "Don't worry. I don't have a single delusion about us working it out. The ship has sailed. I think she and I agree on that. Done deal."

"It's like Sage and me all over again." She shook her head as if to say, *What a shame.*

"Maybe with less of a glorious finale." She indicated Tyler's present state with her chin. "But I don't want you to worry about that wedding."

"Which is in three weeks."

"Damn, you're fast."

She pointed at her growing stomach that had likely taken on size since they'd been sitting there. "I'm in a race, Aster."

"Brynn and I will be fine."

"If you say so."

Aster spent the rest of her day in town. The diner was centrally located and gave her a perfect excuse to walk the sidewalks and mentally reestablish this place as home. She passed a few folks who were surprised to see her back.

"Aster, you're home."

She smiled because it apparently took her leaving for Tammy Littlefield from Spaghetti Straps to finally learn her name. "Hi. Yeah, just back recently."

"For good?" She nodded and rocked back on her heels. "Well,

that's exciting. Did you check out the new candy shop? You can fill up your own bag with whatever you want." She gestured emphatically across the street, and Aster remembered how exciting it was when something new happened in town.

She used to hate how desperate that felt. Now it seemed sweet and earnest. Somewhere along the way she'd softened. Perhaps with age. Perhaps with heartbreak. Maybe the loss of her mother. The end result was that she wanted to check out this new candy shop, which from the looks of the sign was called Edna's Sweet Treats. Well. Who was Edna? And maybe they had a little something in common.

"I think I'll check it out right now."

"Fantastic. I'm a big fan of the gummy fish. Take care, Ashton."

She closed her eyes. Couldn't win them all.

Edna's had gone in where the old fishing supply store used to be. She understood why it had gone under. The closest spot for quality fishing was quite a haul. The candy store was bright, colorful, and packed with options. It immediately lifted Aster's spirits. She imagined Edna was the elderly woman behind the cash register with the tinted glasses and tall white hair. She was chatting away with a customer as Aster perused the aisle.

"I'll be back soon. The clients love the new chocolate mints you sent over, and I'm going to place a formal order."

Aster froze. Brynn was the customer. Her neck prickled with warmth at the sound of her voice. Everything in her told her to bolt, and with a heated face, she tried. She turned to go, panicking more than she would have predicted. The only problem was that the door of the small shop felt woefully far away, and she bumped her shoulder on a jelly bean display, calling huge attention to herself.

"Aster?"

She froze. She wished she was the kind of person who could keep walking and never look back, but this place was too small for that. So she turned back as casually as she could, but the no-big-deal battle was surely lost. "Huh?" She made a point of blinking and refocusing as if she'd totally just realized it was Brynn standing there with a question mark on her face, searching Aster's. "Oh. Hey. Hi." She was a child again. Cheeks ablaze. Stripped of all intelligence and ability. She slid a strand of hair behind her ear and waited.

"Your hair is longer." Brynn smiled. Correction, attempted to smile. It faded almost immediately. She looked like Aster felt, like she'd just seen a ghost.

"Yours is a tad shorter." It wasn't a huge shift, and someone who didn't know every inch of Brynn likely wouldn't have noticed. Aster wasn't them. She glanced away and back, remembering how she used to play with that hair while Brynn rested her head in Aster's lap, lost in the pages of a book. She'd threaded her fingers through it in the heat of passion.

Brynn absently touched her hair. "Yeah. A little. Well…" She lifted her bagged purchase.

"Well…" How odd to share common space with the person you felt closest to in the world and still have them feel millions of miles away. "Have a good day."

"Right." The light in Brynn's eyes dimmed, the formality of their exchange painful. "You, too."

Brynn left the store, bag in hand. Aster remained, wishing that had gone better but knowing there was too much water under that bridge to expect it to. Their past had clouded the entire conversation, weighing them down with awkward regret. They were a broken pair, not that this was news. Even though they'd been friendly, she was still deeply angry at Brynn for exiting their friendship. She imagined Brynn had her reasons for what she did, but at the present time they seemed like so very long ago and baseless.

"Can I help you?" Edna asked, craning her neck. "We're having a twenty-five percent off sale on display case chocolate. The ones shaped like animals are my favorite. Have you seen the chocolate frogs? You don't often see frog chocolate."

"I think I'll come back another time," Aster said blandly. Not even chocolate in frog form could fix her mood.

CHAPTER FIFTEEN

B rynn patted Chestnut the mischievous dachshund on the head. "You stay out of the trash from now on, young man." After treatment on the good drugs for a wobbly tummy and an overnight stay with Freddy, Chestnut was on his way home to keep his owners forever on their toes.

"Thanks, Dr. Brynn," Erica and Ben said, scooping up their boy. They seemed like a really nice family, which reminded her that she was due to meet Tyler for a fitting in twenty minutes. She moved quickly about the office but it wasn't fast enough, which left her racing on foot eight blocks to the small alterations shop. Out of breath and guilt-ridden for running late, she burst through the door.

Tyler turned. "You made it."

"I'm so sorry. Chestnut had me running late."

"He has that effect. It's the adorable way he blinks at you, like you're the only human on Earth and he plans to make you his best friend."

"That's exactly it, he—" She went silent. Aster stood twelve feet away on a small stool in a forest-green off-the-shoulder dress. Brynn's mouth went dry, and her brain stuttered. The seamstress moved adeptly around her, pinning the bottom of the dress as Aster faced the lighted three-way mirror.

"Just running a few minutes late," Tyler said, following her gaze.

"Hi," Aster said, raising a hand.

She looked absolutely stunning, as in push pause on the rest of the world and admire this woman and her God-given beauty, the dress accentuating all the best parts of her like an arrow sign. "Hi back."

"Five more minutes," Gina, the owner of the shop, said from her spot on the ground.

Brynn nodded politely, then attempted to make small talk with Tyler about the wedding, the office, the weather. But it was really just five minutes of Brynn raking in each and every detail of Aster in that dress, like they were leaves in the fall. She stole glimpses of the curve of her breasts, which she remembered torturing endlessly back in the day. That is, until the only night they'd had together, when she'd been free to explore those breasts with great specificity.

"But the weird thing is he doesn't even like chocolate milk."

Brynn blinked because what? She'd completely spaced on Tyler, who she now realized was going on about Sage and milk, and she'd forgotten to listen because Aster was feet away looking like *that*.

"That's crazy," she said with maybe too much enthusiasm, pulling an odd look from Tyler.

"Are you even listening to me right now?"

Caught. Brynn pivoted. "Oh, I think they're finishing up."

"All yours," Aster said, stepping down from the stool. Apparently the changing room was right behind Brynn, which meant they did that little awkward dance until Brynn effectively got the hell out of the way. Who were they anyway? Since when did she and Aster have physically awkward moments? She would have believed it impossible until now. She hated everything about who'd they'd become. She'd love to say Aster had been solely responsible and hand off that blame, but underneath she knew there was culpability on her own doorstep. Maybe even more than Aster's.

She was whisked off by Gina to change in an alternate dressing area. When she returned, Aster was gone, probably ran out of there like the place was on fire. She couldn't blame her.

"You want to talk about it?" Tyler asked, arms folded as she watched Gina tug in the waist of Brynn's dress, similar in color to Aster's but an entirely different cut.

"The milk thing?" Okay, that was a childish avoidance tactic. Even she knew that. This was Tyler, her ride or die. She knew where all the bodies were buried.

Tyler sent her a look.

"Do we have to?"

"As someone who stood here and watched how the two of you just behaved around each other, I feel like we do."

"Fine. What is there to say?"

"No one affects you the way Aster does."

Brynn blinked against the truth of the sentence. She didn't have the energy to argue. "Yeah, okay. So?" This conversation already had her uncomfortable.

"And ever since the two of you have been keeping your lives to yourselves, I've seen a huge change in you, and I don't mean for the better."

"Okay, ouch."

"Did I hurt you?" Gina asked, popping up.

"No, not at all. It's my cruel friend, the bride."

Gina looked at Tyler, then Brynn, then went back to her pinning.

Tyler wasn't deterred. "Do you even remember what being happy feels like? Because I certainly remember what it looks like on you. The smiles when you'd get a letter. The slight blush when you would read one. Your whole being lit up when you reported all Aster was up to in Boston, and when I talked to you when you were there?" She shrugged. "You were hovering somewhere in the stratosphere."

"Things change. We weren't supposed to take things any farther than we did. That's how I look at it. Aster is someone who was very important to me for a time. But people move on."

"There was nothing about the little scene I saw play out moments ago that indicated anyone had moved on. The temperature in the room went up three degrees, and the sad quotient tripled."

"I can make it cooler in here," Gina offered.

"We're fine. But thank you," Brynn said.

"My point is that you're not a happy person."

Brynn gaped. "That's an awful thing to say. Yes, I am."

"See? You don't even know what happiness feels like enough to identify it. You've been *existing*, and for what?"

Brynn had no rebuttal.

"Please listen to me when I tell you that this is your second chance. She's here. She's amazing. And clearly still has some feelings of her own."

"It all feels like too much." The fear, the intensity, the jagged feelings that always overcame Brynn where Aster was involved. She'd been free of facing them for a while now, and it felt like she was staring at the beginning of something terrifying. "I don't know if I can."

"That's bullshit because you're the strongest badass I know. Start acting like it."

Gina's eyebrows went up.

"Are you about to push me like those football players before a big play?"

"No." Tyler seemed to think on it. "I can."

"No violence," Gina said, pin in her teeth.

"Sorry, Gina," they said in unison.

"Plus, we probably won't need violence. If Brynn ever wants to feel again, she knows what she has to do, who she has to talk to, and what she has to fix."

This was a wallop, coming from the person who knew her best these days. "Whatever happened to dear sweet Tyler?"

"She's a mama bear now." Tyler offered a wink.

❖

The wedding wasn't huge or overly lavish. After losing their mom earlier in the year, it didn't feel right, according to Sage, to throw a huge shebang. Plus, he and Tyler had never been that kind of couple. Their love was sweet, quiet, and pure. Aster thought they'd done a remarkable job capturing all of that in the decor and the aesthetic of the event. The ceremony began at seven in the evening as the sun set on the horizon and lightning bugs began to appear. Sixty white chairs were assembled into six rows divided by an aisle. An archway with white twinkly lights covered Sage as he waited for his bride, Aster at his side along with a few of his closest friends.

"You ready for this?" Aster said in his ear.

"Don't make me cry," he said back, but his throat was already strangled, and she knew he had only a few moments before the first tear spilled over. As it should be.

Eric Clapton's "Wonderful Tonight" played as Tyler's first attendant, Eve from the clinic, walked down the aisle, followed by the clinic's receptionist, Joan. The two smiled widely with the perfect kind of softness for the occasion. Aster felt the well of emotion hit before she even saw her. Brynn appeared from around the corner and paused at the top of the aisle looking like an angel. Aster's breath caught and her hands trembled. Refusing to steal a single second from her brother's moment, she used one hand to steady the other as Brynn began to walk toward them with a single long-stemmed rose in her hands. The sky was a cobalt blue, and the music hit its crescendo as if sewn to Aster's own heart. This wasn't fair. This so wasn't in bounds. Images of what could have been floated over her like snowflakes. She wondered what their wedding would have been like. She imagined Brynn walking down the aisle to her. In the small space of time, those fleeting seconds, she allowed herself ownership of the daydream. Enveloped in happiness, she beamed, connecting with Brynn, meeting her gaze for a few treasured beats before restraint took over and she slammed herself back down to Earth. She ached for the other version.

Once Brynn took her spot across from Aster at the front, she tried to focus her attention on Tyler, on the romance between her and Sage and how wonderful the occasion was. She was ripped from those efforts repeatedly because all she could think about was Brynn and her proximity. In spite of it all, Tyler was radiant, Sage beamed, and the ceremony was every bit as gorgeous as they deserved. Aster stood next to her brother as he looked Tyler in the eyes and with a strangled voice promised to love her forever. Such a far cry from years back when he denied there was a romantic feeling in his body for her. How time changed things. Another look across to Brynn, who didn't look away, her expression unreadable.

The ceremony concluded, and the group moved indoors for cocktails and celebration. The mood shifted, reverence out the window and revelry in full effect. Joan and Eve were already dancing as they moved through the buffet line, shaking their asses and hip-bumping in celebration of their boss and friend. Sage had already loosened his tie and lost his vest, a sure sign that he'd be dancing for hours. He'd always been good on a dance floor. Aster played it low-key. She stuck close to her dad to make sure he was okay, his first big family event on his own.

"You don't have to babysit me," he told her around his beer.

"Well, can you babysit me then?" she'd asked quietly. "I'm not great at big events."

He'd smacked a kiss on top of her head, his beard scratching her forehead the way she remembered from her childhood. Having a job was helpful and kept her focus narrow. Any lapse had her skin tingling at the thought of Brynn celebrating in the same room. Brief visual check-ins told her that Brynn was also staying busy, taking her role as maid of honor quite seriously. She brought the couple food, drinks, arranged for each formal event with the DJ, and rarely stopped moving around the room.

"Go dance," her father said, once the dust settled and the formal toasts were done and the party began.

"I'm good."

"Suit yourself. But it's my son's wedding," he said, tossing back the last of his beer and joining Marigold and Sage in the "Y.M.C.A." That made her smile. He hopped and did his best to make that *M*, checking with others on the floor to make sure he had the choreography right. Bless him. He was quieter these days and seemingly lost without their mom, but he was actively trying, and that was important. She'd visited him daily since she'd been back and made meals a couple of times.

Deciding to indulge in a glass of wine, Aster made her way to the bar. There was a cake line, and she had to maneuver her way through the throngs.

"Oh, sorry," she said, elbowing someone behind her.

"It's okay."

She looked back immediately. Brynn. Of course. Maybe it was the sentimentality of the occasion, but instead of walking on, she paused. Only she had no idea what to say. Nice cake? You come here often? Maybe even, hey, remember that time we mattered more to each other than either of us thought possible? Instead, she went with, "I think the ceremony was beautiful."

"It was," Brynn said. "And they're such a great couple." They were trying, the both of them. That was clear. She stepped forward in the cake line. "How are things out at the restaurant?"

"We're closer. Looking at a soft opening next month."

"The town is excited." Her eyes were greener than they'd ever been. The dress brought out their color. "Maybe I'll come out there that week. Check it out early."

It was the first time either of them had hinted at any sort of friendship or sharing of space beyond happenstance. It was Brynn dipping her toe in the water. So why was Aster's immediate reaction to retreat?

"Cool." She looked behind her. "The bar's getting busy. I better grab my glass of wine quick." It was the dumbest response ever, but she was operating under duress.

"Right. The bar," Brynn said. She had her number, and it was dialed to weak.

The night became a bigger struggle than she'd planned. Her heartbreak, an ailment that she'd shelved, was back again in full force. She had a second glass of wine, which these days was a lot for her. Then a third. She wasn't driving. Why not? The world then slowed down artificially. She could breathe, and the little bit of alcohol erased her terror. It also made her do something stupid.

"We should talk sometime," she said, leaning down close to Brynn's ear as she laughed at something Joan said. Why was she doing this? Because why not? What was there to lose? She had a distant idea that she might feel differently in the morning. All the more reason to push through, right?

Brynn looked back at her, struck. She clearly had not been expecting that. Yeah, well. Neither had Aster until a few moments ago. "Okay. We can do that." She paused and dropped her voice. "Are you okay?"

She nodded. "Sublime. Enjoy your night." Aster left them to their laughter, heading for the exit, seeking some air. She could feel Brynn's eyes on her for the entire walk to the door, and now she was a little embarrassed.

The lights from the ceremony were still on in the distance and called her like a beacon. She walked the thirty yards to the rows of empty white chairs set up for happy people celebrating love. The wine had loosened something in her, and she ran her fingertips across the top of one of the chairs, allowing the whole scene to taunt her. She'd never have this because she'd never have Brynn. There was no one else. She'd tried dating, but the inevitable comparison left her incapable of moving forward with any relationship. Her heart wasn't in it, and that wasn't fair to the other person. Not only that, they always knew. Even Nora had backed off after seeing her feelings for Brynn firsthand.

"About that talk…"

"Maybe we could set up a time." She heard the edge in her voice. She didn't like it.

"How about right now?" Brynn asked, taking a seat in one of the chairs.

Aster folded her arms. "Now, huh? Okay. So, what's new?" She smiled at the question. Nothing like a good icebreaker.

"How have you been?" Brynn asked. Only she meant it sincerely. The soft look in her eye, the pity, said she meant since losing her mom.

"Like the world swallowed up the best parts of itself, and now we're all left to grapple for air."

"I'm sorry, Aster."

"I know. For what happened to my family. That's what you're sorry for." It was pointed, and from the look on her face, Brynn knew it.

Brynn sighed. "Aster." She was searching for words. She still looked so very beautiful, and the moonlight wasn't helping. None of that mattered, though, because she'd fucking disappeared two years ago. "I was terrified."

"Of what? Writing a letter?"

"Of getting hurt."

She nodded. There was a time when she'd carried sympathy for Brynn on that note. She'd screwed up, activated a trigger in someone she loved. "The way I handled things back in Boston wasn't right. It should have been an argument. A knockdown drag-out even. It didn't deserve a disappearing act. You left my life *entirely*." She bit the words out.

"I know." Tears pooled in Brynn's eyes. It didn't matter. The feelings long shoved down were bubbling to the surface, and Aster had no desire or ability to block them.

"You came up with the cruelest punishment possible and inflicted it. I didn't deserve that."

"You didn't. I know." Brynn stared at her hands which she opened palms up, searching for what, Aster didn't know. "I got your letters. The ones you sent after I stopped mine."

"Oh yeah?"

God, the letters. The ones where she'd poured her heart out, asked for an opportunity to fix things, and if not that, then just for friendship. A reset on who they used to be. She'd even resorted to texts. She'd not heard a peep back. Yet her brother assured her that Brynn was alive and well and reporting to work every day.

"I don't know what to tell you," Sage had told her on the phone. "Maybe she just needs time. Do you want me to talk to her?"

"No," Aster had said. "Just wanted to make sure all was okay."

She had given Brynn time. She'd waited. She sent a few more letters letting Brynn know that she was still thinking of her, missing her, and ready to talk when she was. It hadn't made a difference. Brynn's social media accounts, which she barely used, had all gone still. But Brynn was out there living a life—she just didn't want to share. Aster had gotten the overwhelming, loud message.

"So you got the letters but just weren't compelled enough by their content to pick up a pen, or a phone. I'd have accepted a carrier pigeon." She laughed wryly.

"I wish I could explain it. The words aren't easy to find and make compelling." She looked off into the distance, stealing a moment. "I think after things went so poorly in Boston, I went home with the knowledge of what we were like...together. I'd never had that information before. I thought we'd be good, but I wasn't prepared for the full reality, for what I felt." She touched her chest, her heart. "After that, the letters were hard because we were both holding back, and I knew that was on me."

"I was doing what you wanted."

Brynn stood, her voice louder. "I know that. I get it." She was clearly frustrated, maybe with herself. "But it was like I couldn't go back. I couldn't figure out how to be your friend, but I couldn't move forward either. I was stuck and lost, and I did the only thing I could. I retreated."

"We could have talked that out."

"I didn't know what to say because every time I tried to formulate an explanation it just sounded so stupid. Even I could hear that much."

"Yeah." Because what else was there to say?

"I'm sorry. I'm just so sorry. I wanted to be there for you when your mom got sick. I was pretty sure that's not what you wanted."

"You do a lot of deciding what it is that I want."

She nodded. "I guess I should stop doing that."

"I showed up at your house, Brynn. You held me as I cried."

She nodded. "Everything sort of fell away in the moment. The fear, the regret, the feeling that I'd let too long go by before saying how sorry I am. I carry around a lot of regret. I've never shared that with you."

Aster didn't say anything, afraid to move a muscle. That sentence had her attention.

"I didn't have the skills back then to cope with the obstacle I encountered when I came to see you in Boston. I wish I had. I'm pretty sure my inabilities robbed me of a lot of happiness. But if I'm being honest, I still feel broken, and I don't know that I'll ever be fixed."

The idea made her heart ache. "That makes me sad for you."

"Me, too. I don't go too many places. I don't stray from the path of my routine. That means I don't do too much living, either. But there's safety there, okay? And I've grown to cherish it, cling to it."

"I know. But to what end?" Brynn was someone who'd dealt with heartache and now went out of her way to avoid it. Made sense. It still didn't fully change where they stood. She wanted to go to Brynn, pull her into a tight embrace, and protect her from the world. It didn't feel like her place.

Brynn seemed to sense her hesitation. "I'm gonna get back. Tyler is probably wondering what happened to me."

"Brynn."

She turned back, moonlight touching her hair. "Yeah?"

"Thank you for telling me. I know it wasn't easy."

"But probably important." Brynn had sucked up the emotion, once again back to the picture of put together. The smile she offered was easy, confident. Aster was now beginning to understand that the veneer was not always authentic. A skill, probably learned over years. "See you in there."

"Yeah. I'm just going to take another minute."

Once alone on the lawn, she allowed herself to breathe, taking deep gulps of air as she paced the grounds, stepping on shadows and feeling way too much. The day had been a big one, and she'd been swallowed whole. She missed her mother so badly her chest ached, but it was a different feeling entirely when the person you desperately missed was standing right across from you the way Brynn had been just moments before. So close, but still wildly far away. Her heart didn't seem to get the memo, reaching for Brynn every second she was near.

One thing was for sure, they needed to come to some sort of understanding about how to exist in each other's orbits because she was back in Homer's Bluff and not going anywhere. The other option was she walk back into that reception, grab Brynn, and kiss her with all the feeling she had bursting inside her. If only option two was that simple.

CHAPTER SIXTEEN

B rynn had wedding hangover. Not from being overserved, because she'd carefully monitored her small intake, but from the over-flowing love and happiness vibes and promises of a life spent together. She'd celebrated those things with Tyler with everything she had in her. Two days later, as she covered Tyler's patients while she honeymooned with Sage in Cancún, the happy, cheerful well had dried up.

"He's sadly overweight," she told Mrs. Donaldson about her beloved Labrador, Hugo. "And it's adding a lot of strain to his joints, which is part of what's causing him to move slowly. He aches."

"Well, he likes his food. What can I say?"

Brynn pulled a weight management sample kit from beneath the counter. "Let's give this new food a try, as well as treat those joints. If it goes well after a week, Joan at the front desk can get you a full supply of the food. Let's see if we can take off four pounds, maybe five over the next six months."

"No, no, no." Mrs. Donaldson recoiled. "Hugo likes bacon and chicken with the skin on."

"I do, too, but it's not the best everyday diet, and we want Hugo to live a long and comfortable life."

Mrs. Donaldson glared, and it made Brynn want to glare right back, and that wasn't like her. But this lady was not listening to reason about her sweet dog, and people were in love in Cancún, and the past was creeping in like a really aggressive tide, and Aster Lavender looked devastatingly good in a green dress. "Could we just give it a try? For Hugo?"

Mrs. Donaldson sighed dramatically and accepted the sample pack.

"Thank you," Brynn said, through the line that had become her mouth. "I think we'll start to see his movement improve."

"Who do we have next?" Brynn asked, Eve accepting the chart.

"Dill Lavender in exam two. Possible corneal ulcer."

Brynn paused in the hallway but only momentarily. She scooped up the file with the intake information and headed straight to exam two. "What do we have here?" she asked immediately upon entering.

Dill, just as she always remembered, began to vertically leap from his spot on the ground as if on a spring. She scooped him up and stared into his eyes. "What did you do to yourself?"

Aster stood. She wore jeans, a navy tee, and a tan military jacket. "He likes to race around the new backyard like a maniac, but the bush might have gotten the best of him. He's been squinting and rubbing his left eye a lot. I think he caught a twig."

"You ran into a twig?" She turned to Aster. "I'm going to use what's called a fluorescein eye stain to get a better look at that eye, okay? And then we'll turn on a special light that will allow me to see if anything glows."

Moments later, once she'd administered the drop that would show her any injuries or abrasions, she flipped off the overhead lights and flipped on the ophthalmic light. "Yep, and there it is, right there on the left. Want to see?"

Aster came around the table in the darkened room and stood next to Brynn, who pointed out how the abrasion glowed yellow. "See that?"

Aster nodded and her hair brushed Brynn's arm. She turned, struck by Aster's partially illuminated profile. They were close enough that Brynn caught the smell of cotton and a hint of cucumber. That hadn't changed.

"What can we do for him?" The concerned look on Aster's face affected her. Her chest warmed at the vulnerability. Such a contrast to Mrs. Donaldson's self-serving hardness.

"I'll send you home with a topical antibiotic. And you stay out of the bushes, or I'm going to tell your other mom what you've been up to."

"You think they remember each other?" Aster asked as Brynn flipped the lights back on.

"I bet so. These guys don't forget much." She scratched Dill behind his ears and watched as he wiggled his little black and white butt.

"It's kind of unfortunate that they're both here in town and haven't seen each other," Aster said with such a businesslike demeanor that Brynn didn't know what to make of it.

"Yeah, maybe they'll run into each other someday."

"We get to the dog park most days around dinnertime. Pickles is welcome to come and play with this guy."

Dill looked over his shoulder at Aster and then back to Brynn, squinting through his scraped eye with hope.

"I should take her more often." Were they making plans without making plans? What was happening, and was this wise?

"It helps him burn off a lot of energy. Plus, he's incredibly social." She laughed. "I struggle to relate, but it's what makes him happy. Who am I to judge?"

Brynn smiled. Aster smiled. They shared one. Beyond familiar and yet so very new feeling. What a combination.

"Should I get that antibiotic?"

"Right. Yes. Just let me…" She grabbed her pad and wrote it up. "Joan can set you up with what you need. Unfortunately, when he's left alone, he should wear an Elizabethan collar to protect that eye. We also carry those if you need one."

"The cone of shame. We have one decorated to look like a box of french fries."

Brynn covered her mouth. "Is that right?"

"Dill prefers as much attention as possible, and it helps."

"A french fry dog? I'm sure it does."

Aster scooped up her dog and the slip of paper. "I know you have your hands full without Tyler, but maybe we'll see you and Pickles sometime. Low pressure. I promise."

"Maybe." She glanced at the wall and back again, giving in to impulse. A rarity. "Hey, Aster? What are you reading these days?"

"*Captain Sussex Takes on the Starverse*, Part Six. I'm almost done."

Brynn nodded, grinned. "So not too much has changed."

Aster shrugged with pride and exited the exam room, leaving Brynn in a better mood than when she'd entered. She'd take any bit of reprieve.

She spent the rest of her day thinking about the invitation to the dog park, deciding she should go, and then changing her mind abruptly. Finally, after the last patient of the very busy day stole a mint from the front and left the building, she sighed. The sheer amount of time she'd devoted to the topic was almost evidence enough for her to go to the damn dog park, neutralize the situation, and find a way to make Aster and her presence in town a lot more commonplace. She simply had to get used to the fact that Aster was around and confusing and still very much the same Aster. She didn't have time to lend her brain to these kinds of hijackings.

❖

Captain Sussex was in no mood for asteroid dodging as Dill made his way up the doggy slide and then down again for about the eighth time. He took a lap around the perimeter, probably looking for playmates. The park was pretty empty today, which meant she was going to need to put her book down and act as playmate in a moment. Dill's barking pulled her focus, and 1.8 seconds later, she saw him tear off like a shot with Pickles streaking after him. In no time at all, the chase was on. Two black and white dogs zipped and zagged and barked and yipped as Brynn walked slowly to the bench, leash in hand.

"She looked a little sluggish when I got home, so I thought I'd take you up on your offer."

Aster's heart squeezed. She was used to that happening around Brynn, but today she didn't police it quite so much. She let it do its own thing, unrestrained from her admonishment. "Sit." She eyed the book in Brynn's hand, nodded to it in encouragement, and cracked the spine on her own novel, returning to it.

Brynn did just that, and from their own sides of the bench, they traveled to respective fictional worlds as the dogs they'd once rescued enjoyed an athletic reunion. The interesting part? Aster relaxed and not just a little bit. Her mind wandered, and her body lost all tension as she enjoyed the nice day and the quiet company. The reading session didn't fix any one problem or erase the hurt she carried, but it did allow her to see that Brynn was the same person she'd always known. After about forty-five minutes, Brynn closed her book as the dogs lapped up water from the doggy-sized drinking fountain. "Should probably head home, figure out my night."

Aster nodded and turned her body toward Brynn. "Why do you always act like life is great?"

Brynn rolled her lips in. She shifted. "This is about what I said to you at the reception."

"A little. Do you not feel safe with me?" She heard her voice weaken on that last part.

"I always felt safe with you." She looked to the sky for answers. "But talking about life and how restricted it can sometimes feel only makes me that much more aware of it."

"For what it's worth, it's okay." A pause. "I get why you do that."

"Yeah?" Brynn seemed embarrassed. She looked at the ground and back up again. She clenched her back teeth.

"But it won't always be this way. I truly believe that."

Her face relaxed. Brynn touched her heart and nodded. She started to say something, but then switched gears. "Thanks, Aster."

"Anytime."

Aster took Dill to the dog park each day for a couple of weeks after that meetup, but she didn't encounter Brynn again. In fact, she didn't see her around town either. Maybe their friendship ended where it was supposed to. She'd make peace with that. Luckily, she had her hands full with the renovation, and now that they were closer than ever to opening, she found her days filled with menu creation, job interviews, decorator consults, and of course working with contractors. She found herself nearly out of her depth and wondered if she'd bitten off way more than she could chew. She just wanted to get back in the kitchen and do what she knew how to do best. Food. The rest of this stuff just felt complicated.

"The restaurant is really coming along."

Aster blinked from her spot on the bench. The day had kicked her ass, and as the sun set she'd decided to zone out with Dill at the park. There was a sluggish cocker spaniel and a very sporty border collie mix happy to see Dill, which gave her a chance to just idle and not use her brain.

She turned around. Brynn. "I'm bad company," she said right off the bat. No reason for pretense.

"Are the two things related?" She unclipped Pickles, who jumped at Aster's knee until she leaned down and let the little girl pepper her face with licks and kisses.

"Your dog is getting fresh."

"Stay on topic."

Aster sighed. Brynn was a hard one to hide from. She knew her too well. "I feel like Marilyn's might crash and burn with me in charge, and then I will have to live with having failed her."

"Your mom."

"Yeah. And I will utterly hate myself if that happens. I gave the restaurant her name. It can't be anything less than amazing." She'd not told anyone how she felt. Not her sisters. Sage. No one. She'd been in Brynn's presence all of two minutes, and the information was falling from her lips.

Brynn nodded thoughtfully and took a seat. "I hear you, and that must feel like a lot of pressure."

Aster's eyes filled. Embarrassing. She quickly wiped away a tear. "Sorry."

Brynn placed her hand on top of Aster's. It helped. "Want my take or just want me to listen?"

"Your take," Aster managed, her voice strangled with emotion.

"You're the smartest person I know. You're also the most talented. If you asked me to pick a person who was born to do exactly this, it's you. But should it fail? You'll press on to a new project, using the gifts you have because you're a dreamer in the most wonderful sense."

Aster swallowed. The words startled her. But they also filled her up. "I don't know what to say."

"Do you believe me?"

"Yes." In fact, she had chills. "How do you do that? Arrive here and in no time at all find a way to say the exact right words I need."

Brynn exhaled slowly. "We've always had that connection. You know that. Doesn't make what I said any less true."

They got quiet, each to their separate metaphorical corners. Aster watched as Dill chased Pickles, dashing in big circles around the grass. He was easily faster but seemed to enjoy the chase. Aster kept her eyes forward. "I've missed you." There was the emotion again. The words were too important.

"I've missed you, too."

She found the courage to look, to meet Brynn's gaze head-on, terrifying or not. "What do we do about that?"

"We're the only ones in our way. But...it's been a roller coaster. I think we both can agree."

"I'm still so mad at you."

"I'm mad at me, too. Boston wasn't ideal, but I should have handled it better."

"So let's stop avoiding the obvious. We have some baggage. We miss each other."

"We're a mess," Brynn said, laughing, which made Aster laugh.

"At least we're self-aware."

Aster blinked, sobering. "Meet me back here tomorrow. Don't disappear again."

Brynn nodded but didn't look entirely convinced. "We could give that a shot. Might be nice."

Aster grinned. "Look how conservative you're being. How am I ever going to loosen you up?"

That seemed to break through the surface again. "That used to be something I'd say to you. How have times changed so drastically?"

"Oh, I'm not sure they have."

Brynn sighed. "Do you ever think the universe has tried to tell us over and over again that we're trouble together?"

"I sometimes wonder if it's ridiculously frustrated at us for not following its signs."

Brynn folded her arms. "Or that."

Aster lifted her book in suggestion. "Shall we?"

Brynn picked up hers. "Let's."

After a few minutes. "You really think the restaurant is going to be okay."

"I know so. Now stop it and read your space story."

Aster grinned into her book, feeling more at ease than she had in a very long while.

❖

Tyler and Sage had purchased a new home shortly before the wedding, one that wouldn't be hers or his but all theirs. The quaint white one-story with the green shutters seemed absolutely perfect.

Brynn marveled at the combination of styles and how easily they flowed together in the space. Country chic was the best way to describe it. Sunflowers, but only a few. A photo of a wagon wheel, but held in a bright silver frame. She'd never seen a place that represented a couple more than this one. She handed over the plant she'd brought them in offering as the tour came to a close.

Tyler, her brown hair pulled into a ponytail, wore large overalls that made her look comfy and adorably pregnant. "Sit, please." She gestured to the table. "I feel like it's been weeks since we've had a non-work-related chat session. Tell me everything. I'm starved for content and gossip." She grinned, and it reminded Brynn that Tyler didn't age. In fact, she still looked like that bright-eyed twenty-year-old she met at school.

"Well, I finally got my kitchen painted."

Tyler frowned and sat back, disappointed. "No. That's not what I meant at all. I need the good stuff. Juicy. What can you tell me about you-know-who?"

"Ah. I see." Brynn smiled because there had been a new development. "We're reading again."

Another frown. "You're reading? Define."

"It was our thing, back in the day. Remember? We would read together. First on the bench in the center of town. Then at each other's houses, mainly hers. That led to kissing. That led to long-distance letters."

"Like in the old-fashioned movies."

"And eventually the best sex of my life. And now we're reading again. Are you following now?"

Tyler's eyes went wide. "*Reading*. Got it now. It's your foreplay." She wrinkled her nose. "You should have just said that. Don't skip the good words."

"Should have just said what?" Sage joined them, ball cap flipped around, tuft of blond hair poking out the front.

"Brynn and Aster are back to their old ways. It's getting hot and literary."

He squinted. "That's good, right? That's what we want."

"Don't let on that we talk about them," Tyler said.

"I already know," Brynn countered. "And is it weird for me to talk about your sister in front of you?"

"No." Sage balked. Grabbed an apple. "I'm a grown-ass man who rides a tractor. I can hear a little gossip about my sister." He took a seat at the kitchen table, reporting for duty. Looked around as if waiting for the gossip session to commence.

Tyler took the reins. "Well, I hear Aster kisses like a dream and can use her tongue like no one's business."

Sage stood again. "Probably a light bulb that needs changing somewhere around here."

Brynn laughed as he fled like a felon. "You're cruel. He was trying."

"What?" Tyler asked. "Now I'll have fresh light bulbs everywhere. Back on topic. So is this reading some sort of preamble? Do I need to congratulate you on a big step?"

"It's some kind of step. Jury is out on what kind." She shook her head, trying to understand it all herself. "It's been like a breath of fresh air just being around her again. I don't want to screw it up, and I don't want her to, either. I'm almost afraid to move. Like the house of cards might come tumbling with the slightest shift. And yet..."

"You're starting to feel the tugging for more than just group reading time."

"Always. That's a given. I can't be within feet of Aster and not want every part of her to be mine."

Tyler rested her chin in her hand. "That's incredibly poetic. Sage never says anything like that to me."

"Don't discount the light bulbs."

"Good point." Her eyes lit up. "We could be sisters in-law if this goes well."

Brynn held out a hand. "No. You're way ahead of yourself, and the house of cards is wobbling as a result. You must stop. Reverse. That's not what we're talking about."

"It's what I'm imagining, and I'm pregnant and uncomfortable and legit always hungry, so it's allowed. Card house be damned. Trumped by the angry preggo lady."

Brynn closed her mouth. Hard to argue with that. "It's just gotten to that point where it feels like something is about to give, and I'm just not sure what it's going to be." She reflected on her time with Aster recently. They met up at the dog park most days of the week unless one of them was pulled for work. They filled the time with books, dogs, talk of their days, and more books. They'd started sitting closer. Gradually. An unspoken decision that threw fuel on the fire that flickered between them. God, everything felt like liquid heat lately. Brynn's face would flush at work when she just thought about taking things further with Aster. Her body would go to Jell-O. Was it possible that passion grew over time like sexy flowers in a garden? Because she remembered lusting after Aster, but it had literally turned into a full-time job.

"I like this ring," Brynn had said the day before, picking up Aster's hand and running her thumb over the silver butterfly pinkie ring. "It's really pretty." It was even more pretty on her. Everything was.

"I bought it to remind myself that I was not the same awkward girl with the inability to talk to people. And that people can grow and change. Do you believe that?"

"Yes. Of course they can. You've changed a lot in the time I've known you. The butterfly is fitting, and that's a compliment." But as they talked, she was taking in the feel of Aster's hand in hers, the weight, the way her fingers, slender with neatly trimmed nails, sent a shiver. She remembered those fingertips against her skin, exploring, tracing torturous patterns. She could feel them now. "Anyway. It's a really pretty ring." She returned Aster's hand to her lap and tried to distract herself with the least sexy thoughts she could conjure. Garbage in the summer. Spoiled milk. Pink and red on the same shirt. Republican politicians having lunch. None of them eclipsed her earlier thoughts.

Tyler brought her out of it. "I don't know where you went just now, but it looked like a really great time, and I would love for you to spend more time there."

"In fantasyland? I live there way too much. Do not encourage me." She placed both hands on top of her head. "I fear I might be broken."

"And I know a great way to get fixed." Tyler bounced her eyebrows. "Fun, too."

"Did you say you need something fixed?" Sage asked, appearing in a toolbelt.

Tyler smiled, fanned herself. Even Brynn had to admit he looked hot. "Those Lavenders," Tyler said.

Brynn slumped back in her chair. "Tell me about it. No one has a chance."

CHAPTER SEVENTEEN

Marilyn's had come a long way. From the worn-down building she'd snatched up from the bank to the upscale eatery she hoped would fill a niche in not only the Homer's Bluff community but the surrounding towns as well. Kansas had a lot of great places to eat, but the rural areas lacked the finesse she'd experienced in Boston, and she knew for a fact that the people would appreciate a nice place to go for a special occasion, a date, or merely to sample some dishes outside the diner's normal fare. Kimble's had had the market all to themselves for way too long.

"What do you think of going with the coconut shrimp and the blackened prime rib for opening night specials?" she asked Wesley, her general manager. She snatched him from Wichita and had been very impressed with his restaurant knowledge and ability to bring Marilyn's together.

"I was hoping you'd go with the shrimp, and the prime rib gives the meat lovers their dream come true. A win-win. Did we decide on napkins folded or rolled with the silver?"

"Folded, please." It felt like the decisions were endless, but they were at the finish line. She just had to keep pushing. While she had herself scheduled in the kitchen most nights in the early days after opening, it was her hope as time went on to hand over more responsibility to her team of chefs. Allow herself the chance to have a life outside of work.

But on opening night, it was like the stars aligned. The people showed up on time for the reservations, her staff put out their best food, and she kept her head down and eye on not only turning out quality dishes but making sure each plate was to her high standards.

"Table fourteen. Last of the night." She snagged the ticket. "Truffle chips and fondue. Two braised short ribs, one scallop dish, and one branzino."

Her small team of chefs got to work, and because they were the last table of the night, Aster threw in a few slices of butter cake on the house, smothered with her special sauce.

As she walked to her car, triumphant and relieved that she'd not fallen on her face in front of the town or, worse, disgraced her mother's name, emotion curled up tight in her chest. She'd asked her family and friends to let her open before coming out, and they'd honored her wishes. Most had reservations for the next day, including Brynn, who would dine with Tyler and Sage at one of their best tables. Her father was all set up with Violet and Marigold, and Ethan had a babysitter for the night. She was truly looking forward to it, especially now that she had her feet wet.

The parking lot was mostly empty, but next to her car sat Brynn's white SUV. She'd know that rainbow license plate holder anywhere. Sitting on the hood, holding a sweating bottle of champagne and two plastic flutes, was the woman herself.

Aster broke into a grin. "You're not supposed to be here. What in the world?"

She hopped off the car in jeans, red sneakers, and a white and blue Cubs jersey. God. That look just wasn't fair. Was there matching lingerie beneath? "It's not like I could let tonight go by without laying eyes on you and saying congratulations."

Aster smiled, her bones going to liquid from the combination of exhaustion and now exhilaration. "You didn't have to."

"No. But I wanted to." The cork popped far into the air, and the bottle foamed. Brynn poured them each a glass. "Plastic celebration for you. And one for me."

Aster leaned in for a sip.

"Not yet. First, a toast."

"Oh, my. Sorry. I almost ruined it."

Brynn extended her glass in the air. "To what I hear from anyone and everyone in lands near and far, the opening of Marilyn's was a smashing success. You, Aster Lavender, are the talk of the town. And this time? Everyone knows your name."

They touched glasses, as Aster beamed from the inside out. She was just going to head home and chill with her dog on the quiet of her couch. This was quite a welcome surprise. Her excitement about the opening commingled with her swirling feelings for Brynn to create the perfect ambitious storm. "Come here," she said, arm around Brynn's waist. She pulled her in, and before she knew it they were face-to-face, staring into each other's eyes before Aster did the damn thing and kissed her long and good, and the miraculous thing was that Brynn kissed her back. The world went still and waited for them.

"Maybe we shouldn't."

Aster worked to catch her breath. "Okay." A pause as they stared at each other, lips swollen, stars at attention. "Should I not have...?"

"I don't know. I don't know a lot of things."

"Then I definitely shouldn't have." She downed the rest of her champagne. "Brynn, I'm really sorry. I think the day had me on a high. I wanted to celebrate. With you. I went too far."

"I wanted to celebrate with you, too," Brynn said, looking lost and scrambling to put things right. Aster wanted to help her, only she was feeling embarrassed and like she was constantly chasing after a woman who clearly preferred that she stay in her own corner, which of course she should. Hadn't she crashed and burned enough for one lifetime? When would she learn?

"And you were sweet to do so. I'm looking forward to tomorrow night. Be sure to order dessert."

"I will. But can we talk about what just happened?"

Aster returned the flute. Hands went to her pockets and she worked on an effective no-big-deal voice. "Let's not. It was a mistake. I won't make it again." Her body was still buzzing from the kiss. Her brain did its best to wrestle control right back. What a battle. Regardless, her buzz had officially been killed, and anger at herself had replaced it.

"Aster."

"Brynn. We can't keep doing this. I can't. If you check the history books, I've never not wanted you. Not for a second. Even when I was furious at you, hurt and reeling, every part of me still wanted you. But I think it's something I need to shelve, and I work tirelessly to do that."

Brynn pinched the bridge of her nose. "This is not how I wanted things to go tonight."

"I'm sorry."

"Don't. You shouldn't be the one to apologize. You should be celebrating your big night."

"I am. I will. But probably on my own." She took Brynn's hand and gave it a squeeze. "You were so sweet to bring me celebratory bubbly. I will see you tomorrow night for a fantastic meal. I really look forward to that, and I care a lot about you, but I can't do this anymore. My heart can't."

She didn't wait for Brynn to respond, and she felt a little bad about that. In a matter of seconds, she was on her way home, frustrated, sad, and done with her attachment to Brynn Garrett. She had to be. It was well past time.

❖

"I think it was the brown sugar pork chop that kept me awake last night," Marigold said as she unpacked a new box of dish towel inventory and made room on the shelf along the wall. The Lavender House was about to be brimming with new products fresh off the lavender truck, so to speak. There was a lot to unpack, catalog, and shelve.

Aster's mouth dropped open. "What? Why?"

"Because it was the best dish I've had in years, and I just kept reliving the experience. My kid sister made that pork chop, designed it, and presented it to me in a fancy restaurant she opened with our mother's name over the top. I was on a high, and there was no sleep to be had."

Aster played back the paragraph in her head, remembering a time when no one really noticed the kid sister playing in the background. And here, she'd kept Marigold up with pride.

"Wait. Are you all misty?" Violet asked, coming closer from where she stood along the shelves near the wall. "MG, are you seeing this?"

"I am."

Aster laughed. "It's been a hard time, and what you said was really nice."

"Group hug!" Violet said.

"No, no, no," Aster said, backing up. "I'll just cry more."

"Sometimes you need to. When I was going through my divorce, you guys group hugged the hell out of me, and it worked."

She surrendered and let the kindness of her sisters wrap her up and hold her tight. The emotion came loose, and she didn't fight. When they released her, she felt like something had unlocked. And then she blurted it all out. "I miss Mom. I'm so happy you liked my food. But I miss Mom a lot. And I kissed Brynn two nights ago, and it didn't go well." She exhaled. There it was. All laid out.

Her sisters exchanged a look and immediately pressed pause on their inventory work. "Well, first of all, slow down," Marigold said. "Let's take that apart."

"I wonder every day what Mom would say or think or do in response to anything and everything. And when that started to fade a little bit, it made me doubly sad."

"Same," Marigold said. "I can't believe we don't have her here with us. She would be so proud of you, Aster. But you know what? I have a feeling she still is. Watching from heaven, tickled to pieces that there's a restaurant named after her, and it's all thanks to you."

"Thanks, guys," she mumbled, really liking that idea, and holding on to the fact that they were all grieving, grappling with this new existence, and experiencing similar feelings. She felt less alone with that reminder and smiled gratefully at first Marigold and then Violet, who had made such wonderful progress in just the couple of years since Tad had her in shambles. They would be there for each other. She vowed it here and now.

"As for Brynn Garrett and you..."

"You mean Tyler and Sage part two?" Violet asked with a wink.

"I don't know whether to be offended or honored," Aster said.

"Neither. You're still untangling the knot," Marigold said, matter-of-factly. "Listen, I may be the only one here who's never been in hard-core love, but I do think it gives me a certain perspective. When a love is deep, it gives you a lot of rope to play with, and so many people spend time tying it in a knot. That's you and Brynn, a complicated little knot that is not at all a lost cause. You're almost untied, Aster. I've seen you two at the park when I drive by, sitting together on that bench, reading your books. Hell, the town should name that bench after the two of you."

Aster was surprised by the optimism. "Really? You don't think I'm an idiot? Because I felt like one two nights ago."

Marigold nodded to Violet, offering her the reins. "Vi, want to offer your thoughts?"

"Most definitely." Her sister fluffed her dark hair and took two steps forward.

Aster nodded. "I'm ready."

Violet offered a soft smile and a dramatic pause. "Be patient."

Aster waited.

Violet stared back at her.

"That's it?" She gestured to their sister. "Marigold offered an entire dissertation with analogies and imagery. Yours is just *patience*?"

"Mm-hmm," Violet said. "And Mom would agree with both of us because we're both right. You're not yet out of the knot, and be patient so you can get there."

"I love you guys, but I don't know. It almost feels like I'd be setting myself up again. The ball's in her court. And she doesn't play a lot of ball these days."

Marigold held up a hand of pause. "I know you don't know. But we do, and we're older."

"Wiser."

"And big basketball fans." Marigold placed a hand on the hip of her flared jeans. "Give Brynn the space to play. That's all we're saying."

Violet stood next to her, forming some sort of older sister wall of knowledge. "And you should listen to us instead of your overfunctioning giant brain, smarty-pants."

"I'll give it a try," Aster said, curious about the prospect and truly wishing her sisters were right. "You've given me a lot of metaphors to consider."

"You're welcome," Marigold said and slid a box her way. "Also, I'm gay. Not sure I mentioned that."

Freeze. "Wait, what?" Aster asked. Her mouth was open, and she was quickly trying to catch up. Violet smiled knowingly. She already knew. "MG, are you serious right now?"

Marigold nodded and shrugged, her eyes going misty. "I think I had to really get to know myself before telling you guys. Losing Mom made me realize how short life really can be. We're here once, and now it's time to be the person I am. No holding back, right?"

Aster's heart swelled and filled with love. She threw herself into her sister's arms and hugged her tightly. "I love you. I'm so proud of you."

"Thank you," Marigold whispered. "Send me your tips."

"You got it," Aster whispered back. Marigold released her and looked around the place, clearly not wanting to make a big deal out of the moment and moving them out of it. "Now pitch in like the Lavender sister you were born to be."

Aster laughed, and she and Violet exchanged a warm smile. "The least I can do."

❖

Brynn's trip to Marilyn's had been eye-opening for a number of reasons. She'd been in her head, confused, and beating herself up about that kiss, and namely her inability to press forward. With her brain fuzzy and busy, she'd arrived for dinner, finding Tyler and Sage already seated at a round table near the center of the room with an exceptional view of the kitchen, which was open for the diners to enjoy the show. She liked that very much about the restaurant.

The dining area was one large room with large black beams across the ceiling in a crisscross. The tables were also black with white table-cloths, a nod to the color scheme of Hole in One, perhaps? But an interesting thing happened. As they opened their menus and settled in, everything in Brynn relaxed. She stole glances of Aster in her chef's coat moving around the kitchen. She seemed to be handling the tickets and expediting food to the servers tonight. Seeing her in her element, in control and so blatantly succeeding at it, made Brynn's heart swell and settle.

"She's my person," she said quietly to Tyler, who followed her gaze. "Just look at her."

"It's really impressive," Tyler said, beaming. "That's little Aster back there being a boss."

Brynn gave her head a shake. "What is wrong with me?"

"You're untying a knot," Sage said loudly from behind his menu, storming the conversation when she hadn't even realized he'd been listening.

"Excuse me?" Brynn asked, confused.

"Something Marigold says when she grabs you by the ear. You got all knotted and now you're untying, and as soon as you do, you can live happily ever after like us." He dropped his menu. "Wait. It's *H-E-A*. You can be H-E-A like us. Something like that. Did I get the letters right? Pretty sure I did. She's right, though." He smiled at Tyler. "We're H-E-A." He kissed the back of her hand sweetly, flashed his Sage dimples, and immediately went back to his entrée perusal.

Brynn looked to Tyler in mystification because surprisingly everything he said made sense. Crisp and clear.

"I don't know what to say about that. He has his helpful moments," Tyler said. "And he knows when to listen to his sisters, which goes a long way. I'll give him that. His mother raised him right."

"I'm no fool," he said behind his menu, which pulled a laugh.

"I think it's untied," Brynn said with an amazed nod. "The knot."

Tyler leaned over and put an arm around her shoulder. "We were all just waiting."

"Now what?" Brynn frowned. "Aster's over the back-and-forth. The me and her roller coaster. She said as much the other night."

Tyler took a sip of water and set it back down again. "All you have is your honesty. Tell her how you're feeling. Be direct and specific. Aster prefers specific. She wants details."

Brynn nodded. "I can do that. Right now? Should I stand on this table and declare myself to the diners?"

"No," Sage said, concern on his face.

"She's kidding," Tyler told him. "And maybe let's wait for a more opportune moment."

Brynn smiled, on a high. She ordered the scallops, mushroom risotto, and a glass of house red. When their table was up, Aster brought their entrées out personally.

"Welcome, officially, to Marilyn's. I hope you enjoy the food. Brown sugar pork chop for Sage with rosemary potatoes, rattlesnake pasta for Tyler, and the scallops and garlic noodles for Brynn."

"This is amazing," Brynn said, unable to contain her pride.

Sage nodded heartily. "Kid sister, I'm impressed. And hungry. I might order another."

"We can fulfill that request." Aster folded her arms and nodded. That was Aster, always conservative. Her eyes went wide when Sage, probably unable to control himself, leapt out of his chair and enveloped her in a giant big-brother hug. She laughed as he released her. "Well, enjoy. I better get back." With a wave she was gone, but not from Brynn's radar. She could have sat there all night watching Aster in that sexy chef's coat. Maybe one night, she'd buy a drink at the bar and do just that. She'd screwed up the other night in the parking lot, but she had her whole life to put things right, and it was time to do just that.

As she ate her perfectly seared scallops, she enjoyed every moment of her first time in Aster's restaurant. But it didn't just feel like one new beginning—it felt like two. Maybe that parking lot kiss and the days of recrimination that had followed had been just what she needed to finally free herself of Marigold's metaphorical knot. Freedom tasted really good. Now, at some point soon she had to see a woman about that HEA...

CHAPTER EIGHTEEN

The home Aster had purchased for herself when she returned to Homer's Bluff was a six-minute drive from Brynn's place on Baker Street, and Brynn felt every second tick by on the drive. From the street, she took in the house, which seemed much larger than Aster's old place, and quite a bit nicer—a white two-story with a large front porch, pristine light green shutters, and a matching, much taller door than she was used to. It was clear Aster was doing okay for herself. But then, Brynn never doubted her potential. With Aster, the sky was the limit in so many different ways. She was special and wonderful, and Brynn didn't want to go another day without celebrating that.

Brynn, with butterflies in her stomach, made her way up the walk. It was late morning, and Aster might actually still be asleep, given it was her day off and she now pulled later nights because of the restaurant. She didn't want to disturb, so she left her note carefully on the door with a piece of Scotch tape she'd brought with her. As she walked back to her car, she looked up at the dark clouds swirling. They had not been part of her plan, and she gave them a hard, threatening look. "Don't," she said and gave her head a shake.

Late that afternoon, she argued with herself over which outfit to wear for the occasion and finally settled on her light denim jeans and lacy white cotton top that always seemed to pull compliments. Hair went partially up in a clip, leaving the rest down and flowing freely. A touch of cleavage. That would work. She chose a silver necklace with a small heart that hung not far from hers. Moral support. If she was about to put it all out there, she would need it. Brynn was confident this was the exact path she was destined to be on, but it didn't make the journey to get there any less terrifying. She'd seen a door close in Aster's eyes the other night, and now she had to see if there was hope.

She'd gone out of her way today to show Aster that she was serious, that she meant what she said, and that Aster could trust what they had. Was she prepared to fail? Yes. But she was also full of so much hope it almost bubbled out of her chest.

She scooped up Pickles, who stared into her eyes curiously. "It's going to be a very telling day. Say a prayer for me?" Pickles tucked her head onto Brynn's shoulder and closed her eyes.

"Good call. Let's snuggle here together and see what happens. Today is a big day."

❖

Aster had very little to do today, and it was a blessing and a curse. She needed a break from Marilyn's to regroup and gather her energy to return the next night. In the meantime, she trusted Wesley to keep the place afloat and running with her vision intact. They already had a dream of a partnership. He truly understood the business and her own personal style.

So that meant the day was hers. Groceries were scarce, and she decided it was in her best interest to pick up a few things, so midafternoon she hopped in her car. As she backed out of her driveway, something pink on her front door snagged her attention. She frowned, hopped out of her car, and found a handwritten note: *Can you come to our bench in the center of town at five tonight?* It was signed with a scripted *B*.

Aster paused, her everything disrupted. What was going on? Did Brynn want to relax with a book? Why send a handwritten note when a text was so much more efficient? And did she want to spend another few hours reading next to the woman she craved more than water? It sounded like another adventure in torture, and she promised to stop submitting herself to that. She pocketed the note, content to send an excuse. But as she went about her day, she just couldn't seem to do it. The note had her interest piqued. And like any good action-adventure reader, she had to find out more.

At five, she found herself walking through town, hands in her pockets, as the storm clouds the weathercaster had warned them about assembled overhead. Did Brynn have on a hood, she wondered as she approached the bench from behind. She had her book tucked into her jacket in case the sky opened up, and Brynn had likely prepared as well.

She stopped a few feet from the bench. "This seat taken?" she asked.

Brynn turned, and Aster practically leapt out of her skin because it wasn't Brynn looking back at her but Sage, wearing a green zip-up hoodie. "It's not," he said with a grin.

She pulled the hood off his head, leaving his blond hair standing straight up, and studied him. "Why are you here?" she asked, glancing around for evidence. Around them, the citizens of Homer's Bluff dashed into shops before they closed or headed to Kip's Diner for one of those greasy burgers that were so addictive. No clues.

"I'm merely the very handsome messenger." He stood, unzipped his hoodie, and presented her with a rose and another pink note. "Have fun, killer." He gave her shoulder a soft slug and jogged across the street to the diner.

Aster, still bewildered and now incredibly intrigued, took a seat.

"Hey, Aster," Heather said as she closed up Bella Beautiful for the day. "I about died for your pork chop the other night. Bringing my friends next week."

"Thank you. I look forward to that." She still grinned each time someone used her name, a sign that things had certainly shifted for her in Homer's Bluff. She held Brynn's note to her chest as she watched Heather walk the other direction down the sidewalk, wanting to be alone before she read it. Finally, she unfolded the pink paper that, was she imagining, or did it smell so much like Brynn herself? She pressed the paper to her face and inhaled, affirmed in her suspicion, which made her stomach tighten.

On to the words, which appeared in handwriting she knew as well as her own.

Dearest Aster,

I'm well aware that I owe you some letters. Here's one. My life changed forever on this bench. For the first time, I met someone I had no idea what to do with. I couldn't decide whether to kiss you or spend the rest of my days learning

everything about you. Now I know it was meant to be both.
I think about those early days a lot. Stealing glances at
you while you read aliens and space wars, my skin tingling
because you were so close. I want to go back there. I miss us.
  Will you meet me at the kennel?
  All my love,
  B.

The swirly *B* got her every time. Aster closed her eyes and
absorbed the words. She was shocked to see them, and at the same
time she'd known them her entire life. Her heart longed to reach back,
but she'd had happiness snatched away from her before. She knew one
thing for certain. She was headed to the kennels. A clap of lightning hit
as she stood, and that made sense. Today felt weighted, important, and
boring weather would not have done it justice. "Bring it on," she said to
the sky as she turned and headed back to the town perimeter.

The veterinary clinic was only a few blocks away, and she made
her way there quickly, needing to see Brynn's face. She needed clarity,
understanding, and maybe a little grounding. When she arrived at the
clinic, Joan, still seated at her desk in the lobby, pointed down the hall
to the kennels. Aster nodded and made her way there as memories
flashed. When she entered the room lined with dog runs, two of the
inhabitants greeted her with their own chorus of barks. No Brynn. In
fact, there was no one in the room at all other than her, a cocker spaniel
apparently named Tiger Shark with a shaved left paw, and a mixed
breed with sweet eyes named Kevin.

"For you."

Aster whirled around and found Tyler in a lab coat holding out a
folded pink note. "Thank you. Is she here?"

Tyler pretended to consider the question with a whimsical back-
and-forth at the ceiling. "No. But you're to read that right here."

Memory lane, this room. Every time I'm in here (and
that's daily), I remember the night we spent getting to know
our dogs for the first time and truly learning about each
other. It was also the first time I stayed up all night because
of you, but it certainly wouldn't be the last. I learned how
compassionate you were over those scary hours, and just

how big your heart was. I love that about you. In fact, I love
everything. Meet me at the playground?

Before dashing off, Aster took a moment in the space. She smiled
at the run where Pickles had licked Dill's little head until he finally
picked it up all by himself. She looked back at the wall where she and
Brynn had sat side by side, keeping vigil and growing closer. Emotion
swelled.

"Don't you have somewhere to be?" Tyler asked, appearing in the
doorway, hand on her hip.

"I guess I do," Aster said, pulling herself out of the weighted
moment and into the present. "I'm off. Want to come?"

"No. I think this journey is just for you."

She hugged Tyler as she passed and held on for a beat. "Thank
you."

"Anything for my favorite duo."

Not surprisingly with a storm threatening and drops hitting on and
off, the playground was mostly empty when Aster arrived just a handful
of minutes later. A determined mother pushed a toddler in a swing, but
the jungle gym, the basketball hoop, and the walking trails had been
abandoned. The slide, however, pulled Aster's focus. Yep, someone
sat at the very top with a splash of blond hair. Her heart sped up, and
she started walking, a million opening sentences auditioned. As she got
closer, it was clear to her that this was not, in fact, Brynn. But perhaps
another messenger?

"Well, hey there," the very familiar voice said, whirling around.

Aster laughed at her good friend and former employee. "Tori. You
got roped into this, too?" She squinted. "What in the world is going on
with your hair?" Her red locks were missing in action, replaced by the
blond that had faked Aster out.

Tori ran a hand down the blond hair. "Bought it just this morning
in preparation for my role. Like it?"

"You're a striking blonde. Just a little jarring."

"Gotta dress the part to further the mission. I have a note for you."

"I wondered if you might."

Tori slid down the slide, popped up, and presented a pink note. "I
also dropped off a fresh dozen for you at your place. Piggly Wiggly day.
I know how much you miss it."

"You really did that?" Aster beamed. "You just made my day."
"No need to exaggerate. We know who really deserves that credit.
Give her a chance. She's one of the rare ones," Tori said, squeezed her
arm as she passed, and flitted off like a little blond delivery fairy who'd
just clocked out.

Brynn was certainly rare. Taking her time, full of thoughts and
feelings that battled and churned, Aster found a spot on a swing and
unfolded the note, sinking into swirly script like a warm blanket.

*You once knocked me on my head on this playground.
I saw the grown-up side of you, and it drove me absolutely
crazy. You made me question everything I thought I knew
about life, love, and what it was I wanted for myself. I still
think about wearing your jacket that night and how close to
you I felt. This place will always be special to me. I relive
that night often. A true favorite. Meet me at the dog park?*

Aster folded up the note and placed it in her pocket with the
others. She'd saved every letter Brynn had ever sent her. Even in her
anger, she hadn't found the strength to throw them away. Those words
still meant so much to her, and now she would add these notes to the
collection. As she ran her thumb over the stack in her jacket pocket,
she was hit with a burst of energy. She was eager to get to the dog park
and see what waited for her next, hoping that this time it might be the
woman herself. She needed to see Brynn, to look her in the eyes and
see for herself.

She walked quickly to the dog park on the west side of town as the
last little bit of daylight held on. The raindrops were on pause, but the
clouds still loomed dark and foreboding overhead. She watched a bolt
of lightning dance across a cloud as she rounded the corner. Sitting side
by side on the bench she often shared with Brynn were Marigold and
Violet. They were shoulder to shoulder, drinking warm coffees from
Lick Luster, who'd opened a coffee bar in the back. In the play area, she
saw Pickles and Dill mixing it up.

She inclined her head. "How in the world did you get my dog?"

Marigold grinned proudly. "I stole him. I'm the best kind of ninja.
You should have seen me."

Violet shook her head. "You gave us the spare key to your house, goofball."

Right. She'd forgotten that part.

"And little Dill wanted to be part of the fun today. He's giving his mama some sass."

Aster grinned at her guy. "He's always had a little too much confidence."

They nodded in near unison at what had to be a joint thought. "Sage," they all said, followed by a laugh.

"This is for you," Marigold said, presenting the pink note as if it was fragile, a valuable. "And Aster? We like Brynn a whole lot, but we love you more than anything." Violet nodded her agreement. "We support you every step of the way. Whatever your future happens to be, we have your back. Team Aster over here. Hell or high water." Aster's eyes instantly filled with tears, and a lump arrived in her throat because those words sounded very much like her mom, whom she missed so badly it nearly killed her. But the new understanding that her sisters were here for her, to step in and be her cheerleaders, was a truly happy thought to take in.

"You guys are great," Aster choked out. "And I think I really needed it this week." She didn't have her kitchen chats with her mother, or the hugs that always propped her back up when things got tough.

"We don't have a choice. We all have big shoes to fill now," Violet said, her own eyes red-rimmed with emotion. "But we're going to be each other's rocks and fill them."

Aster nodded, truly feeling their love as well as relief. She was so very relieved to know they were there.

"My door is always open for both of you," Marigold said. "You guys know that, right? I don't care if it's two a.m., you just come on over."

Aster nodded. "Mine, too."

"Same," Violet said, touching Aster's hair and sealing their pact.

"And I'm setting you up soon," Aster said, pointing at Marigold. "We may have to venture out of Homer's Bluff, but I'm going to help you find your person."

"Deal. But for now, we got a couple of dogs to play with," Marigold said. "So don't mind us. Get out of here and get to reading."

Aster, feeling lighter for seeing her sisters, confident and renewed, grinned and took the bench they'd left for her. She turned to the latest note.

Aster,
*   When you returned to Homer's Bluff, I panicked. The idea of being around you again was terrifying. But right here in this spot, I remembered all over again who we were. Us. Two people drawn together in the most inexplicable of ways. I was often supposed to be reading my book when instead my mind was consumed with nothing but you. I relished sitting so close to you again, marinating in the feelings that only you have ever inspired in me. I've known for much longer than I've admitted (even to myself) that we belong together. How about one last stop? Meet me at the fairgrounds?*

Aster needed to remember to breathe.

The fairgrounds were a head-scratcher. Unlike the other locations, she and Brynn had very little history there. The open space was perfect for festivals and the occasional carnival that passed through, but on the average, the land stood empty. She said farewell to each sister with a tight hug of gratitude. They promised to keep the dogs safe until their owners were ready for them. Feeling a little wobbly and nervous, Aster made her way to the fairgrounds as each memory she'd revisited filled her up and swarmed her senses with overwhelming nostalgia. Each one was important, but as a group they painted a picture of something pretty special.

When she arrived at the fairgrounds, her gaze was pulled immediately to a grouping of white and purple dogwood trees because with that kind of color, how could it not be? Standing in front of them, waiting patiently, was Brynn. She radiated hope in spite of the fact that she looked about as nervous as Aster felt. She wasn't sure what they were about to say to each other, but she had a feeling it was worthy of showing up on a pink-noted adventure. Brynn raised her hand as Aster approached. Her heart thudded with each advancing step. She was moving toward something big, unpredictable, and wonderful. This was her lightning dancing across the sky. Brynn was.

"I hope I didn't wear you out too much," Brynn said.

Aster took her in. After the notes, the words, the nostalgia, she just wanted to soak up the sight of her. "Hi. Just a little. It was nice, though." She heard the softness in her voice, reserved for Brynn and their moments together. It was all swirling together now.

Brynn took both of Aster's hands in hers, and that helped everything trickle to a stop. Their eyes connected and the world hummed pleasantly. "I don't know if you know what it's like," Brynn began, "being terrified of the thing you want more than anything else."

Aster shifted. "A little. Yeah." She wasn't giving a lot. She knew it. But at the same time, she needed to hear the words from Brynn first.

"From the beginning, I knew you were important. It was like the universe drew this big arrow sign over you, and even then I wasn't sure where you fit into my life. Reading buddy, fellow animal lover, confidant, best friend, object of my overt lust. Which was it?" Aster couldn't smother the smile. "Love of my life seems to fit best. It encompasses all those things and more."

Aster felt those words squarely in the center of her chest.

"I let you go once, and I don't plan to do that ever again." She squeezed Aster's hands. "And when I pulled away from that kiss the other night, it wasn't because I had doubts. It was because I hadn't had a chance to say all of this. To get my head around it all so we could do this right." She exhaled and took a beat, her voice getting quiet. "To show you how wonderful you are."

"Yeah?" Aster began to give in to the hope nestled behind her heart.

"I noticed this grouping of trees at last year's Autumn Harvest Fest and thought they would make the perfect spot to get married." Aster's lips parted. "Since then, I've envisioned us here, saying I do, and promising each other forever. That's been my favorite fantasy. But, Aster, I want the reality of you. Us. I love you and always have." Brynn searched her eyes. "Now I just need to know from you if there's enough space for another chance. A real one this time."

"Can we go back to the I love you part?"

She touched Aster's cheek. "I do. I love you. Always."

Aster covered her hand, and the last little piece of her unlocked. "I love you, too."

The smile that slowly took over Brynn's face was one she would always remember. And just like that, she was up on her toes and leaning in for a kiss Aster anticipated with her everything. Her arms moved around Brynn just as a clap of thunder hit, their own version of applause. The rain that had teased all evening began to fall, a sanction.

"We should get out of here," Aster said. "But it might be the most beautiful spot I've ever seen."

"We'll have to come back someday."

Aster kissed her one more time. "I have a feeling we will."

CHAPTER NINETEEN

Neither one of them had brought a car to the fairgrounds, which meant it was them against the rain as they set out to Brynn's place, the closer of their two homes. They started off at a steady walk, holding hands the way Aster had always wanted to. They stole looks at each other, basking in the relief that finally being together brought. When the rain picked up, so did their pace. But when the sky opened up on them, pouring down like no tomorrow, they had no recourse but to run.

"Ahhh!" Brynn yelled as her foot caught a puddle, soaking her foot and ankle. Thunder muffled her complaint, and Aster gaped, then laughed.

"What is happening right now?" she asked as the storm pelted them with big, wet drops. Another clap of thunder. "Come on. I got you." She tugged Brynn along, looking back to see her blond hair drenched, her white top clinging. It wasn't a bad look.

"There's apparently a party happening in the sky, and we're without umbrellas."

"Cruel and unusual!" Aster yelled. They were two houses from Brynn's, clothing stuck to their skin as they laughed, shivered, and scurried the rest of the way down the slippery sidewalk. Aster didn't care in the slightest. This was a day that she would remember for the rest of her life for all the right reasons.

When they arrived under the cover of Brynn's porch, they reached for each other instantly, lips clashing and clinging in a dance so wonderful, Aster lost track of time and reason. Everything had come together, and her heart soared to heights unimaginable. Was this real? How could she live in this moment forever?

"Come in," Brynn said against her lips. "We can warm up. Dry off."

But Aster's eyes were on Brynn's perfectly swollen mouth and the way little tendrils of hair framed her face and curled slightly from the rain. More thunder cracked, mirroring the intensity of her feelings, her desire. "I'll follow you."

Brynn's house was dim when they entered. She turned on a single lamp and smiled. A chill hit Aster, her wet skin and clothes catching up with her. "Let me get you a dry robe. You can snuggle up with a glass of wine and warm up while I change." She poured Aster a glass of red, retrieved a white fluffy robe that smelled like her, and disappeared into the bedroom for what felt like a decent amount of time. Aster hung out in the kitchen, sipping the wine and enjoying the feel of Brynn's robe against her body. She'd hugged it to herself more than once by the time she heard Brynn.

"Aster. Come find me."

Brynn's confident, even voice sent a shiver, and she set down her glass. Around the corner, she found Brynn's bedroom, a room she'd only glimpsed in the past. But no sign of Brynn. "Where are you?" she asked.

"Just had to get into something dry."

Aster opened her mouth and froze because Brynn was lying. She'd had to get into something sexy, and if anything was dry it was Aster's mouth.

"What do you think?" Brynn asked, one arm going up on Aster's shoulder. The white satin shorts and the matching shirt she'd left hanging open had Aster stalled. She fixated on the exposed skin, the inside curve of her breasts peeking out.

"I think you're the sexiest woman on earth."

She'd brushed her hair, taken it down, but it was still wet. Why was that doing crazy things to Aster? "Want to take it off me?" Brynn asked, running her finger down Aster's collarbone. She pulled in air, legs shaky.

"Yes." Aster touched Brynn's hair. Found her eyes. "I've missed you. Touching you. Staring at you without apology."

Brynn nodded. "Me, too."

Her fingers gently swept aside the one edge of that satin shirt, revealing her breast. Aster dipped her head and placed a kiss there softly to a quiet moan from Brynn. Aster lifted the breast, generously taking more of the nipple into her mouth, sucking softly, moving her tongue in a circle across its surface. She straightened and slid the rest of the shirt off Brynn's shoulders, taking in the damn sight of her. Gorgeous. Waiting. Aster gently turned her around and kissed her neck from behind. She reached around her body and cradled her breasts as she kissed the underside of her jaw. Brynn pressed against her and somehow expertly found the tie on that robe, prompting it to fall open. Brynn turned in her arms, slipped her hands inside the robe, to her back, and then to her ass. She stepped into Aster's space and pulled her hips to Brynn's. Fire. There was nothing like this. She was drunk with desire and determination and awe. She stepped right out of that robe, letting it fall to the floor. She felt Brynn's eyes on her body, everywhere. She reached between Brynn's legs and touched her intimately through her clothes and watched as her eyes slammed shut and her lips parted. The bed was right there, but she walked them to the wall, driven by instinct and raw need. With Brynn's back against it, she slid her shorts down to her ankles and, with nothing between them, pressed her body to Brynn's and kissed her thoroughly.

But she needed more. She needed all of Brynn. She let her hands roam over her hips, her stomach, her breasts, and her thighs encouraged by the sounds Brynn made, at first quiet moans of encouragement that had shifted to whimpers when her need increased. Aster caressed the inside of one thigh then the other before coaxing them apart. As they kissed, Brynn nodded. Permission. Aster pulled back from the kiss, tilted Brynn's chin until their eyes connected, and slid her fingers gently inside, thumb stroking. As Brynn began to move against her hand, Aster matched her rhythm. Outside, the rain continued, underscoring their dance. Brynn's eyes were a deeper shade than normal, having gone dark with desire. She pulled Aster closer, wordlessly asking for more. She obliged, moving faster in and out until in a beautiful thrash, Brynn went still and shuddered silently, grasping Aster tightly at the shoulders, her nails digging in, producing a welcome burst of pain and pleasure across Aster's skin.

"Too much," Brynn breathed. A smile. "That was too much."

"It wasn't enough," Aster whispered in her ear because she had so many plans for Brynn, her body, theirs together. She cupped her ass and kissed her lips wildly, her own arousal acute and raging.

Brynn didn't hesitate, going up on tiptoe to match her intensity full-on. She had Aster by the face as she explored her mouth with her tongue, moaning against it. "I've wanted you naked for so long," she whispered against her mouth before going back in. "These breasts. Mine." A hot shiver shot through Aster at the thought of being owned by Brynn, but nothing could be more accurate. Brynn owned every part of her and more. Brynn bent her head and pulled a nipple into her mouth as Aster saw white. The passionate, open-mouthed kisses to her breast brought Aster down, literally. She was sitting on the bed before she knew it, her legs too wobbly for support. Her center ached and her thighs trembled.

"There's a fire when we touch."

"Every damn time," Aster said, nodding, their fingers playing, intertwining, and letting go again.

"When was your last time?" Brynn asked, resting her palm on Aster's stomach. She loved the casual touches of intimacy. The way Brynn claimed her.

"Oh. That would have been you," she said, cradling Brynn's cheek.

Brynn seemed struck, in absolute awe. Her eyebrows dropped. "Really? All that time in Boston. All those women you worked around. You never…"

"No. Some tried. But I just couldn't. Not after we were together. I only wanted you after that, even through my anger."

"I just never imagined that." She rested her cheek on the pillow absorbing. "Not that I'm complaining." A smile.

"What about you? Were you seeing someone or…" She braced herself for the answer. Of course, anything Brynn did on their time apart was fair, but the details would be hard to think about.

"No." She exhaled slowly. "I tried to imagine myself dating again, but I knew better. My last time was in Boston."

Aster nearly couldn't believe it. "We waited for each other."

"That's what you do when you're in love."

"We had to untie the knot."

Brynn gasped. "Someone's been talking to Marigold."

Aster laughed. "You've heard it, too?"

Brynn nodded. "And what a knot we were in."

Aster slid down the bed onto her side, placing them face-to-face. "Not anymore." She placed a soft kiss on Brynn's lips. "I'm never letting you go again. I'm making you breakfast every morning and kissing you every night."

"Promise?" Brynn asked.

"On the planet Pentagargo."

Brynn laughed loudly. "You are such a nerd. But you're my nerd. A sexy one." She eased a leg between Aster's. "And really hot in my bed. Without clothes on."

Everything in Aster woke the hell up. "I feel like you're coming on to me."

In answer, Brynn lifted her thigh, placing it more firmly between Aster's legs, and pressed upward. "I don't think I'm the one who's going to be coming."

Aster felt the familiar stirring hit, and she rocked her hips softly.

"Just so you know, I'm about to have my way with you again." The authoritative way Brynn said that had her wet all over again. Warm breath, lips, pressure, passion, the brush of skin came together in a haze of her undoing. Brynn played her body like a gifted musician bringing her to the brink and pulling her back in again until she shot like a star in a wash of wonderful.

"I can safely say that you're worth every second of the wait," Brynn said, falling next to her. She studied Aster's face and slid a strand of hair off her forehead.

"We're lightning, you know that?"

Brynn lifted her head and met Aster's gaze. "We are?"

"Alive, unpredictable."

"Beautiful," Brynn countered. "I like that. That's us."

"It's a good mascot. I mean, if we're not going with carrots."

"Tough call, but no."

In the early morning, Aster sat on the edge of Brynn's tub, wearing the white fluffy robe and drinking coffee as Brynn showered nearby for her day of work at the clinic. Lucky pets. Her body was very aware of all they'd done together the night before, satisfied and a little tingly in the best way possible. Through the glass she watched fondly as the water fell from Brynn's skin, the most gorgeous woman in all the world.

"You're back," Brynn said over the water. "Where did you go?"

"I told you. I made you breakfast. Big benefit of falling in love with a chef. But you have to come eat it before it gets cold."

Brynn stepped from the shower and opened the bathroom door. "You're not kidding. You really did make breakfast. Bacon, even!"

"I had to. I love you. Bacon confirms it." It was really that simple for Aster. Brynn slid into a robe, and they had the most wonderful breakfast together, full of conversation, soft touches, and decadent food. When it was time for Brynn to leave for work, Aster stood with her on the porch, looking out on Baker Street where it had all started back in the day.

"Surely your new next-door neighbor doesn't live up," Aster said, checking out her old place, ruminating on all that had changed in her life since back then.

"Bubba? No. I've yet to want to take my clothes off when in his presence. There's always tomorrow, I guess."

Aster laughed. "You stop that right now."

"And now I want to take my clothes off." She placed a soft kiss on Aster's lips. "Bye, baby. I'll come by the restaurant after work."

"I was hoping you'd say that."

Aster stood there and watched as Brynn walked to her car, bowled over by how natural it felt, their very domestic morning together. Right then, she knew without a doubt that this was the first one in a lifetime of mornings they'd share. "Hey, Brynn." Brynn looked up, car door in hand. "Favorite book lately?"

"How about just a story?"

"I'll take it."

"I really like the one about that last Lavender sister. What's her name? Anyway, she leaves town, she comes back, and she finally settles down with the woman who plans to love her until the end of time. It's a really good one."

"A page-turner?"

"The best kind. I love you. Have an amazing day until I see you."

"I love you, too." Aster blew a kiss and watched as Brynn's SUV headed off down the road, knowing innately that she was the luckiest lightning chaser ever. She'd captured it forever in Brynn, and she was never letting it go.

EPILOGUE

One year later

Aster checked the rib eyes, pleased with their progress. The sear was about where she wanted it, and the juices were sealed up nicely inside. She took a deep inhale, loving the aroma of steaks on the grill, excited to be preparing them for the family gathering she and Brynn had decided to host last-minute at their place on Baker Street. The backyard around her bustled with springtime activity as her siblings and their families made use of the spacious yard as they snacked on the appetizers Aster had whipped up on the fly. She smiled as she watched Brynn, wearing cutoffs and a flowing red shirt, move around between the small groupings, making sure everyone's drink was full and that they didn't need anything.

"You should relax. Enjoy yourself," Aster whispered in her ear as she passed. "I got this."

Brynn flashed her a winsome smile. "One more lap and I will do just that. I set out a pitcher of fresh lemonade with strawberries, and I'm going to enjoy a glass. I'll bring one for the sexy grill master, too." She let her hand trail down Aster's back as she passed, dropping coyly to her backside for the briefest of moments. Brynn looked back, proud of what she'd accomplished.

"You're bad," Aster mouthed.

Brynn laughed and nodded slowly in agreement. They'd spent a lazy morning in bed. Morning sex had become a favorite, with Brynn most commonly taking the lead. Aster had been woken that morning by lips on her shoulder making their way to her neck, while a skilled pair of hands snaked under her tank top from behind and found her breasts. She smiled at the attention. "Someone woke up rested."

"What?" Brynn said, kissing her earlobe. "I just really like you."

"Get on top," Aster said, giving Brynn a tug. Her very favorite position. Something they very much agreed on.

"Your wish," Brynn said, and they were off.

She loved weekends and the adventures they brought. Like this one. With nothing on the agenda for their Saturday, she'd turned to Brynn again after lunch as they read books together on the couch.

On one side of the yard, Ethan and Sage tossed a junior-sized football back and forth, wearing matching baseball caps turned around backward. Tyler looked on with baby Wrigley on her hip, the light blond cutie trying to grab hold of every person who passed.

"Sorry about that," Tyler told Marigold as Wrigley grabbed the fabric of her shirt. "She's handsy."

"Most action I've had in months," Marigold said. "Give me that little girl. We want to stroll and see the family. Find ourselves a bite of Aunt Aster's famous chocolate chip cookies."

Tyler handed the toddler over and accepted the margarita that Brynn had waiting for her. She did a little dance as she took a sip. Brynn laughed and kissed her friend's cheek with a smack.

"You doing okay, Dad?" Aster asked. He stood off to the side with a beer in hand, watching the action.

"Oh yeah. It's a nice one out. It's fun to see everyone enjoying themselves." He grinned. "This was a good idea. Need any help?"

"Can you watch the steaks while I check on the oil for the fries I cut earlier?"

"Oh. Yeah. I know steaks," he said, his voice dropping an octave as he took control of the grill. "You've come to the right place."

He'd really come out of his shell recently, assuming the doting parent role in a manner Aster never would have predicted. He called each of his kids regularly, invited them over for football games or lunches he'd thrown together all by himself. But Aster had a feeling he was getting a little unseen help from the sweet angel looking down on them all. She knew she was, as well. Her mom was with her still, guiding her daily at the restaurant, encouraging her on the harder days when Aster missed her so much that she couldn't breathe. Aster was grateful for that.

Inside, she found Violet slicing a fruit plate, always one to take the initiative.

"Thanks, Vi. One less thing."

"It's what Mom would be doing if she was here. Jumping in and helping out."

"You're right. Thank you for standing in." Aster gestured to the backyard. "Cruz seems nice."

Violet followed her gaze to the man she'd only recently started dating. "It feels early to bring him to family stuff, but I think it might be a worthy cause."

Aster liked seeing Violet happy again. "He seems gentle. Kind."

"That's an understatement." She turned, her back pressed to the counter as she explained. "Ethan adores him. They have a lot of fun together, and he's the first person I could actually see myself with since the divorce." Her eyes went wide. "Speaking of, did you hear that Tad got drunk at a country club in Wichita? Broke a bunch of glasses and threw a chair. He had to be escorted out by three security guards, kicking and screaming the whole way. Asked them if they knew who he was, while the whole club watched. Someone put the video of the whole thing on Instagram."

Aster grinned. "I did and loved every second of that gossip. Glad to hear it's true."

"It's more than true. His father was so embarrassed that he cut him off and fired him, too." She made a little rhythmic clapping gesture. "God takes his time, but he gets around to most everyone. For good or bad."

Aster raised the fry basket and gave it a shake. "You know, I think you're right."

"Even you and Brynn getting your happily ever after. And now a little one."

Aster went still. She turned to Violet. "Wait. How did you—"

She smiled softly. "I've been pregnant before, Aster. I know what it looks like." She watched Brynn through the open back door. "She's glowing. It's really the most beautiful thing."

"I think so, too," Aster said. "We were going to wait and tell everyone once we're a little farther along. A few more weeks."

Violet made a lock and key motion in front of her lips. "They won't hear it from me." She pulled Aster into a tight hug that brought tears to her eyes. "I'm so happy for you that I can't see straight. Anything you guys need, you call me."

"We will," Aster said, over the moon at their most recent news. It had taken them a couple of tries at a clinic in Kansas City, but when the stick showed two lines, Brynn had leapt into her arms and kissed her into next week.

"What's with all the love happening in here?" Brynn asked from the doorway.

"Aster was just making fries while I teared up like a lunatic. No worries. I'm done now. I'll leave you two lovebirds custody of your kitchen now."

"What was that about?" Brynn whispered when they were alone.

"I will tell you later."

"Will you also rub my feet later? On the couch. With a movie on."

Aster kissed her nose. "I would love to. It's a date."

"And I should warn you." Brynn's green eyes danced. "The hormone train I'm on is a little ridiculous. I may or may not keep my hands to myself. You're wearing the jeans that do me in. Probably just to torture me because you knew other people would be here and there was nothing I could do about it."

"You found me out." Aster smiled because pregnant Brynn had quite the sex drive, and regular Brynn was already pretty ambitious. "I promise to let you take me out of them if that's what you want." Just the sentence alone had Aster looking forward to later.

Brynn kissed her cheek as the dogs dashed through the kitchen, made a fast and furious lap, and dashed back outside again, clearly enjoying their day. "Good. Now I think the steaks are calling. Your father is staring at them like they might sprout wings."

"He takes his job very seriously."

"I see now where you get it. Now let's go spend time with these amazing people in our backyard. There's a cornhole tournament sprouting up, and Tyler and I are gonna take the whole thing. Vets united."

Aster laughed. "I won't tell Sage."

Brynn paused, door in hand, and looked back. "We're gonna have a family, Aster." She said it quietly, but with so much feeling that Aster's heart practically burst.

"I know. It still doesn't feel real. I honestly can't wait for the rest of our lives."

"Look at us. Who knew the power of an everyday bench?"

Aster placed a hand over her heart and watched the love of her life rejoin their family on a wonderful spring day. There was a time when Aster thought life was boring if it wasn't constantly throwing her curveballs. It turned out, she was simply missing her person, who would never be anything less than exciting in Aster's eyes. Brynn, quite simply, made the world feel colorful and bright. And now they would walk through it together. Forever and always.

About the Author

Melissa Brayden is a multi-award-winning romance author, embracing the full-time writer's life in San Antonio, Texas, and enjoying every minute of it.

Melissa is married and working really hard at remembering to do the dishes. For personal enjoyment, she spends time with her Jack Russell terriers and checks out the NYC theater scene as often as possible. She considers herself a reluctant patron of spin class, but would much rather be sipping merlot and staring off into space. Bring her coffee, wine, or doughnuts and you'll have a friend for life. www.melissabrayden.com.

Books Available From Bold Strokes Books

Closed-Door Policy by Erin Zak. Going back to college is never easy, but Caroline Stevens is prepared to work hard and change her life for the better. What she's not prepared for is Dr. Atlanta Morris, her gorgeous new professor. (978-1-63679-181-4)

Homeworld by Gun Brooke. Headed by Captain Holly Crowe, the spaceship Velocity's crew journeys toward their alien ancestors' homeworld, and what they find is completely unexpected—and they're not safe. (978-1-63679-177-7)

Outland by Kristin Keppler & Allisa Bahney. Danielle Clark and Katelyn Turner can't seem to stay away from one another even as the war for the wastelands tests their loyalty to each other and to their people. (978-1-63679-154-8)

Royal Exposé by Jenny Frame. When they're grouped together for a class assignment, Poppy's enthusiasm for life and love may just save Casey's soul, but will she ever forgive Casey for using her to expose royal secrets? (978-1-63679-165-4)

Secret Sanctuary by Nance Sparks. US Deputy Marshal Alex Trenton specializes in protecting those awaiting trial, but when danger threatens the woman she's falling for, Alex is in for the fight of her life. (978-1-63679-148-7)

Stranded Hearts by Kris Bryant, Amanda Radley & Emily Smith. In these novellas from award-winning authors, fate intervenes on behalf of love when characters are unexpectedly stuck together. With too much time and an irresistible attraction, anything could happen. (978-1-63679-182-1)

The Last Lavender Sister by Melissa Brayden. Aster Lavender sells her gourmet doughnuts and keeps a low profile; she never plans on the town's temporary veterinarian swooping in and making her feel like anything but a wallflower. (978-1-63679-130-2)

The Probability of Love by Dena Blake. As Blair and Rachel keep ending up in the same place despite the odds, can a one-night stand turn into forever? Or will the bet Blair never intended to make ruin their happily ever after? (978-1-63679-188-3)

Worth a Fortune by Sam Ledel. After placing a want ad for a personal secretary, a New York heiress is surprised when the woman who got away is the one interested in the position. (978-1-63679-175-3)

A Fox in Shadow by Jane Fletcher. Cassie's mission is to add new territory to the Kavillian empire—murder, betrayal, war, and the clash of cultures ensue. (978-1-63679-142-5)

Embracing the Moon by Jeannie Levig. Just as Gwen and Taylor are exploring the new love they've found, the present and past collide, threatening the future they long to share. (978-1-63555-462-5)

Forever Comes in Threes by D. Jackson Leigh. Efficiency expert Perry Chandler's ordered life is upended when she inherits three busy terriers, and the woman she's referred to for help turns out to be her bitter podcast rival, the very sexy Dr. Ming Lee. (978-1-63679-169-2)

Missed Conception by Joy Argento. Maggie Walsh wants a relationship with Cassidy, the daughter she's only just discovered she has due to an in vitro mix-up. Heat kindles between Maggie and Cassidy's mother in a way neither expects. (978-1-63679-146-3)

Private Equity by Elle Spencer. Cassidy Bennett spends an unexpected evening at a lesbian nightclub with her notoriously reserved and demanding boss, Julia. After seeing a different side of Julia, Cassidy can't seem to shake her desire to know more. (978-1-63679-180-7)

Racing the Dawn by Sandra Barrett. After narrowly escaping a house fire, vampire Jade Murphy is unexpectedly intrigued by gorgeous firefighter Beth Jenssen, and her undead existence might just be perking up a bit. (978-1-63679-271-2)

Reclaiming Love by Amanda Radley. Sarah's tiny white lie means somehow convincing Pippa to pretend to be her girlfriend. Only the more time they spend faking it, the more real it feels. (978-1-63679-144-9)

Forever by Kris Bryant. When Savannah Edwards is invited to be the next bachelorette on the dating show *When Sparks Fly*, she'll show the world that finding true love on television can happen. (978-1-63679-029-9)